ROUGH SEAS AHEAD

ROUGH SEAS AHEAD

• • •

Philadelphia Crime Series #4

David S. Tanz

ISBN: 150881080X
ISBN 13: 9781508810803
Library of Congress Control Number: 2015903903
CreateSpace Independent Publishing Platform
North Charleston, South Carolina

Other Books by David S. Tanz

A Shot of Brandi (Crime Series #1)
Silk on the Rocks (Crime Series #2)
A Toast to Justice (Crime Series #3)
Reunion

"I don't care if you ever come home, I don't mind if you just...keep on rolling away on a distant sea, cause I don't love you and you don't love me"

Eric Clapton, *Promises*

PART ONE

CHAPTER 1

As the sun erupted from a still gray Caribbean backdrop, its rays began to stretch out in an aurora of pastel shades. It reminded Vandergriff of a French impressionist painting, like random brushstrokes might appear upon an empty canvas beginning to take life. Lt. Terrance Elberry shot a quick glace over his left shoulder, focusing on Captain Vandergriff. Jon Vandergriff was the younger captain on the PacLantic Cruise Lines two ships, which was an up and coming challenger to its big three competitors. Glancing down at the digital readout on his navigational screen, he rattled off the slight change in headings so that the ship would ease into the port in Phillipsburg, the capital city of St Maarten. As the crew stood assembled on the bridge before docking, as they had done countless times, something just did not seem right to Elberry.

"Captain, are you sure you don't want me to slow her down a bit as we guide her into to port. You have taught me well and it would be my pleasure."

"Thanks for the offer but I got her right where she belongs and she is in good hands. There are no rough seas ahead," replied Jon, in an even, yet forceful tone.

Elberry consented, deftly hiding his concern which had stemmed from the previous evenings celebration of Captain Vandergriff's 40th birthday gala. April Minot, the current social director of the ship and his fiancée, had toasted so many times that she had to be carried off to her stateroom before she totally disrobed. Jon was too blasted to even notice, hiding his habitual, almost obnoxious overprotectiveness and jealousy of his current lover. He caught a short catnap before resuming his duties, but the crew, especially Elberry, had seen their superior out of control in the past and knew the consequences of a major screw up. Elberry rattled off the information appearing on the large computer screen. It included the strength of the current, its direction, the speed of the ship and the ships depth, amongst a slew of other information. At that moment, both a warning light and digital voice relayed critical information that the ship was veering off course into shallower waters. Vandergriff squinted at the monitor, looking for the automatic control sensor that would right the errant course. In his usual sober state, he had never had cause to use this particular function, but his mind and reflexes were substantially impaired. Elsberry shot his hand toward the stabilizer, but it was swatted out of the way, as Vandergriff placed his ego above that of the passengers and crews safety. The sheer power of the ships engines was no match for the tug boats that were guiding her into port.

With no time to react, the vessel veered slightly to the starboard side. There were several piers that extended out from the shoreline in Phillipsburg, all varying in length. Being slightly off course, the cruise liner plowed over one of the piers that had been driven into the seabed, hitting it with such force that the ship began to tilt. The impact caused both a lurid crushing noise as well a force which tossed objects that were not secured to defy gravity. Loud foghorns began to sound, alerting the passengers and crew of possible danger. A loud and voluminous digital voice interrupted the warning signal, advising the passengers and crew to don their life preservers and follow the same instructions they had practiced during the mandatory muster drill. Response would be slow; it was just around 5 A.M. and many of those aboard were still fast asleep. As the captain and crew began to prepare for the severe impact, the passengers began to emerge from their deep sleeps within their stately cabins. Crowds of people began to fill the port side, as the starboard side began to tilt at a more sever angle downward. Screaming now drowned out the instructions that were blaring from the multitude of loudspeaker that occupied the decks. Those who were unable to get a secure grip on the railing or any sedentary part of the ship helplessly tumbled, as they slid helplessly on the recently polished walkways. The ship finally stopped. Screaming continued as the dim lights of fishing crafts and all available sea-worthy vessels headed toward the massive cruise liner.

Arguments on the bridge had now subsided as the staff shifted into damage control mode. Flashing red lights and loud sirens emanated from emergency vehicles that now dotted the coastline which appeared teasingly close. The crew began to herd the scores of passengers into the small motorized crafts which were designed for such an occurrence. The well trained staff preformed as they had been trained, attempting to minimize the panic that consumed those aboard.

The medical staff of six was overwhelmed by the outcries of those who had been injured or lie helplessly scattered randomly on the deck. Life boats were dropped into the dark waters, while at the same time; countless ladders were lowered as well toward the approaching rescue boats. And although it seemed like an eternity to most, it was less than an hour before all of the crew and passengers were standing on dry land. They stared in disbelief and awe at the mega-ton vessel that lay motionless offshore. The continued blare of sirens still pierced the pre-dawn silence, shuttling those who had been injured away to the nearest medical facilities. As these horrific events unfolded, the backlash of what had just unfolded had even yet to come.

● ● ●

More than a thousand miles away, Milton Phelps was awakened by his distinct ringtone of his I Phone, as it played a familiar melody. "Beyond the Sea", a sixties hit from Bobby Darin, mirrored the theme song used in the company's slick television ads. This particular call would have devastating implications unseen by so many.

At 38 years young, he had made his millions over a decade earlier. He had grown up in Connecticut, with one brother and a widowed father who had been a lifetime fisherman. He had attended Boston University, where he majored in economics with a minor in geography. He had hopes of turning his father's small fishing business into becoming one of the larger fishing purveyors of the rich New England seafood corporations. Each summer he would work with his father and crews, as they captured haddock, tuna and the multitude of shellfish that populated the Atlantic Ocean and shorelines. He planned to combine his growing education and more modern business savvy to transform his father's old fashioned methods in to a large fishing conglomerate.

The next several years after graduation, he plied his newly found economic formulas with his knack for seizing opportunities within the fishing industry. Early on in the growing business, he was able to buy out some of the old companies prior to any conglomerates. These larger corporation like Gorton's, were more interested in swallowing up established mid-size companies rather than the smaller mom and pop type operations that he was much more familiar with. Within several years, he had increased his sales and employees tenfold, along with a growing distribution network up and down the eastern seaboard. In year five, he started to get noticed, being courted by larger corporations making him generous offers. It was in the fifth year that his father advised him that he should sell out before the rough fishing life would seep into his soul and get him "hooked" into a life that ocean would inflict upon his soul. Before any decisive decisions could be made, fate stepped in. The salt had etched lines of age and experience into his eternal sun drenched features, now gently laid him to rest as he passed in his sleep.

Without his father's presence or input, he chose to ignore the generous offers he was being barraged with. His mounting ego, coupled with his stellar successes, were not enough to thwart off the deluge of corporate America. His steadfast refusal to merge or be bought out, eventually led to the companies downfall. Contracts were drying up, as well as his reliable methods of transport. Trucks with large loads were being stolen and shipments delayed, causing spoilage of his product which depended so much on the speed between the catch and getting to market or to the end user. Within two years, the business was no more. Even with financial help and suggestions of his brother, he could not reverse the downward spiral of his once successful corporation. Not wanting to deplete a comfortable seven figure saving he had squirreled away, the company followed the path toward complete bankruptcy. Both the advice of his father and brother and now seemed too correct in hindsight.

His brother George had taken a similar path in both education and success, but chose the field of international investment banking. He too had attended Boston University, and then remained at BU, getting a Masters in economics from there. It was ranked in the top 25 graduate programs by U.S. News and World Report, a fact that he assumed would enable him to be grabbed up by a top banking concern. Unlike his brother, his love for the sea did not extend much past his teens, seeking rather a lust for both knowledge and money. He had graduated in the top three of his Master's program and was swooped up by a large international banking firm which fulfilled his current dream. In the years that followed, he submerged himself in his work, leaving little time to pursue a social life and more time to challenge his brain and slowly emerging ego.

CHAPTER 2

With the salt of the sea now coursing through his veins, Milton needed to enter a new arena that would keep him near the ocean. It was now a part of him.

He was still in his late twenties, when he ventured out on a cruise, designed to relieve the onset of depression coming from the loss of his business, as well as to put him back in touch with his roots; those being fashioned by the salty ocean air and the beauty of intricate shades of blue that the water took on at its ebbing moods. This particular cruise took in the Baltic. It departed from Southampton, England and its ports of call included Barcelona, Rome, Gibraltar and Lisbon. It would give him a taste of new places, adventure and foremost, an idea of where his next business venture might be.

It was in Florence that his life would take on a new perspective. He had signed up for a day trip which would include a tour to the Renaissance city in the heart of Tuscany. The city was rich with museums, cobblestone streets, beautiful cathedrals and crowded outdoor markets.

The first stop was the Galleria degli Uffizi, the city's most popular tourist destination. Masters such as da Vinci, Michelangelo, Botticelli and other historic master artists fill the gallery with artwork one only sees in books. Having taken several art appreciation courses to fulfill his college requirements, he always had an interest in seeing these masterful works first hand. Now he had arrived,

The bus dropped about two dozen of those passengers who had signed up for this particular excursion. The group was met by a well-seasoned guide, fluent in English, Italian, French and Spanish, who would guide them through the treasured halls of the masters. The anticipated tour would begin in the Hall of Tiziano that hosted the works by Titian.

Born in 1448, Tiziano Vecellio was a great master who was sought after by all of the rich and famous European courts. He was known for his use of color rather than drawing, going against the majority the opposite style that was strong in Florence. His portraits were strong in vibrant colors and included such subjects as dukes, duchesses and even the current Pope.

It was while his art appreciation was lost in the fluid brushstrokes and, that his focus was broken by a soft, sensual voice that seemed to appear from behind.

"He is such a master of different shades of red as well as his detail for the female body", the voice expressed, the volume barley louder than a whisper.

He turned, noticing an attractive woman, long brunette hair falling slightly below her shoulders, along with piercing hazel eyes.

"Indeed," he replied, adding "Venus of Urbino was a gift from a duke to his young wife. Not only has he captured the eroticism of Venus, goddess of love, but is also said to have many hidden meanings."

"I am very impressed with your knowledge of both art and eroticism," replied Adrianna, the woman who had not yet given her name. "Are you an art dealer or critic?' she added with an obvious curiosity.

"I could try to impress you and say I am both," he said, a wide smile forming across his mouth,

He held out his hand and made an introduction.

"Milton Phelps," he chimed in, continuing with an obvious enthusiasm toward her. "I had taken some art courses my sophomore year at Boston University and just wanted to see what I had only known from my textbooks. The pictures were small and did not give the masters an iota as such is done by viewing them in real life.

"Adrianna Zola and it's a pleasure Mr. Phelps," she replied adding, "and I attended Emerson University in the great city of Boston like you."

They shook hands, the conversation now straying from the original admiration of the great master.

"Then why hadn't we met before in that great city?" he asked, still having yet to let go of her hand.

Gently pulling it away, she queried, "I graduated in 1997, moved away for a short while and now I have moved back."

Her explanation was brief, leaving room and setting Milton up to pursue her obvious interest in him, as well as his in her.

"And I currently reside in Boston, the Back Bay area over on Exeter", he said smiling, knowing that a connection was beginning to emerge.

Pressing on in exploratory conversation, she agreed to abandon the tour at lunch and find some quaint outdoor café where they both could continue the flow of their chance meeting. Hell, Italy *is* known as a romantic playground, she rationalized and accepted the offer.

After continuing the morning portion of the tour, the two new acquaintances shared stories and brief experiences of their pasts. They laughed quite a bit, as they began to discover a common ground as well as a growing attraction. The latter being more of an unspoken understanding, though neither made mention of it. She quietly thought to herself how nice it was having a conversation in real time, with a real person, rather than all of those lonely souls who depend on their smart phones for such matters.

After splitting off from the crowd, knowing they had to be back at the bus to return them to the ship, they wondered through the unfamiliar streets of Florence. They found a small Trattoria, nestled behind the tacky leather boutiques near the St. Lorenzo street market. Staring at the menu and pointing to interesting dishes, they were waved to an unoccupied table that was stationed below an ornamental awning bearing the colors of the Italian flag. A waiter quickly approached, a white napkin draped over his arm as he filled their glasses with San Pellegrino, the Italian equivalent to Perrier. The waiter offered menus along with a brief description of the daily specials, his broken English barely passable enough to interpret what he was saying. They pointed to two dishes that were recognizable, and Adrianna chose the wine. As time passed, their comfort level intensified, sharing more personal history as they warmed up to each other, barriers disintegrating. By the time the meal was over and the wine drained, their fingers were intertwined as they stared across the table at one another.

Their fingers still interlaced, they arose and walked toward their destination point for the bus to transport them back to the cruise ship. Before the bus pulled up, Adrianna leaned in and placed her soft lips upon his, followed by their tongues extending and swirling around in a sensual gesticulation. A connection had been established, and the romantic backdrop of the European canopy could only lead to...

● ● ●

When they finally arrived and passed through security, they agreed to meet for dinner at one of the more romantic venues the cruise ship had to offer. They opted for the steak and seafood restaurant. The chemistry and desires were now escalating and seemingly beyond their control. The candlelight dinner only added fuel to their growing passions. He had a 20 ounce rib eye and she a stuffed lobster, the gourmet meal only heightening their desires. The connection they had made was both unexpected and welcomed. And they both knew it was mutual.

That evening they consummated their unexpected afternoon meeting with a night of passionate love making. It appeared that their emotions and connection had carried them to the next level: not as a random act of casual sex, but rather a foundation for what the future might hold. They both craved to please each other, unselfishly doting upon each other as they explored their sensuality in an uninhibited manner. Although yet to delve into their past relations, it really didn't matter at the particular moment. They both knew it would appear with time and when it was meant to be,

During the remaining days of the cruise, they spent almost every waking moment together. They confessed their pasts, their faults and their desires. And it seemed that everything they were discovering only added to what would eventually bring them together. Within a year of their first chance meeting in the romantic city of Florence, they tied the knot and took up residence in the city of Boston. The only request he insisted upon, in a rare lighthearted moment, were that she become a fan of Red Sox Nation. He joked as he presented her with the classic black cap with the font they created, now known as "Dirty Sox".

CHAPTER 3

During the next half dozen years or so, Adrianna continued her work as a decorator in Boston and its suburbs, making quite a name for herself. Architectural Digest even devoted a short three page spread to several of the homes she had redecorated in Beacon Hill, mixing what they called "Colo-deco, which was a blend of the rich woods and sharp textures mixed with black and white checkerboard and bright colored zebra patterns. Only a state that backed McGovern over Nixon for President could get away with that type of bold, liberal art forms."

Milton on the other hand, began to dabble in day trading, in the risky areas of futures, options and precious metals. He now had a plan that would keep the salty air of the sea he loved so much, as part of his lifeblood. Before his father had passed, his brother had schooled him in regard to investment strategies. But his brother George never quite forgave him for his father's death, saying that if had been less egotistical and stubborn; he would have accepted an offer and all would have lived a longer and more comfortable life. What George didn't know was that he taught his brother too well in the realm of financial investing.

Over the next five years, Milton parlayed his low seven digit savings almost six-fold. He could now realize his plans. His dream was to invent a new type of cruise line that would create various interests and uniqueness which the big three cruise lines only offered bits and pieces of. He studied the list, constantly adding, deleting and expounding upon unique interests of the population. He held the paper and examined the variety of themes that he would initially offer:

Professional Athletes
Spicing up a marriage
Film Stars up close and personal
Best-selling authors
Porn stars
Comedy Icons
Famous chefs and hands on demonstrations
Magicians teaching their secrets
Wine tasting and collecting

These were the categories he would begin with. During the past several years, he began making connections; networking and talking to booking agents and the like. With his increased bankroll, he was able to make connections that he never thought possible. He was a risk taker and had the full backing of his wife and partner. The cruises would sail every other week, needing time to change themes and décor. Who else other than Adrianna would be adept enough to pull something like that off, other than his capable and creative better half? He knew it would work.

It had taken the early years to find financial backing and more importantly, a vessel that he could convert into his prototypical cruise ship. Building one was out of the question, due to time restraints and cost. In year four he had found one and Adrianna worked with the architects in order to design it so that it could change venues as easy as a chameleon.

By his 33rd birthday, he was now ready to break into the market. He lined up his advertisements, using print and television as his main media channels. The first cruise would need to be a blockbuster, so he went with theme using famous stars and directors of the stage and screen. Knowing it would be the most costly; he also believed it would garner the most publicity. When he finally put the nearly 500 cabins on the market, they were sold out in less than two days. You would think the Beatles and Stones were the main attraction!

The first cruise went off with only a minor hitch when one of the top performers learned she had sea sickness, having never been closer to the ocean than a beach shoot for a Sports Illustrated famous swimsuit issue. Actors preformed scenes from their classic movies and did improvisations suggested by the awe struck passengers. Workshops in acting, makeup and directing were held. Live news feeds were beamed back to all the major networks along with photo shoots provided for all major publications. It would be an understatement to say that Phelps was on the way back from failure, a step above rags, to riches.

As several years passed, Milton was able to purchase a second ship from a small European company that had gone into Chapter 11. This particular ship was used for conventions, as hotels usually do, as well as being rented to large corporations for sales meetings and reward trips. It consisted of close to 300 staterooms and its menu and activities ran the gamut depending on how much the hosts were willing to spend. It too turned out to be a major success, and he devoted his time to managing both venues, expanding both their popularity and revenues.

The first venue was a complimentary cruise which invited corporate companies that specialized in the area of event planning for midsized to larger corporations. The short list included party planners from large hotel chains such as Hilton, the Marriott and Westin, who would share in part of the profits for booking the PacLantic line. Hollywood studios and movie production companies, along with television names such as HBO, Cinemax and Showtime were also invited. The ship could be used for both publicity parties as well as filming. Phelps also took a stab by inviting some of the larger Broadway production companies; both serving as a stage for performance as well as specialty cruises which might feature three hot ticket shows, all performed in the span of one week for the artsy crowd. It seemed the use of the ship was endless; and would earn a reputation as a hot ticket and high priced item.

As success grew over the next several years, Milton was growing in popularity and wealth, while his brother George began to foster an emotional cocktail consisting of part jealousy, part admiration and to a larger part, hatred. Not once had his brother offered him any type of chance for investment, nor had he extended any type of reconciliatory actions. The wedge of their father's death had created a growing fissure between the two brothers that seemed to parallel the San Andreas Fault. There was no one to specifically blame, as neither had made any attempt at suturing the deep wounds that had been caused by the event.

Adrianna on the other hand, was having the time of her life. Who said that a honeymoon has to end? Having been named Vice-President of operations and been given a fifty percent share of the corporation, she kept her soul involved in pulling together what was needed by each corporation that had reserved the ship for each of its different settings. Over the years she had developed great relationships with specific companies needed to furnish each distinctive offering that had been planned. She knew who to contact for gourmet foods, designer settings or specific types of entertainment. Loving the newness and challenge, she excelled at making each journey an extraordinary, if not a memorable and lifelong eternal experience for all of those who attended.

TMZ and Entertainment tonight jumped on the PacLantic bandwagon. You didn't have to be on dry land to misbehave, although when Lindsay Lohan made her debut, the good silverware was locked up and there were no vehicles that she could operate to collect another DUI. Justin Bieber was banned outright; he wasn't old enough to drink and his entourage had rap sheets longer than the ships round trip course in nautical miles.

And Milton had done his due diligence, obtaining Panamanian registry for the two vessels. There were major economic advantages, as there was no income or withholding taxes payable by non-resident shipping corporations. Along with that, provisions were made which eliminated the necessity to have the ship dry docked prior to registration. In simple English, it was the cheapest way to register the ship and pay the least amount of dollars to operate it in international waters.

Life had been good to Milton and Adrianna up until the early morning call that awoke him from a deep sleep. You can use whatever cliché you choose; what goes around comes around. Shit happens. It is what it is. However, in the long run, it would change the course of many people's lives over the period of time that would follow this disastrous event.

CHAPTER 4

Milton answered the call on the fourth ring, not used being awakened at 4:30 in the morning. His senses began to return as he answered with an abrupt, "This better be good."

On the other end was Douglass McCain. Although his title read that he was" Vice President of Operations" on his business card, in reality he was Phelps's go to guy, the fixer. He handled problems that arose and were deemed just below a level that his trust enabled him to make decisions without disrupting his boss and mentor. But this particular problem did not fall into such a category.

"Milton, we have had an incident with the Adventurer", he gingerly began, not wanting to begin with creating a concern which he knew would happen soon enough.

The "Adventurer" was the second ship in his line which catered to the corporate market.

Without an immediate response from his boss, he continued.

"The incident occurred several moments ago and it involved the Adventurer. It seems that the ship somehow ran aground as it pulled into St Maarten and although we have no fatalities, rescue ships have extracted a number of passengers who have been injured. We don't know the severities and such as of this moment, but I have some of our people on the scene as we speak."

Phelps shot up, putting his feet on the floor and left the bedroom. His senses began to return, as his mind race to deciphering the tidbit of information that he just ingested. He thought coherently and then spoke.

"Find out what the hell happened, how it happened and assess the damage. Get your ass on the next flight down and talk to our P.R. people. We have to get this shit under control before the press makes it out to be the next Armageddon. *Do it now,*" he barked, his mind processing the implications as well as the solutions.

Cruise ship disasters and mishaps were not new or uncommon to the nightly news. In 2014, a South Korean ferry led to more than 100 deaths due to negligence and poor reaction from the crew. But that was only one disaster. In the past several years, cruise ships have been struck by viral and bacterial illnesses, fires, missing passengers and environmental hazards. Phelps was lucky that there were no fatalities during the mishap, but he very well knew that lawsuits and bad publicity would follow this tragedy. But the bottom line was that he had learned long ago, that the public has a very short term memory for such events, especially when no one is killed.

Adrianna reached her arm around to feel for Milton, gesturing her hand in various directions to locate him. After several seconds, she noticed he was no longer next to her and called his name. The only response given was that he was on the phone and would be right back. But she knew him well and she noticed his tone was off. She climbed out of bed and found him in his office, the phone still pressed against his ear. Leaning against the doorway, her mind now cleared and began to listen to the full conversation, trying to piece together what was happening in real time. It did not sound good.

Milton was now on the couch. With remote in hand, he turned top CNN and watched intently to see if the story appeared. It did. The reporter, a tan skinned attractive woman stood before the camera, the disabled ship in the background. Staring into the camera, she began to speak, her facial expressions deriving those of concern.

"Early this morning, the cruise liner Adventure, one of two ships in the up and coming PacLantic cruise fleet, collided with a pier during its docking approach. At the present time, there have been no reports of fatalities, although several dozen passengers have been transported to local area hospitals for various injuries. Local police officials are on hand, awaiting investigators specializing in maritime mishaps. Our inside sources tell us that the crew of the ship has been led away in order to be questioned in detail, regarding the events that led up to this occurrence. Our reporters are standing by to bring you the latest facts regarding this case."

The camera faded as the anchor switched stories, reporting on yet another school shooting; in where else but California.

Adrianna approached and joined him in the large family room on the overstuffed couch that faced the television. She put her arm around him and squeezed him just enough to let her know she was there for him. The room was large with 30 foot ceilings, the windows decorated with stained glass scenes portraying several of the Beatles classic album covers. It was a mixture of modern and classic art deco, two of Adriana's favorite motifs. Thrown in for good measure were a couple of Titian copies, just to remind the couple of how and where they had met. She leaned her head on his shoulder and glanced up at him before speaking.

"Do you care to share the events du jour with your loving partner?" she queried, kissing his neck softly, in more of a supportive than a sexual way.

Turning toward her, he exhaled a deep sigh, a trait she had observed when he wanted to sugar coat the true facts. She gazed deeply at him and waited for the response.

He began to relay the series of events as he knew them, interjecting the implications of all possible accounts of the mostly negative outcomes that might arise from this ongoing event. She was attentive, not inter-rupting his ramblings, waiting for the time when she could interject a positive remark which might ease the aftermath of this disaster. The fact that no one had died up to this point was one of the few factors that gave him some solace. They were both mesmerized by the footage of the ves-sel as it struck the pilings, being caught on the video monitors at the port as well as numerous android phones. It was only a matter of time before it would go viral on You Tube as well as international news.

The camera then focused in on interviews with the first sets of passengers who had been able to get on the primary lifeboats that had been launched. Reporters rushed to mob those being led off the lifeboats. Many of the major cable networks had yet to arrive, but there were still crews from France and the Netherlands that covered local stories as the island flew two country's flags. It would take an hour before the passengers and staff was standing ashore. The last to arrive were the captain and his officers, who shielded their faces, heads down, as they were led toward a small cluster of official looking buildings that housed the cruise line offices.

The silent and embarrassed crew was met by Sam Graymore who immediately gave them instructions. He stood at 6'3" tall, had windblown blonde hair and dressed in a dark blazer with the company logo on the pocket. They had met him several times before when they had experienced some minor issues. He was professional, blunt and did not like to be interrupted. He began to speak to the crew when they all seated at a long table in a small conference room.

"Before we get into details, I want to say neither I nor my superiors are happy with this event. But before we pass judgment or take any actions, you will all be interviewed by the PacLantic attorneys and public relation representatives who should be arriving in a short time. *Do not, I repeat do not discuss any of these events with anyone outside of this room. Do you all understand me?*"

He was more forceful and confrontational, than sympathetic and concerned in regards to the major fuck up that had just transpired. He continued.

"Doug McCain will also be arriving and as you know he reports directly to Mr. Phelps. Up to this point there have been no reported fatalities, although there are several dozen people at various medical facilities on this island. Gentlemen, you all better pray to God that no one dies, or you will all be held accountable, "he lectured, continuing in a blatant condescending manner.

Elberry was the first to glance up, his eyes meeting the piercing stare of Graymore. He spoke, his voice a mixture of timidity and remorse.

"If I may sir, I would like to express our deepest apologies and concern for all those entrusting us to their safety. We expect nothing less than to accept any of the consequences or ramifications that our actions have caused."

Graymore thought it a bit odd that Elberry and not Vandergriff was speaking for the group. He was not the highest ranking member of the crew nor was he the most seasoned. This fact alone raised suspicion that something was just not right, and he did not want any accusations of something being covered up. When the legal team arrived, they would drill down to the bottom of this catastrophe and learn the truth as to the specifics of the cause. Until then, he would make no assumptions or accusations until all the facts were gathered and sorted out. He was not looking forward to the outcome. The P.R team would have to spin this better than a carousel on steroids.

● ● ●

Just then, McCain's name appeared on the caller I.D. that Milton seemed to be gripping on to for dear life. He put the phone to his ear.

"Talk to me", he barked, McCain knowing the foul mood that his boss was capable of whenever a circumstance or event was something he could not control.

"I just boarded a charter to the island. Graymore is down gathering information and I told him to isolate the crew and not say a word until legal gets in touch with them. I should be there in shortly over an hour."

Sam Graymore was in charge of public relations, flying to wherever the ship docked. He handled the press releases, interviews and any type of problem which might arise during the ships stay at any particular port of call; currently stationed in St. Maarten. For him, this event would be a first and he was strangely up for the challenge.

'It's been taken care of Mr. Phelps," he quickly responded. And although he been with the man from the infancy of PacLantic, the name

Milton was never used, no matter how many times they had socialized. It was the control freak kind of thing.

● ● ●

During the next hour, pastries and coffee were brought into the conference room as they awaited their interrogatories. All those who had been on the bridge were seated along with the chief steward and those in charge of the evacuation. Their number totaled thirteen. How lucky could they be? Most sat with their heads down, silently staring at their coffee cups or just closing their eyes. There was no doubt that each was anticipating the questions that they would be asked, as well as constructing the answers they would provide. Even Madame Marie, Bruce Springsteen's famous fortune teller from Asbury Park, New Jersey's boardwalk would not be needed to predict the outcome. All fingers would be pointing at the error and post hangover condition of Captain Jon Vandergriff.

All heads peered up as three forceful knocks on the door erupted the stillness. Graymore opened the door without even asking who it was. Pulling it open, he stepped aside and three individuals in designer clothing entered the room. There were two men and one woman. The leather briefcases and attaches confirmed their assumptions that it was the legal team for PacLantic. They were followed by two of St. Maartens finest who took positions outside of the door as it was closed. When the door closed, Graymore face turned unsympathetic and he began to speak.

"First, let me introduce you all to our legal team," he began. His open hand was directed at the first individual, who took a small step forward.

"This is Chris Banner. He specializes in maritime law and is an expert in regard to laws that govern and protect companies that are outside of our country's jurisdiction when a criminal act has been committed there are accusations as such. Miss Jenny Farmer specializes in cases that involve possible criminal lawsuits involving negligence that might and probably will be levied against our corporation. Last is Mr. Fran Medford.

Fran specializes in litigation regarding civil lawsuits which will definitely follow this incident. At no time, and I repeat, no time," his voice elevating threefold, "will any of you talk with anyone other than me or these three individuals in this room regarding the series of events that recently took place."

After the brief but poignant introduction, all heads were again lowered, their eyes not wanting to make contact with the new players that had been added to the "game". To put it mildly, they were all nervous and in all probability, scared shitless.

The group was split up and assigned to give interviews to the legal team. The building contained several small rooms and they were led away one by one as Graymore guarded the others with a watchful eye. There was little conversation, only time for introspective thoughts and the uncertainty of their futures. These interviews lasted for different durations, and as the attorneys interviewed the employees from the bottom up in terms of rank and importance on the ship, they were then driven away to an unknown location to be kept under the watchful eyes of PacLantic security. And of course, away from the media.

As if rehearsed, although it was not, by late afternoon, only three remained. Vandergriff, Elberry and second lieutenant, Joseph Wooster would now be interviewed separately, none knowing what the other would say.

During Wooster's session, he was asked to recount the series of events that had led up to the tragedy. He did not appear nervous, being rather willing to recount the events, giving much forethought in his attention to detail.

"It seemed like just another routine docking," he began. "There was nothing out of the ordinary in regard to currents, weather conditions or wind speed. There was another ship several hundred yards behind, but they had cut their engines, having arrived about a half hour ahead of schedule."

Wooster paused as he noticed Farmer taking dubious notes as she honed in on every word and inflection. Without looking up she asked,

"Please tell me about any conversations or behavior that was out of the norm as the ship approached".

Wooster gathered his thought before continuing. He showed no signs of trying to sugar coat the facts, Farmer supposed to herself. He came to a crossroads, doing and saying the truth or protecting the man he had worked with and respected over the past several years

"As we approached, Elberry commented on the direction and speed the ship was heading. Hell, he offered to take over, but Jon wouldn't hear of it." Pausing with a deep breath, he went on.

"Truth be told, it was the Captains 40th birthday the night before, and I am not sure he was, how can I put this. He might not have had all of his reflexes and senses that he usually demonstrated during the docking procedure."

Farmer interrupted.

"So what you are saying is that he was incapacitated? Drunk? What *are* you saying?" she asked in a curious, yet stern fashion.

Putting his hand over his eyes and head down he answered, his voice now barely audible.

"Yes, whatever you want to write down. He was just not his usual capable self and not in full control of his senses. There, are you happy now?" he said.

"And was he hung over from his birthday festivities or not?" she continued in a bit of terser tone.

Wooster looked up, meeting her eyes with an almost helpless expression, and confirmed that yes, he was indeed hung over.

Farmer reached out and her hand grasped his wrist. In a compassionate and appreciative way, she thanked him for being honest and assured him that his level of responsibility would be held at a minimum. After several more brief questions, she arose and walked toward the door. After opening it and speaking in a low whisper, the security agent from PacLantic informed Wooster that he would be transporting him to his temporary residence. As he exited, she thanked him for his honesty and concern.

In an adjacent room, Elberry sat across from Medford, who was already on the sixth page of notes adorning his legal pad.

Elberry had as well chosen to relay what he believed to be the untainted facts. He was still a bit miffed about the conflict that his superior had shown regarding his ego versus that of the passengers and crews' safety. His honesty and recollection would later confirm the story given by Wooster, regarding the state of mind that Vandergriff had been in during the docking procedure. Because the crew had been sequestered before any discussions could be had, he had only hoped that the stories given by his fellow shipmates would coincide with his. Deep down, he was confident that they would.

When the interrogation was finally done, Medford called for the security team that would transport Elberry back to his location. When Banner had concluded his questioning of Vandergriff, the three would have a relaxing dinner at Rare, the prime steakhouse on the island. After an aperitif, they would relay the facts to Phelps.

Banner had been given the assignment to interview Vandergriff, due to his seniority and penchant for getting to the bottom of things. During the question he made notes not only of Vandergriff's response, but also of his body language.

He began with Vandergriff's background, as well as his rise to the position of Captain of the Adventurer. He hoped that by playing up to his ego and accomplishments, he would diminish any possible defense mechanisms and make him feel more at ease. It would prove to work as it always had. He was now ready to get down to the hard facts.

"Run me through the procedures you followed as you guided the ship in," Banner asked, his voice soothing and non-threatening.

Vandergriff knew he was responsible, mounting a halfhearted defense with Elberry, knowing he had probably been blamed for the collision already. He would have to choose between admitting to the facts or the possibility of being caught up in a lie. With much thought, he chose the former. He began to speak, his voice steady and his words attempting to minimize his culpability.

"Plain and simple, Mr. Banner, it was my ego and lack of judgment that caused this accident. The previous evening I had celebrated my 40th birthday with a bit too much spirit. Combined with my lack of sleep and poor judgment, I miscalculated my bearings and caused the accident. What can I say? I and I alone are at fault and will accept the consequences. All I can ask is that you express my concern for all those who I have hurt, and that you represent me in a way to cause me the least amount of suffering you can. I will live with this for the rest of my life."

His request was genuine, as well as his admissions. It was a good start. The public relations people would spin his actions as best they could and to leave out the fact that he was intoxicated. That would need to be covered up. It would take weeks to brief the crew and authorities in such a way that they would compensate those who were injured, as well as preserving the integrity and reputation of PacLantic. That was why he was here.

Back in Beantown, George was thoroughly enjoying the show of his brother's woes as it unfolded on every news station. He was sipping a glass of Makers Mark as the story of yet another cruise ship disaster gobbled up time on the major networks. This one was special. It was to become his brother's personal demon. This was his one and only sibling. The one who was still The one who he blamed for his father's death, the one who he schooled in finance and the one who didn't have the decency to offer him the chance to invest in his venture. Not that he would have anyway, and this unfolding event made him even happier that he had not invested a thin dime.

"You seem to be enjoying the show. It's rare I get to see the spiteful side of you." At 5'9", with mid length blonde hair stylishly grazing her shoulder and hazel eyes that glistened, her looks were spectacular. Angel, the woman he had mentored in his current investment company, also had brains, cunning and drive. Neither wanted to claim exclusivity in their relationship and the passionate lovemaking sessions that they shared gave them all the more reason to circumvent marriage. Hell, why ruin a good thing, they would always joke.

"Am I that easy to read?' he asked in a sarcastic manner, knowing that they were so on the same page, and at times they finished the others sentence.

"It's almost more enjoyable than getting inside information on a hostile takeover," he retorted. Traders knew that kind of information was as profitable as hitting the lottery but without the astronomical odds.

With the following day being July 4th and falling on a Friday, the markets would be closed, enabling them to savor the flow of information that was emerging by the hour. He smiled, trying to picture how his hard skinned sibling was handling the news.

During the course of the next several weeks, events unfolded faster than Watergate and Nixon's resignation. Milton Phelps substituted his high budget television cruise ship ads with those of a sensitive and caring CEO who promised "innovative safety standards, stricter background checks on staff and a free week aboard PacLantic Cruise Lines for any future problems that may arise." Those who knew the man well believed it was an Oscar winning performance. With the Adventurer scheduled to be in dry dock for 6-8 weeks for repairs, Phelps upped the talent and amenities on the Prestige, his flagship of the small fleet. He was a survivor and this was his virgin entry into the long list of cruise ship disasters in maritime history. Business did hit a low, but that was blamed on a second ship mishap on a competitive line, occurring weeks later, and injuring twenty. Like all stories before, it would only be a short matter of time before the public forgot. The American public was pretty damn good at doing that.

● ● ●

Less than two months later, the actual trial began in St. Maarten. The license plates on all vehicles read, the "Friendly Island". Time would tell how "friendly "the jurors would be, as well as to whom.

The prosecution, represented the sovereign nation as well as those who would suffer losses in business revenue, both present and future, aimed at proving the guilt of the company. With that would follow massive fines and the payment of the merchant losses, bad publicity and the actual repair of the port area. They were also seeking criminal charges against some of the crew, needing to hold someone responsible for the act of criminal negligence itself.

The defense believed its best court of action was to settle the damages out of court and arrange a plea for Vandergriff, the actual perpetrator of the criminal act. Graymore had discussed this with Vandergriff. He would serve as the sacrificial lamb. They would plea him down to reckless endangerment and destruction of government property. In return, he would plead guilty and be fined, which in turn PacLantic would cover. Additionally, a two year prison stay would be tacked on. He would in turn, surrender his Captains license and not be qualified for any reduced time for the standard "good behavior". Behind the scenes, Graymore promised he would remain on half salary during his incarceration, keeping that fact private.

After much soul searching, he came to the realization that he had to take the offer. If convicted he might see a longer sentence, stiffer penalties and no source of income from anyone.

Before opening arguments, the defense called for a meeting in the judge's chamber to discuss the arrangement the two sides had agreed upon. With that news, the trial was briefly halted and then followed by a statement read by Vandergriff admitting his guilt. The prosecution accepted all of the concessions agreed to by both parties and the judge read the penalties into the records. Another story would emerge soon enough.

George and Angel were both outraged by the decisions, as were many of those following it on Jane Velez and Nancy Grace. He so wanted to see his brother ruined. During his childhood years, his brother was always the tougher and more popular of the two. He rarely lost a fight or any of his popularity amongst his peers. George was always the smarter and he would use this asset do what the judicial system failed to do, and that was bringing his brother down.

PART TWO

CHAPTER 5

Almost 2 years later

Vandergriff had spent the better part of the past two years minding his own business. A blow to his ego and romantic anticipations were dampened early in his incarceration. After countless letters and phone calls, his onetime soul mate, April Minot, gave him the brushoff in the standard" Dear John" letter. She proclaimed that his selfishness and ego did not figure into her long term plans. He was also blamed for his lack of chivalry during the birthday blast that caused this whole incident, by not coming to her aid and staying with her in her time of need. Time of need was a euphemism for drunken stupor, he thought to himself. Who needed that selfish, self-centered bitch, he rationalized, which lessened the impact on his now shattered ego. The problem was that he truly did love this woman and over the next couple of years, he would realize all the mistakes he had made during their relationship. Dwelling on the past and what could have been would only produce a no win situation. And little did he realize how the hurt he had caused her would lead him down a new road that would alter his life. She didn't love him and he had lost his love for her.

Soon to be reaching mid-life and turning 42, he was at a loss as to direction his life would take after his release. He had only known one trade, that of a seaman. Both the publicity and damaging reputation would be an impossible obstacle to overcome after his release. Both his face and reputation were tarnished, making it impossible to peruse his lifelong passions. He needed to find a way to endure, to make a living. Being a survivor, there was no chance in hell he would not bounce back and forge a successful new profession. He would reinvent himself. The only problem so far was how and as what?

● ● ●

That morning, George had dropped off Angel at Logan International Airport for a flight down to Miami, as Vandergriff was being housed at the Federal Correctional Institute in Miami. It was a low security facility opened in 1976 with a population that hovered around 1000. Some of the more notable inmates, past and current included Manuel Noriega, the former dictator of Panama, convicted of drug trafficking, money laundering and racketeering. (No, he wasn't the malevolent dictator whose wife had all those shoes.) Other alumni included some mafia figures from the DeCavalcante crime family in New Jersey. Were they from exit 14 or exit 14a off of the New Jersey Turnpike? Another alumnus was Bill Campbell, former Mayor of Atlanta, who had been convicted of tax evasion. Vandergriff was small time compared to those celebrities that Lifetime movies are made of!

Fate has a way of interceding into one's life at the most unfortunate times, and even once in a while at the fortunate ones. Since we all know that there are no such things as a coincidence, Vandergriff was soon to a victim of such circumstances. He wouldn't haven't even believed his future if it was found in a fortune cookie.

Inmate #10181957 was paged to the visitor's area during one Sunday afternoon. Since April Minot, as well as his fellow crew had abandoned him, he was totally clueless as to his who that guest might be. He was taken from his cell but not before he was adorned in leg irons and handcuffs that was attached to a chain around his belt. He was led down a long hallway consisting of those ugly concrete blocks painted in a color best described as "exorcist green". The door into the waiting area buzzed the security lock open and he was led into the common area filled with a host of visitors. The guard led him to the end seat, where he glanced up at his visitor.

Across the Plexiglas that ran up to the ceiling, sat a quite attractive lady. She had a black pageboy haircut, hazel eyes and dark red lipstick covering her puffy lips. Angel had donned a wig, but didn't bother adding any type of contact lenses that would alter the color of her distinctive eyes. George had supplied her with a fake driver's license and credit cards for back up identification. Although George didn't own a cruise line or rub shoulders with celebrities, he had made the acquaintance of a sufficient number of friends that were more let's say, "Under the radar" in their endeavors. He had a good network of connections over the years, making a fair number of recipients some big bucks based on what some might interpret as "insider trading."

Vandergriff was speechless, not knowing who this looker was, and for that matter why she was here. He just stared, waiting for her to introduce herself and do some explaining.

"Hello Jon. Would you prefer me to address you as Mr. Vandergriff? My name is Carolyn West and I was sent here as an intermediary for someone who is interested in meeting you and possibly contracting you for your experience in the area of your maritime expertise." She was both very general and consciously non informative in what she would say.

She remained gazing at him, trying to get a read on what she had just offered, but a look of puzzlement adorned his facial features. She continued.

"I prefer not to talk too much as I am not aware who may be listening to us. Rather, I will give you the number that you should contact me at after you are granted your freedom. Once outside this, this place, "she said with a not so obvious disdain, "we can further discuss this issue."

She waited for a response, knowing that her offer was not only brief but very unclear. He stared at the number she held up to the glass, giving her a look that confirmed his memorization of it.

"You have my interest Ms. West."

"Call me Caroline please,"[1] she interrupted, wanting to preserve his interest in her.

"Okay Caroline. You have obviously told me nothing. I get it. But I have no place to go, no one to work for and, and I love your eyes."

She smiled.

"Good, then I assume I will hear from you within the next several months. I look forward to discussing some propositions with you," she whispered, knowing full well that her female signals were being read loud and clear; at least clear in her mind, but misleading and unclear in his.

Later that evening, Angel, minus her jet black hairpiece, sat by George's side and enlightened her lover and partner in crime on the day's events. He also had some news for her. Milton's recovering cruise line had been given a shot of Adrenaline when one of his devoted passengers and off center actor from a television sitcom had volunteered to put up the cash and partner with him for two more ships. She joked, asking him if one of the new themes would include a "cocaine and drug sampling "venue. He quickly responded quoting his favorite songs by the Eagles.

"There were lines on the mirror, lines on her face. He pretended not to notice, they were caught up in the race."

They both laughed, but if the deal went down, it would rejuvenate his mindset as well as his bank account.

George continued, waving his arm and indicating his anxiety of what had transpired during here day trip to Miami.

"Should I begin with my return flight, where a four hundred plus pound excuse for a man, who not only had dog breath, but who kept snoring? Or the fact that they ran out of Pringles before they had served us in first class?" she added comically just for the hell of it. He smiled, but gave her a rueful stare encouraging her to continue.

"I think it went perfect. I followed our plan to the T. I was a bit flirtatious, but not anxious. I gave him the vaguest of details in regards to what we need him to do, as well as why we chose him. Stressing the fact that he would be all but banished from being within fifty miles of any body of water, I hinted that we may be able to change that reality."

"And his response?" asked George, now impressed with her results.

"My female intuition tells me that he is interested, actually quite interested. Our little meeting will give him something to look forward to between now and his imminent release back into the world of high unemployment. He *will* chase after the bait we just threw into the ocean's depth, pardon the pun."

"Excellent my dear Angel, which is just another reason I adore you so much" he whispered, but was funny how the word "love" never entered into his adornments.

"Now it is your turn to do something for me. I have had such a long day, jetting down on one of your schemes," she began in a manner which he had known all too well.

She slid upward on the couch, squirming as her back arched and her hands begin to unbutton her tight black jeans. He grabbed the bottom of her pants cuffs and helped her remove them, listening to her breathing begin to grow louder in the wake of anticipation. In a soft voice, he completed the song that they had quoted earlier.

"They had one thing in common they were good in bed, she said faster, faster, the lights are turning red."

For the next hour they made love, their passion surpassing any teenage couple who might have experienced their first encounter in the backseat of a car. For them it was the passion and the excitement of life that made them click. They were truly pursuing the path of "life in the fast lane".

CHAPTER 6

During his final two months of his incarceration, Vandergriff did his due diligence to find out more about this mysterious Carolyn West, the woman who had visited him unexpectedly. She had appeared out of thin air. Not actually bearing gifts, but rather offering a somewhat sketchy plan for his future.

He immersed himself in the prison library, searching the computer for any information on this woman. His resources were limited, as the computers in the prison had so many blocked web sites as to what he could search for. He tried various spellings of Carolyn, of West and even employment sites relating to maritime job offerings. All of his searches came up with the same results. He could not find a trace of anyone that resembled her, but then again, he didn't really know *what* he was looking for. There were no pictures or descriptions even remotely similar to the unknown vixen. Neither the guards nor his fellow inmates could offer any help, asking them if she was familiar or had visited previously, trying to scam any of the other inmates.

He also placed a call to Elberry, the only part of the crew he was in minimal contact with. After the deluge of the ship disaster, Elberry had received no criminal or civil penalties, but he was prohibited from serving on any type of cruise or charter ships that carried passengers. His license was suspended for ten years. It might just as well been one hundred.

With the salt of the sea running through his veins, he moved west to Louisiana and took a job as a mate on a shrimp boat, fading into a life of anonymity. He remained in the shadows long after Forrest Gump had given shrimping in the Gulf its fifteen minutes of fame. The reason he had remained in touch with his ex-captain was a subject he had put a minimal amount of thought into. It was probably a mixture of sympathy, friendship and camaraderie that comes with spending long hours at sea. Regardless of why, he was willing to sacrifice a small amount of time for the man who absorbed the brunt of the blame. Shit, he *was* the cause that had altered many people's lives.

● ● ●

Vandergriff was now counting the hours to his release, his anxiety split between freedom and his meeting with the unknown. At about the same time, Milton and Adriana Phelps were in the process of christening their new additions to the PacLantic Fleet. The Adventurer had suffered only minimal damage for the severity of its actions. The small tear in its hull had not taken on too much of the corrosive salt water and had been able to be towed into dry-dock where the repairs took slightly under a year.

The Topaz was the third ship, a smaller passenger carrier by today's massive standard. It carried 400 passengers and had a crew numbering slightly under 150. The ship could be termed the "economy vessel" in its fleet. It offered rooms ranging between $39 per night, and topping out at $999 for the two bedroom top deck suite. The catch was that everything on the ship was a la carte, and nothing was included. Meal plans and food choices offered a wide range of meal plans. Excursions, alcoholic libations and even Wi-Fi came at a price. The only things which were offered gratis were the seats in the casino and the sunrise over the ocean.

The other was the 2 ½ Carat, the name chosen by the ex-Hollywood sit com actor, due to his substantial investment in the two new ships. Its itinerary focused more on singles, top musical groups and those who have been recently become tabloid phenoms. Passage was toward the higher end range, but PacLantic touted the voyage as one which would stay with you for a lifetime…and possibly even longer.

Stringent and in depth scrutiny was given to every square inch of the whole ship. Safety standards exceeded the recommended minimums and the crew was hijacked from existing competitors, albeit at much higher salaries and more lucrative benefit packages. Television ads flooded the cable networks on all the food, travel and leisure activity stations. Print ads joined the media blitz in magazines that related to those similar markets. Milton even took out several half page ads in the expensive advertising **PEOPLE,** in exchange for a paragraph in **the "People to Watch"** section. After the launch ceremonies, which looked like a presidential convention, Phelps invited some local celebrities, upper management and fifty of his closest friends to a privately catered event at the Fontainebleau in Miami.

Built in 1954, it is one of the most historic and architecturally noteworthy hotels in Miami Beach. It is located in the heart of Millionaires Row on Collins Avenue. Jerry Lewis starred in *The Bellboy*, used as the backdrop in the 1960 film. More well-known is the scene where James Bond is engaged in a high stakes gin game with Aurelius Goldfinger prior to Oddjob painting Bond's attractive assistant in gold paint. On December 2, 2008, it was added to the U.S. National Registry of Historic Places. What better place than this landmark to draw even more attention. Milton and Adriana were back. And back to the style they had been accustomed to.

Fifteen hundred miles to the north, George and Angel were sipping some single malt scotch when one of those fluffy entertainment stories appeared on the 50" plasma screen. Red white and blue ribbons were streaming over heads as a large crowd had gathered to watch the ceremonies. Wearing a scowl, George pressed mute and stared at the crawl below, his eyes darting from right to left. "Milton Phelps and PacLantic were celebrating the launch of their two new ships. It was less than two years ago that his signature cruise ship had plowed into the port of St. Maarten, injuring dozens. The incident was the one of several that had occurred in a short time span, forcing the cruise companies to adhere to tougher standards and regulations."

The broadcast abruptly ended, followed by an Amber alert, the license plate now engulfing the whole screen.

"Can you please explain why that sorry ass brother of mine always seems to land back on his feet," George said indignantly to Angel, shooting down the remainder of his drink.

Grabbing his wrist, she turned to console him. Staring into his eyes with an empathetic gaze, she began.

"Shame on you for not being pragmatic here, my love. We have been planning and planning our grand scheme which will put an end to your selfish brother ever getting back on his feet again. Neither financially nor emotionally will he be able to cope with what we have in store. So stop sulking and pour us another drink."

Whenever Angel took more of a dominant measure in their relationship, he seemed to snap out of his negativity and regain his confidence. It wasn't that he was subservient to her. On the contrary. They were wired with some of the more ominous personal traits such as greed, lust and pride, leaving room for more on the pathway to the seven cardinal sins.

George arose. He slowly walked to the bar in the corner of the living room and picked up the bottle of Laphroaig Scotch. At 40 years old and a price tag of six hundred dollars, it was a fitting choice for the pair, even if they didn't know life was again imitating art. This single malt was the favorite spirit of Trevanian's assassin Jonathan Hemlock in the movies, *The Eiger Sanction* and *The Loo Sanction*. The former movie starred and was directed by Clint Eastwood. It was a story about a classical art professor who doubles as a professional assassin. He is later forced out of retirement to avenge the murder of an old friend. Hell, it's just another one of those movies where art imitates life.

For the next hour, she lay with her head on his shoulders, his arm draped over her elbow, hand resting on her thigh. With the sound still muted on the television, it was now set to one of the travel channels, as they fantasized about their imminent success regarding the downfall of his brother's soon to be nonexistent empire.

CHAPTER 7

The heavy metallic key was slipped into the lock and was turned clockwise, making the familiar clicking noise that signified his cell door was about to be opened. Vandergriff's, cellmate, Enrico Carrazo shook his hand and hugged him, whispering something to into his ear that produced a wide grin.

"And don't forget to tell my old lady what I told you, bro. I know she will get a kick out of that. And oh yes, tell that cranky bitch I still love her."

"My pleasure, bro," echoed the response from the departing Vandergriff, proud of the new expressions he had learned during his incarceration. It was hard to believe that the blonde haired, fair skinned, blue eyed Nordic had now shed some of his stoic image. His two years in prison had not only taught him a lot, but also furnished him with some of the "street smarts" that he was never schooled in. The blend of various ethnicities, both social and economic that populated the prison, may have been one of the only positives that arose from his prison stay. In the early weeks of his detention, he spent an overabundance of time replaying the events that landed him there. That was followed by beating himself up due to his stupid and selfish actions. It was the blend that melded various individuals that brought him out of his depression and self-pity, and for that he had grown and was thankful. He was still the same deep down inside, but now had a "new set of eyes" in which he could process the world around him.

Feelings of nervousness, anxiety and the unknown all merged within his brain. He felt a slight tremble, accompanied by a chill, as he stood before the desk stationed by the exit of the prison. Next the guard called his name, and he was given his personal belongings that he had surrendered when he was processed at his time of being shuffled into the general prison population. An envelope was passed through the window containing his passport, personal documents and some money he had accrued during his tenure there. One hundred and thirty eight dollars was all he had amassed for his two years of labor. It was the amount he would spend just going out for cocktails with April Minot.

April had vanished and never reappeared during his time in the joint. He neither expected any type of loyalty from her, nor any commitment to wait. It was what it was, and it was now time to move on. In ten minutes his processing would be complete and he would walk through the double set of gates that had penned him inside the wall of his temporary residence for the past two years. What waited beyond those walls would begin a new chapter in his life. Or maybe they would not.

● ● ●

Angel Almar, a.k.a. Carolyn West, checked herself one last time in the reflection cast by the lighted mirror facing her that she had unfolded from the driver's side visor. She was seated in a rented black BMW, showing that she could afford it and hopefully adding a bit of exclusiveness to her act. Grabbing her lipstick, she applied a finishing touch of the Claret shaded color she had chosen for the occasion. After all, appearance *is* everything. Tamping her lips, she nodded slightly to herself, indicating she was happy with the final product. She re-adjusted the rear view mirror and checked her watch. It was about 3:00, the time she would meet the man who would carry out her and George's disreputable plan. At least she would do all in her power to see that he did. Leading him on would be as easy as being the only entrant running up to the stage in a million dollar lottery presentation. It would coincide with his yearly salary if he took the pair up on their offer.

Her car was parked across the street, facing the driveway and exit area that he had told her to meet him at. Several people emerged together but Jon was easy to spot. He was half a head taller than all of the rest, and his blonde hair tossed in the ocean breeze. As she had rehearsed in her mind so many times prior, she started the car and slowly rolled up to the release area, lowering the front passenger window so that she could get his attention. She did. He nodded, greeted her with a "Hello Miss West", and she waved her arm toward the seat. He slid in, acknowledging her, not just for being the only individual he knew in Miami, but the only one who gave a damn to pick him up. Her brain processed the naivety and boyishness he exhibited, and she smiled to herself.

"It was my pleasure, Jon. I am looking forward to our long lunch at the beach. I hope this will work out for both of us," she said, her voice lowering an octave as her teasing declaration ended.

Pulling out a folded envelope, she deposited it on his lap. It was a stipend for his time that he would give her at lunch.

"Go ahead and open it. This is just my employer's stipend for the time you are giving me at lunch. There are by no means any strings attached."

Upon opening it, he counted, finding fifteen crisp one hundred dollar bills. He said nothing for the moment. Then he spoke.

"The truth is Ms. West..."

"Carolyn, call me Carolyn. And tell me the truth Jon. May I call you Jon, or?"

"Jon will be fine, he responded, his face slightly distorted as he looked for the right words.

"Since you came to visit, I must admit, I am very confused. I tried to find you on the internet, asked some inmates, guards...and found nothing."

She let him continue, wanting to see both his level of curiosity, as well as body language.

"I don't believe you need my services for any maritime work, and that is where my skills lie. Do you want to write an article on me for some American trash tabloid? Do an interview? Are you a reporter?"

She glanced at him and smiled.

"No, no and no. It's none of the above. But I would rather talk to you over lunch. I can answer all of your questions in due time. Is there any music or station you would like to listen to? We should be at the restaurant in two minutes."

Jon said no thanks, and turned his head to watch the passing landscape, as his mind tried to process the unfolding scenario.

Minutes later, the car pulled up to an upscale oceanfront seafood bistro, aptly named" Le Poisson Bistro". A valet opened the passenger door, while another opened the drivers. He slid out, not being used to this type of service. He smiled, thinking that he liked it.

Immediately a tall, slender hostess greeted them, asking if they had a reservation. Carolyn said she did, gave her name, and were ushered over to a more remote ocean view table. She slipped the hostess a twenty, making it obvious so that Jon would notice. She needed privacy. Her sunglasses still hid her eyes and removed them only when the waitress appeared to take their drink orders and recite the daily lunch specials. Without pause, she ordered a dirty martini with blue cheese stuffed olives. Not having had a drink in two years and restless to cut to the chase, he told the waitress to make his the same.

Peeking above the oversized menu, she commented, "You probably haven't indulged in any type of gourmet meal that you had grown accustomed to in years," she hinted. "Do feel free to indulge in any entrée. Whatever you might have a craving for. Remember this is a business expense and it *is* my treat."

Before he could reach a decision, the waitress appeared with their cocktails. Lifting her glass, Jon followed suit as the glasses gently collided in a toast he assumed she would make. She did.

"To both you're newly found freedom as well as, at least hopefully, a fun and profitable working relationship. Cheers!"

"Cheers!" Jon echoed taking the martini to his lips and savoring the experience he had been deprived of for two years. As the vodka flowed, it brought a smile to his lips, accompanied by the good memories he had remembered while under the influence. He had tended to drink in excess, which was the source of his major fuck up and subsequent incarceration. Testing his willpower was proving to be a worthless challenge and he had only been released several hours ago. "WTF", he thought to himself.

The waitress, Cate, returned with another round of drinks. She placed them down and asked if they had decided.

"I'll have the Cobb salad and an appetizer of the stone crab claws please, Carolyn assuredly stated.

Jon hesitated briefly. He looked up at Cate, dictating, "If you please, I shall have a dozen of the Eastern oysters please, and if it's possible, the vegetables rather than scalloped potatoes, please," he politely requested.

After the second drink and prior to the arrival of the appetizers, Carolyn saw her opening. She began her well planned pitch.

"I would first like to apologize for all the secrecy and drama I probably left you with at our initial meeting, because I assumed that there were listening devices planted all over the visiting area. I really couldn't talk and I just wanted to meet you in person."

"No apology needed", he began. "I must admit you do have my interest, but in what, well, I don't even know."

"I totally understand,' she countered.

Just then Cate appeared and placed the appetizers down. Her eyes met Carolyn's, her slight nod indicating to bring another round. Prying a man with alcohol was not even a challenge.

She stared at him, breaking a crab and began, but not before it slid between her pouty lips. He stared.

"I was hired by a company who specializes in investments, I.P.O's and buying established business. Who I work for and what I am looking for are not really important to you. Nor am I at liberty to disclose."

He held her gaze as she continued, silently savoring the salty oyster which he was thoroughly enjoying. She did not want to get him too buzzed so as not to understand her offer, but rather just enough so he would feel worthless enough and accept her proposal. She continued.

"My client believes that PacLantic Cruise Lines is a viable company, but not in its current state. The owner is an egotistical maniac who craves too much attention and lacks the foresight to compete with the big three. I believe he would not sell, based on his history, but that is unimportant to you as well. Are you with me Jon?"

Jon was paying attention, his mind beginning to form a picture as to where she was going with this proposal. His involvement and place in the scheme of things, he was still yet unable to piece together. He nodded to acknowledge he was following.

Her eyes narrowed and the soft look on her face now hardened.

"Before I continue, I want your assurance that what I am about to say to you will go no further than this table," she began, her voice lowering and the words becoming more emphatic.

"I understand," he said, staring right back at her. The alcohol now fueled his courage rather than compromising it.

"I will now make it crystal clear why you are sitting here. PacLantic could have just as easily come to your aid after the disaster you were involved in. Instead they decided to put the blame squarely upon you, making you the sacrificial lamb, as the proceeded into damage control mode. Yes you were guilty, but after all the years of service that you gave the company, it is a sad fact that their appreciation was never expressed. How did that make you feel?" she said in a more subdued manner.

He had spent the last two years asking that question. Yes, he was bitter and she had struck a nerve. She knew she had. As his pale Slavic skin tone began to redden a bit, and a scowl of anger grew from his face, she knew. She continued.

"My client wants to give you the satisfaction of, how can I say it, showing your appreciation and giving them back the pain that they put you through during the whole fiasco."

He now had his arms folded in front of him, leaning in closer and his attention fully absorbed by her words.

"Using your familiarity of the ship, your disfavor for your past employer and our resources," she stopped and took a sip of her martini for effect. "We want to hire you to take passage on each of their vessels and commit a series of acts that will cost the company both bad press and enough damage to tie them up in port. We do not want any harm to come to any of the passengers but rather to Phelps and his shareholders. When the public finally abandons their interest in his cruises, my people will swoop down and buy him out for pennies on the dollar."

She raised the glass, took the last sip and continued in the same scheming manner.

"If you accept our offer, you be handsomely compensated. You will be given a new face and a new identity. But more importantly, you will have settled a score and at the same time, be given new purpose. We are asking a big sacrifice on your part and unlike your former employer, we will give you all the tools and resources that you need to be successful."

She leaned back in her chair, just as a teacher might do after giving a passionate lecture and waiting for comments. But he did not move. A torrent of information had just been infused into his thought patterns. His mind began to process the emotional and moral implications if he accepted her offer. He shook his head abruptly, as if it might scramble the puzzle pieces of this offer into one cognitive thought, one immediate answer. But it did not.

She leaned forward as if she was about to speak, to try and close the deal or overcome any objections. As if he knew what she was about to do or say, he uncrossed his arms and waved her off, not wanting her to speak.

Then Jon leaned forward, his voice just above a whisper, and he spoke.

'Whoa, let's hold on for a minute please. I have just spent two, pardon my French, fucking years deprived of my freedoms, not knowing what I am going to do with my life, and boom, you hit me with what feels like an atomic bomb. You Americans are so subtle!"

He sighed, his outstretched hand still waving side to side, indicating that he wasn't quite finished yet.

"I must have time to consider my options here, and besides, we have not talked about any concrete amount of money that you will compensate me with. That is an important factor for me to consider."

This statement alone told her that she was on the right track and he was seriously considering her proposal. She feigned interest and concern as she gazed back at him.

"I will need a few days to think this over, as you may suspect. If I do accept this offer, I will devote all of myself to accomplishing what you ask. If I do not accept, I will abide by your request for privacy. This meeting never happened. Is that acceptable?" Jon asked.

She was a bit surprised at first in regard to the logic that he had quickly mustered in lieu of all of those drinks. And at the same time, was impressed with both the interest and clarity in which he expressed his concerns. Yuppers, she had made the right choice, said the right things, and in the long run, knew he would be a more than willing participant. She said she would give him forty eight hours to make a decision. If he agreed they would meet again and if not, go their separate ways.

Her flight touched down at Logan shortly before eight. She had texted George that her 'interview' had been completed, gone as well as hoped for, and would fill him in on the details on the way home. She mistrusted cell phones, as we all should.

Her Southwest flight touched down several minutes before the scheduled ETA. After deplaning, she extended the handle on her 20" rollaway luggage bag and briskly walked toward the exit, highlighted with large TSA arrows. George had pulled his car into the cell phone waiting area and waited for her text. Upon receiving it, he drove the half mile to the arriving passenger area just as she exited the building. She still wore her disguise, and he momentarily fantasized about picking up a stranger at the airport, taking her home and then having his way with her. Ah yes, the mind is a terrible thing to waste.

Carolyn, who was really Angel, removed the wig, wanting to return to her real life persona. George was slightly disappointed, his fantasy now deflated.

"Damn I liked that look. It kind of conjured up a nice airport fantasy thing, lonely flight attendant, ya know," he said with a distant look.

She scowled, not even wanting to go there.

"In fewer words than how I spent my summer vacation, how did it go?" he asked. His true anxiety was well veiled.

"I gave him the forty eight hour deadline as per our discussion, so I will have a definitive answer by then. I also gave him the cash, which was just the right amount I believe. He has nowhere to stay, so some of his windfall will cover a hotel. If he wants to add to that the style he was used to, it will eat up a fair amount. If he wants to dine as he had in the past, that will eat up another couple of hundreds. And if wants to find a woman, well then bingo, two days later he has the mere pocket change given to him for making license plates or whatever they do these days in prison."

George smiled, liking the woman's perspective on a drunken sailor attitude one might have after experiencing a loss of freedom. His six figure income can only immediately replaced by what we are offering him. And hopefully he picked up some nasty ideas while doing his time, and is now corruptible."

"We shall see what we shall" sea", he mused, removing his hands from the steering wheel and emphasizing the work sea with air quotations. "Get it?" It was a typical poor attempt at lame humor in Angle's mind.

"I think that was clever," he chortled, until a poke in his ribs from Angel made it clear that she wasn't amused.

"And by the way I am famished. The Ritz Bits didn't quite cut it on the flight home, and wouldn't ya know, they ran out of Pringles again," she stated with faux seriousness.

"How does a quick detour to Chinatown sound. We can grab some soup, dumplings and some Peking Duck?"

"That sounds divine," she sighed and George proceeded toward the off ramp to his favorite destination as Angel called ahead. They would get home, feast on the favorite and wait until Captain Jon made his choice. They would remain positive and least of all, not even mention or acknowledge that his brothers cruise line had now doubled in size.

CHAPTER 8

Julian Gando sat at the bar, crowded with suburban diners who had come to satisfy their carnivorous instincts. He loved the Capital Grille. His left hand was wrapped around his seven and seven, the drink that had been popular back in the 70's but still held its popularity with the *Goodfellas* and *Godfather* crowd. His right hand plucked a well done potato chip from the wire mesh basket that occupied every four foot space along the dozen or so seat bar. As he crunched down on the salty thin chip, he peered toward the entrance while he awaited the arrival of his dinner guest. The revolving door turned and he gave a slight wave as Paul Gasparo entered the building.

Gasparo stood slightly less than six feet tall, was in late forties and had a wiry yet muscular build. His face was etched with lines that reflected experience rather than middle age he was now numerically categorized by. He acknowledged Gando with a short nod and then proceeded over towards the hostess station. Watching from the bar and as the hostess grabbed two menu's, Gando threw a twenty dollar bill down on the bar and joined his guest as they were shown to a table. The table was located at the rear of the dining area. The seating space consisted of a high back leather semi-circle that was situated in a more dimly lit area of the expansive room. The men slid into the outer perimeter of the booth, and were handed menu's as the server introduced herself. Gando, apologizing for his terse interruption, asked that she bring him another seven and seven, along with an order of fried calamari with hot cherry peppers. Gasparo ordered an Amstel Light and a shrimp cocktail. Hell, the bill was on the government and he worked hard enough to rightfully earn a treat from the taxpayers.

"Glad I don't pay any taxes or I might send a complaint to your superiors," he said jokingly as he extended his hand to greet Gasparo.

Gasparo extended and shook his hand with a macho tight grip, then grinned, finding Gando's comment slightly amusing. The man across the table was his witness and Paul his new 'handler' as they were called. Paul was assigned to Gando after the recent attempt on his life. He had been assigned to keep track of Gando and watch his back. After the most recent attack where he had been shot and almost killed, Gando rightfully questioned not only the capability of the Witness Protection Program, but also of those who were responsible for looking after him. He knew they would not be around 24/7, but this had been the second attempt on his life, the other occurring in Philadelphia, when he had decided to turn states evidence.

The food and drinks quickly arrived. Gando took another swig of his cocktail before plunging his fork into the tender calamari and then gently bathing it in the accompanying marinara. Another sip of whiskey and then he said to Gasparo.

"Okay Paul, what's on your mind?"

Gasparo knew that Gando would not be happy about the upcoming conversation. He began.

"So the agency thinks it better if we move you out of Florida and to another location."

He watched Gando but received no verbal or facial response. All that appeared was just the plastered smile of one who was enjoying his food, while he digested the words as a chess player might do his next dozen or so moves. He continued, taking out a small notebook in order to refer to some previous thoughts he had jotted down.

"We prefer not to keep you on the eastern seaboard where you might be more easily accessible", he said pausing. He then added "and to remove the target that you seem to wear so prominently. We were thinking maybe outside of Chicago, maybe Seattle, or possibly Kansas City.

The program director thinks that you might blend in a bit better in those localities."

Still there was no response. He had expected their dinner meeting to go something like this. He knew that a contract was still in force, and the feds wanted to protect him from both any hired assassins, as well as from himself. They knew all too well of whom he really was and also what he was capable of doing if they were to lose track of him.

"Talk to me Julian. Where will you feel both safe and comfortable? Work with me here," Gasparo asked in a slightly annoyed fashion.

No response came from Gando until the last of the peppers had been consumed and the remaining marinara sauce sopped up from the plate. He removed the napkin from his lap, brushed it lightly over his mouth and returned it to his lap. He leaned in a bit closer and stared at Gasparo.

Mr. Gasparo," Gando began, the fact that he used the mister rather than Paul was an indication of where this conversation might be headed. "I am not a cat with nine lives, had having used up two already, and mind you, both of which since I went straight," he emphasized, "and both were while I was under the watchful eye of this so called witness protection. And now you expect me to *follow* procedures and go back in the program. Really Paul?"

Gando's displeasure with the program as well as his lack of safety was of major concern and he expressed his concerns as such. He had an agenda, and remaining with the Feds was clearly not in his plans. He rambled on, his intensity taking on a tone somewhere between disdain and anger.

"To put it bluntly, I am done with you guys. I would rather take my chances and watch my own ass. Tell your bosses that Gando is done. He is done with being watched and done with any illegal activities. I am going to live my life out the way I want to and *where* I choose. Seattle? Kansas City? Really now, he paused briefly and then added, "Can I make this any clearer?" Talking in the third person was a nice touch he thought, a little more dramatic.

Gasparo played back in his mind, all the scenarios he thought that Gando would object to. This had been one of them. He organized his thoughts and pressed on, much like a boiler room salesperson reading off of a script. He continued.

"You Julian are our responsibility. Part of the arrangement was that you remain in witness protection until the program, and only the program, decide that your safety is no longer in jeopardy. It is obvious that you are still in harm's way."

Their conversation was temporarily interrupted two separate servers appeared. One placed the Kona Delmonico in front of Gasparo, and the Porcini rubbed Delmonico found its spot in front of Gando. A side of creamed spinach also found its niche in the center between the two. When the servers asked if there was anything else needed, Gando held up two fingers and nodded, indicating another round of drinks for the pair. She then disappeared into the crowd of diners.

"Salute", declared Gando, a not so subtle hint that he wanted to change subjects. It didn't matter as Gasparo was far from done.

"Listen", Gasparo began, his tone combining a mixture of reason and logic. Their conversations were becoming a volley of inflections. "We have learned from our mistakes and plan to add manpower in order to increase your safe keeping. Shit, you have given us more information and factual references so that we can take these assholes down. Just hang in there with us and I swear to you that as soon as your safety is in check, you can, as they say, feel free to roam the country."

Gando slid his serrated knife over the tender cut of beef, stabbed a little creamed spinach on the crowded tines, and savored the taste. He smiled, tilting his head in a mock confused fashion and spoke.

"Listen Paul, you're a smart guy and more than competent as well. The problem is, Gando paused for effect, "the bottom line is simply I want out. Yeah, it's the fact that I feel unprotected, and yeah I know we have an agreement. Simply putting it, you guys have not lived up to your end and now I will do the same. Didn't Sammy the Bull opt out of the program before his time, and he killed a lot more people than I had, *and* not all were the bad guys. Crello and I just made a deal, and we have sold the restaurant. I am sorry Paul, but it's time for me to get out of Dodge."

News of selling the restaurant was unexpected, yet realistic in regard to the recent attempt on Gando's life. Gasparo briefly put himself in Gando's position and realized he might have made the same valuation.

The two men cut their steaks, sipped their drinks and pretty much remained silent. It was like a chess match, as each tried to think how the other would react if Gando's statement transformed into reality. Gasparo knew the danger of losing sight of Gando. The fact was he was a killer, had no ties to anyone and was experienced at flying under the radar. And Gando knew that if he remained with the program his freedom would be limited, he would be constantly watched and he would not be able to peruse his plans for the future.

Gando placed his knife and fork down on his cleaned plate and caught a glimpse of Gasparo looking up. He began to speak, his voice soft spoken and non-committal.

"Let's do this. It's Wednesday night. Give me a sleep on the pros and cons of both my concerns and options. And of course those of yours. We will have dinner on Saturday and we will come to an agreement. Maybe you can get your people to loosen some of the restrictions a bit, as well as their hard ass approach. They will also need to be more cognizant of my and Jake's safety, seeing as they have screwed up twice and that is unacceptable."

Gasparo interrupted, holding his hand up as if directing traffic. He leaned in closer.

"And it will be necessary for you as well to meet us in the middle. We will need updates several times a week on any suspicious activities you might notice as well as your current associates. I agree. We both have been a bit lax in holding up each of our ends of the bargain. But don't misconstrue this as a sign of weakness or overcompensation. We still must strongly insist that you stay with the program at least for the time frame as agreed upon in your plea bargain. Am I clear on this?"

Gando leaned back and nodded, suggesting they grab a shot of brandy before concluding their meal. They did. Both arose from the table, Gasparo picked up the tab and they walked toward the exit. Both had as much trust and belief in the other as they had before dinner, which was less than minimal at best.

● ● ●

After Gando had the valet deliver his car, he then slid in the front seat and pulled out the cell phone from the middle console. He never brought his phone with him during meeting with Gasparo. His privacy was one of those things he would not share with the program and he knew how nosy Gasparo could be. He punched the Bluetooth connection and spoke.

"Call J.C.," he said, with a clear and distinct voice. The device was sensitive and incorrect calls were more common than correct ones.

After two rings, Jake Crello picked up, anxious to see how the meeting with Gasparo had gone.

"How was dinner, Julian? Hope you ran up the taxpayers bill," Crello asked, more concerned with the meeting than his gastronomic experience.

Gando smiled to himself, always knowing what Crello had *really* meant. Crello could be ha-ha funny, as Joe Pesci famously questioned Ray Liotta in one of the more poignant scenes in *Goodfellas.*

"It was great and pretty much predictable as usual. I only wish that our conversation had matched the food.

"How so, Crello countered.

"Gasparo is not too enthusiastic about loosening his and the feds reigns on me just yet. And his face contorted a bit when I mentioned selling the restaurant, but I mentioned it was your decision and I fought you on it."

"Nice. But did it fly?"

"Yeah right, like a bird with a broken wing."

"Go on," said Crello.

"The long and the short of it is this. They want me to move to a less conspicuous city. I won't even tell you where, nor would I send my worst enemy there. But we had planned for this outcome, so we are still in the stronger position. How did things go on your end?' Gando asked.

"I spoke to my cousin Mike and he had some good info for us," Crello replied with an upbeat tone.

Mike "the Spike" Peretti was not really his true cousin, but brothers friends. In the large extended picture, he was pseudo distantly related, but not really. He worked for a small crew out of Jersey City but was also familiar with a group of Goodfella types in the tri state area. Connections run deep. As with all connected types, Mike had gotten his moniker from interesting yet unflattering circumstances.

He stood about 5'8", slightly below average for today's male and not a truly desirable height by female standards. He sported the Michael Douglass look from Wall Street, but lacked the good looks. His nose was a little too large for his face and his mouth a bit crooked when he tried to smile and look sexy. The name "Spike" was attached to his name, not because of the rhyme, but rather that his method for hooking up with women. He had a reputation of spiking potential conquests drinks with roofies, making it a slam dunk in getting women to "accompany" him home. True, they performed only marginally better than a corpse, but his over active hormones didn't really care. Not what one might call a true Romeo! Still, he was reliable and more than able when it came to the respect and admiration that he admonished on Crello.

Gando paused and told Crello he would arrive shortly and discuss the matter in person. Although his car was swept for bugs on a regular basis, he did not want his grand plan to be overheard by the Feds just in case.

Gando arrived at Crello's condo shortly after their phone conversation had ended. He had noticed no tails or cars that followed too closely. Experience had made him a cautious man whose street smarts had been programmed into his psyche since he had started his criminal activities.

Crello's second floor porch light flickered twice, as he saw Gando pull up into the parking area. Gando killed the engine and hopped out of the car, giving a quick wave to his buddy. He climbed the stairs, entered and the door was locked behind him. Crello had a 7 & 7 waiting in his hand and Gando smiled and accepted. Gando made his way to the recliner, knowing that his best friend wanted to hear about the full meeting and he as well about the plans they were formulating. Under Gando's advisement, Crello had the condo swept for listening devices as well on a consistent basis.

"My gut instincts tell me that he knows I am going to leave the state soon and vanish, Gando began. "I could see it in his facial features, his body movement. He might have feigned concern and interest, but I could see the wheels spinning. We plan to meet on this upcoming Saturday so we can solidify a secretive exit from this place, but I just know that he doesn't trust me."

"Your record speaks for itself," commented Crello, raising his glass and toasting in respect to his best friends propensity for flying under the radar.

The two sat for a bit, sipping their drinks. Crello grabbed Gando's glass, refilled it and set it back down on the coaster for him. He leaned in while speaking in a soft voice out of habit, always suspicious, as if someone were listening. Taking out a royal blue folder, he began to relay the plan to Gando in more details and with a firm timeline. If all went as planned, Gando would be up in North Jersey within twenty four hours.

CHAPTER 9

Wednesday night, and it was crunch time for Captain Jon. The forty eight hour deadline weighed heavily on his moral, financial and ethical threads that pieced him together. It was right vs. wrong. It was making an income vs. where to get his next meal. It was doing something illegal vs. legal. But tipping the balance was the facet of revenge. The right side of the page was blank in that area.

The list filled a page which he had the old two columns, which we have all used to weigh out what we perceived as important decisions. The left column had a plus sign, which had been written with many strong lines over it, while the right side had a negative sign enveloped by parentheses. That might have had a subliminal instinct in regards to which side of the paper would contain the longer list.

He left the small table in his Extended Suites 'work area' and readied for dinner. He would be meeting the woman he knew as 'Angel", aka Carolyn West, at the Capitol Grille for his life changing decision. By the time he showered, shaved and the cab arrived, he was still ambiguous as to what the final outcome might be. And if any of you followers still believe that there is no such thing as a coincidence, he would be occupying a table less than forty feet away from Gando and Gasparo. Holy shit, Batman!

As his cab arrived at Boca Center, a huge upscale mall not unlike any other one in any major city, he paid the driver and got out. He noticed that she was waiting near the parking valet stand, smoking a cigarette and sporting an accordion file tucked under her free arm. It wasn't the latter two attributes that garnered his attention, but rather the sequin jacket, leather mini skirt and low cut, almost opaque blouse that won out. If it was meant to influence his upcoming decisions, it categorically had. A slight bulge had now emanated from his male agenda.

As he approached, he shook his hand from side to side in what she viewed as a nerdy gesture. Her eyes would have rolled back in her head had it not been for the mood she was trying to create. She ignored his outstretched hand and planted an ever so light kiss on his cheek, in the most sensual yet non sensual way she could. One of those just enough- not too much- make you feel confident, type of kisses. The bulge she noticed confirmed her formula of balance yielded the desired results.

A doorman with a deep Florida tan and surfer type features pulled open the heavy doors with the same smile he had worn several hundred times an evening. Angel slipped him a ten, making sure that Vandergriff knew that she was flush with enough cash to display her overt generosity. She gave her name at the hostess station and was escorted by a' Stepford' type looking waitress, a generic brunette who walked like she had graduated from some schools that trained high end chain restaurant employees. Or even worse, like a Rod Serling character from *The Twilight Zone.*

Jon swung around the table to pull out the chair for Angel, doing everything except handing her a menu. She thanked him as the waitress queried as to what cocktail they might before choosing their fare. Without any hesitation, Angel placed her order, requesting a dirty martini with a couple of blue cheese stuffed olives. What the hell, thought Vandergriff and asked the waitress to bring him the same. This pleased Angel. What was that saying? Imitation is the best form of flattery?

She began with some small talk, preferring to wait for the alcohol to kick in, just in case she needed help from the distillers of Kettle One. The drinks appeared shortly thereafter and were placed correctly in front of the pair

They clinked glasses and his eyes glazed over her, and then began to make a bee line slowly descending down to her cleavage. And although she was well aware of his actions, she ignored it and threw her chest out a tad more for effect. He was so easily led on and as malleable as Play Dough.

"To a long and profitable relationship in as many ways possible", she declared, not leaving any room for objections. A classic Dale Carnegie sales technique.

"Cheers", Vandergriff replied, nodding in agreement. Was it the list or the monetary benefits or the revenge factor? Maybe even the cleavage…not. Whatever his motive, she was happy that she hadn't had to go through all the objections he might have harbored. All she would have to do is go through a brief overview of her expectations of him and the first task that he would be assigned to in the grand scheme hatched by the minds of George and Angel.

Their glasses were drained and if on cue, their original server had appeared placing a second drink in front of each, as well as the daily specials.

Angel ordered first, noticing that Vandergriff was still intently studying the menu. It was a far cry from the baloney sandwich or over salted dry egg noodles, which had been his main staple for the past two years. His craving for high end gastronomic delights of which he had grown accustomed to during his years on the high seas, were sorely missed. With little hesitation, Angel ordered.

"I would like to start with the Lobster and Crab Cakes and for the entrée, the Filet Mignon and an order of the truffle French fries please," she said softly.

Nudging Jon's hand, with two fingers, she distracted his intensive perusal of the menu, and asked if he would like to share a wedge. He looked up almost startled from the menu, as if it were a novel. She repeated her request and he obliged with a slight nod.

"And for you sir," came the waitress' semi upbeat request.

"I shall have a shrimp cocktail to begin and the surf and turf for the main course young lady," he said, smiling and handing the large menu back to her.

With the orders and pleasantries out of the way, Angel got down to business. It was almost if her pleasant and teasing manner disappeared as would a leopard in a Penn and Teller stage production. She began.

"You know the basics of what your job will entail, but the specifics will be doled out to you as we actually get closer to its origin."

Vandergriff held up his hand, motioning for her to slow down. He too had thought this out, and did not want to be steamrolled into anything too quickly.

"You will have to a bit more specific than that. I must know more than bits and pieces of what you expect from me, if I am going to sign on. As a captain, I was used to planning routes and alternative measures for different scenarios. Because what I am doing will be risky, I will need to have back up plans in place, rather than to haphazardly improvise." He leaned back and folding his arms, waited for her reaction and reply.

"That is a fair request," she shot back. "You will be taking risks and I understand your concerns, but at the same time our rule of thumb is to accomplish a means to an end. If that means we may need some improvising, then so be it. But they all must be approved by both me and my client."

With a serious and satisfied look, he nodded.

During the course of the meal, they spoke in low voices, not wanting to advertise their malevolent blueprints. She was surprised to see little objection when she mentioned the demand that he undergo plastic surgery to change his appearance. After all, he had been broadcast worldwide after the disaster. The result was Vandergriff had racked up closer to fifteen hours of fame, rather than the standard fifteen minutes. He effortlessly relented to that request. After all, he would feel safer, and his agreement to this scheme was due in a large part about starting over.

'Just make sure they keep my good looks intact," he said, not in a cocky manner but more of a boyish one.

"Uri Savitt is one of the best surgeons around. He is well used by the Israeli government to disguise members of the Massad if they have been exposed, captured, or have become too well known in the espionage arena. My employers are well connected, and you must trust us that we have your well-being at the top of our priority list."

He believed her, at least for the present time. Before leaving the restaurant, she removed the doctor's card from her small purse with her fingertips touching only the corners. No prints left would mean the absence of any trace evidence. Thank God for CSI and NCIS. These shows teach everyone how to be a criminal, she thought.

As they left the restaurant, she had a cigarette while waiting for the valet. She would take him home figuratively, not literally as he may have been expecting. On the ride back it was agreed that he would see Dr. Savitt for the surgery on Monday. She reassured him that he would have some creative input regarding the design of his new face through a computer generated graphic program. That put him a bit more at ease. And to discourage any advances or an aggressive male hormone attack, she mentioned that after he was dropped off, she needed to get back to her client with the details of how their meeting went. Disappointment was reflected in his look, but he mentioned he understood. Business before pleasure. She was given a friendly kiss on the cheek and promised a call to inform her when and where the surgery would be scheduled. The pieces of the puzzle couldn't have been falling into place any easier.

● ● ●

"So did he *really* buy the bit about you needing a few more days to make your decision?' Crello asked with incredulity.

Gando smiled. He was ready to begin the long night

Tonight was the night that the plan to throw some red herrings into the mix and get Gando on a plane back up to New Jersey finally had arrived. It was complicated but they had so many angles covered that they were almost overly confident.

Although Crello was several inches shorter than Gando, he put on his newly acquired elevator shoes that added 2.75 inches to his height, making him the exact size. His outfit had some stuffing under the shirt as Gando was a bit wider in girth than he was. He slipped on the trousers that both had purchased together, adding to the likeness. Since it was nearing midnight, the Miami Marlins hat that he commonly donned, would have the brim slanted down in order to hide the features of his face.

Gando stood out by the back screen door which opened to the cookie cutter sun rooms which was a staple at almost every residential complex in Southern Florida. He took an aluminum baseball bat to the black door handle, and with one powerful blow, dislodged the lock from the flimsy aluminum door. He had wrapped in a cloth to muffle the noise, which worked minimally at best. He then returned to the patio and slammed the bat into the side of the reclining lounge chair one time. Pulling a syringe from his pocket, he filled his mouth with the full 12cc contents. The contents were a syringe of blood he had drawn from a vein in his arm. Taking a position on the chair, he swung his head around as he opened his mouth, the blood flying in every which way. He repeated this process, making sure to spit some onto the dented part of the bat, adding an even a greater brushstroke of realism to crime scene. He then tilted the round table down so it leaned on its side. He did not want to overdue his staged crime scene. He liked it. It was a blood spatter masterpiece.

"Yo Jake, check it out," Gando called in a low voice. Crello stood at the patio entrance, not wanting to contaminate the scene or get any blood evidence on his person or clothing.

"Nice work Picasso. Ya did a helluva nice job. But all the red is so boring. What? No brain matter or chips of bone fragments in your canvass just to give it a more realistic kinda of feel?

Gando laughed.

They both stood there for a log moment, admiring the blood spatter patterns as if it were a Rorschach diagram.

"It is pretty damn realistic. All we have to do now is sit back and wait for the feds to find it," Gando added, as he dropped his empty high ball glass on the floor for a little added realism. It was like he was just resting on the patio when one or several intruders disturbed his peaceful reclusiveness.

Phase two incorporated the fact that they had kept a watchful eye through the upstairs windows, seeing if a pattern existed during the spotty surveillance of the witness protection agents. They had been doing this since they had purchased the condo. Although there was no time stamp on their random surveillance, the pair knew that they usually spotted within an hour give or take after midnight, and an hour or so before sunrise. It was shortly before midnight and the agents had still not appeared.

The plan was running in a flawless motion. Crello grabbed his small airplane carry on and headed out the front door. Gando would watch until Crello got in the car, signaling him with the flick of an upstairs light when the predictable black Ford Escape took its 5 mile per hour jaunt toward their condo.

Several minutes later, the light flickered and Crello pulled away from the curb. As he sped up, so did the tail car. Crello had made a reservation to fly from Miami to Chicago under Gando's WPP alias. He knew it would show up on the Feds radar and they would be waiting at the airport and by the terminals. To complicate things more, he had made a similar reservation to fly from West Palm to New Orleans on a chartered jet, also using the same name. This action would double the number of agent tied up in the stakeout and the tail. Brilliant plan again. He would alternate his routes in order to obscure his followers as to which airport was his final destination.

Now Gando began his journey. The rented car that he had reserved had been picked up and deposited in a strip mall ¼ mile from his residence. It was under the name Chris Walters, pretty generic and through Crello's connections. He had obtained a passport, Florida driver's license and two prepaid credit cards with his moniker.

As he walked to the car in the light mist and coastal winds, he grew a bit anxious about his upcoming plans. Other than revenge to be administered to his hunters, a visit to Rutts Hut in Clifton New Jersey was a must. Rutts is a New Jersey institution, opened as a roadside stand in

1928. Their signature dish, the 'Ripper', is a deep fried hot dog that splits open when they emerge from the deep fry basket. It was a taste that brought back his youth and fond memories of growing up in the Garden State. It came as no surprise to him, that while watching a PBS special on hot dogs, Rutts was listed in the book *1,000 Places to see in the U.S and Canada before you die.* He would see it again, but he was damn sure it was not his time to die.

He arrived at the car and threw his carry on in the seat passenger seat. It would be about a half hour trip to the airport and he would return the car to a remote parking area before taking a shuttle bus to the U.S. Airline terminal and the awaiting red eye to Newark. Peretti would be waiting at the airport to pick him up and deliver him to one of the many chain hotels that surrounded the large airport. Gando was back in business. And would be back to his old habits that made him who he was.

During the roughly two and a half hour plane ride, Gando replayed some of his earlier memories of his New Jersey youth. He remembered working out Standardbred horses at nearby horse farms and then sneaking out to Roosevelt or Yonkers raceways to watch and bet on some of those that he had driven in the old wooden sulkies. His youthful school trips to Palisades Amusement Park and the 'older teen hotties' in their scantily clad bikini tops. His two years spent at a small college in upstate New Jersey. But more vivid were the memories of how he had hooked up with the 'wrong crowd' and eventually ended up in his present vocation. It had started with stealing products from tractor trailer trucks that parked in the large rest areas on the New Jersey Turnpike, eventually leading to small town numbers and protection schemes in towns outside of where he had resided. He could have flown from Florida to Australia several times before he would be able to recall all of the questionable and illegal activities that he had participated in.

The plane finally touched down and his thoughts returned to the business at hand. He needed to meet Peretti at the terminal pickup gate and get some rest. Upon exiting the plane, he grabbed his suitcase at the luggage carousel and stepped out into the New Jersey aroma that he remembered. He drew in a large intake of the morning air, a mixture of jet fuel and neighboring chemical processing factories. He loved the rough smell of the pollution and light smog, not for the olfactory pleasure, but rather more as a reminder of his earlier days. Most of us would probably preferred the acidic odor of fresh coffee beans as Juan Valdez might have in one of his large coffee plantations way south of Newark, New Jersey. But not Gando. The air and the familiar ground he stood upon invigorated him.

PART THREE

CHAPTER 10

Stephen Davis sat at his large desk strewn with personal photos, open case folders and a beat up laptop that had seen better days. His landline phone was cradled between his ear and chin, keeping one hand free to scribble down notes on his legal pad that were being dictated to him by the frantic caller.

"And when I knocked on his door it was open. It's never open. Mr. Gando is such a nice man. But the odor, it was something I had never smelled before. And none of the neighbors say that they haven't seen him or his wife for days, and."

"Slow down ma'am. Just speak more calmly and give me your address, so that I can send some of my people over. And please, stay out of the apartment until someone of authority arrives. Will you do that for me please?" Davis' voice seemed to have a calming effect as she gave him all of the pertinent information. The call would normally be handled by the homicide division, but because the address was in South Philly and the name of Gando had come up, he grabbed the hysterical women on the other end.

He looked up as the rest of the team was waiting for the lowdown.

"Dubbin and Kelly. I want you two to run down to South Philly and check out what might be a dead body, or a dead animal," he added

As they approached, he tore off the top page of the pad and handed it to them. Unlike a doctor writing out a prescription, he had meticulous handwriting and took copious notes. Dubbin grabbed the paper, threw on her OCTF windbreaker and headed out of the office with Kelly in tow.

When they arrived on Snyder Avenue, a small crowd had gathered. One patrol car had just arrived and had dutifully begun to take names and notes in regard to any possible witnesses. Miss Galliano, the woman who had called it in, assumed the approaching male and female, who wore badges draped over their waistband, were the detectives in charge. The air through the slightly opened door carried the odor of death. It is said it is an odor that is said to be unlike any other, one that is never forgotten. Dubbin removed the recently mounted crime scene tape, had the porch area cordoned off and then gently began to push the door open. Neither detective had drawn their service weapons. They knew that if any foul play were involved, the doer would have been long, long gone by this time.

Recognizing the rancid and familiar odor, they entered slowly, holding a cloth against their noses and breathing through their mouths. Upon arriving in the living room, Kelly nudged Dubbin and pointed to a pair of legs that protruded from behind a small alcove. As they approached their eyes almost simultaneously were drawn to the man's face. Or at least what was left of it. Just as mob legends and Hollywood portrays, the face was such that even his mother wouldn't recognize him. It was clearly a signature mob hit.

As if scripted for television, the CSI team entered, carrying the forensic bags that have become as familiar as the ba-bum from Law and Order. One technician began taking pictures of the scene as the other rolled out some tape to obtain a working set of fingerprints. Kelly turned to enter what he believed was the master bedroom.

"Yo, we have another one in here. It's a woman and it looks like she took several shots to the torso. Call the boss and fill him in. I'm gonna check the rest of the rooms."

Dubbin called Davis and before she uttered a sound, he picked up she heard him ask, "Is it Julian or no?"

"I can't really answer that yet. His face is totally blown off but he doesn't have the same build. And I thought the feds still had him under their wings in Florida."

'Those guys in the witness protection are outright idiots. They couldn't even count the vehicles in a one car funeral."

A bit of an old cliché but she got his point.

"CSI is taking prints and we should know in a few hours. Kelly says there is also a woman here but they are printing her too. Looks like a contract hit, ya know, the guys face is missing."

Davis could only surmise that some rogue mobsters wanna-be's had been out hunting for the bounty on Gando's head and had no clue that he had been whisked out of Philadelphia. Interestingly enough, it was only a mile or so from where Gando and his girlfriend, Bryant Merril had once resided.

"I just placed a call to Gasparo in Florida, but it went to his voice mail. He can tell us if Gando is still down there or not. Let the techs do their thing, check out the scene and come back in. We can sort things out when we get the prints back and the call from Florida".

"Okay chief," Dubbin responded, knowing he preferred that salutation rather than boss.

Because Gando was in witness protection and had committed a majority of his crimes in the Delaware Valley, his prints had almost been memorized by the fingerprint team. When the CSI team returned with the set of prints from his ten digits, Harley Rushmore, the resident expert immediately knew that they were not a match. Davis had been next to him when he got the news.

The prints belonged to one Jules Gando, a postal worker, which made his prints accessible in the system. All government workers were printed and their prints stored in AFIS. The woman was confirmed to be his wife, Jennifer. Now Davis was left with a murder that was the wrong victim, but it also left him on the hunt for a greedy member of organized crime running around his city.

"Thanks, Harley. I owe ya one for speeding this up for me."

Harley nodded and Davis turned to return back upstairs to his office. He knew the case would make headlines, stirring up memories of the homicidal statistics that were almost, yet not quite as common, as a

Philly cheesesteak. It would be his job to solve the case and put the city at ease. Seventeen days had passed with no reported homicides, tying the record from decades earlier. One more day and they would have passed it.

● ● ●

The next morning, Gando awoke from his king sized bed at the Airport Hilton in Newark. Although well sound proofed, he had been a light sleeper, mostly due to his survival instincts, but the dim roar of jet engines speeding down the runway, had just enough bass to break his REM sleep.

He had arrived safely and incognito. Crello's plan was brilliant and worked like a charm. He had led the Feds on a wild goose chase between the two local airports, allowing Gando to get the last flight out to Newark the previous night. Peretti had waited at the Hilton just to make sure he arrived safely from the shuttle bus which dropped him and his carry-on off in front of the entrance. He felt safe, as the the flight was full and his new identity had got him through the TSA.

Gando checked out the bright numerals on the digital clock. It read 7:02 which was about the time he would normally stir from sleep. Peretti was due back at 8:00, with coffee and cannoli's. There were just some things that were indigenous to a certain locale. You wouldn't get a cheesesteak in Kansas, a crab cake in Montana, nor true cannoli in Florida.

Gando was ready to shower when a knock emanated from the door. Actually three light taps. The voice that followed announced that his morning papers were here and would be left at the foot of the door. He had requested the New York Times, The Newark Star Ledger, the Miami Herald, and the sorely missed Philadelphia Daily News. At one time, he had dominated the headlines with his damaging testimony against the remaining New York City mob bosses. "Gando Gabs" and "He Talks and Walks", were two of the more pulp type headlines. But Gando wasn't one for publicity and when he was caught, he was forced to deal with it. But after entering witness protection and getting some surgery done, he fell back into the anonymous lifestyle which he worked hard to achieve.

Gando arose and proceeded to head to the bathroom for his morning shower and shave. He turned the shower knob ¾ to the limit on the red marking and entered the sliding door. The warm water felt good, and in a philosophical way, he viewed it as cleansing him of his recent Floridian exile and preparing him for his next venture. The highly chlorinated New Jersey water felt familiar to him. Although not a religious man, his mind occasionally drifted to the more metaphysical reasons for his being. "Enough", he thought and directed his mind toward just enjoying the pulsating stream of water that soothed his jet lagged body.

Emerging from the shower, he slipped on his boxers, slacks and solid black shirt. As if staged, the door knocked and he headed toward it. The only two people that knew his whereabouts were Crello and Peretti. He slipped the 9mm Glock into his waistband just in case. But this was also due to the fact that he long ago had been wired to err on the side of caution and self-preservation.

"It's me, Peretti, Mr. Walters", the low voice came from the door, accent dripping of 'North Jerseyeese'.

Gando opened the door, took a quick glance down the hallway and invited Peretti in. Peretti headed toward the round table and deposited a cardboard tray containing four coffees and white box labeled *Calandra's Bakery.* The box brought a smile to Gando's face, recognizing the name from his childhood mixed with images of his father walking in with the box that hadn't changed in its fifty year history.

"How did you know to stop at my favorite bakery, Peretti?" Gando asked in true amazement.

"Gimme some credit Mr. G. I' was born and bred in Jersey, ya know." Any New Jersey native is given the option of using the "New". Using the word Jersey is more hip and acceptable.

Gando nodded, then gave Peretti a firm handshake and motioned him to sit at the table. He did, as Gando proceeded to open the pastries.

Before removing the biscotti, he savored the aroma from the box, again hitting him in the face with reminiscences of his youth.

The two made some small talk. Gando relaying the cat and mouse game that he and Crello played with the feds, before getting down to the business at hand.

"Yeah, my uncle Jake is a real character, ya know, Mr. G."

Gando took notice of the Mr. G which he didn't mind, but he hoped the "ya know" phrase would soon vanish as they began to talk and plan. The phrase sounded like Fargo meets Newark, minus the "don't". Forgetaboutit, he told himself.

Peretti cleared his throat as he pulled several ill folded sheets from the inside of his leather coat. Crello had given him a job to do and he was prepared to give Gando the findings of his 'expedition'. He began.

"There ain't a lot of patterns that this guy seems to follow, ya know, he is pretty damn careful".

Peretti and his small group of five had been tailing Aldo Mancini, son of imprisoned mob boss Peter Mancini, whom Gando had rolled on in what seemed like a lifetime ago. Both he and Marco Bracci had conspired with their sons to put out a hit on Gando, forcing him into Witness Protection, and hence the move to Florida. There had been several failed attempts on Gando's life and the word on the street was that the bounty on his life was nearing one million dollars. Now Gando would be taking the offensive, his goal being to eliminate those who were conspiring to execute his eventual demise. Now he was back in the game, in his comfort zone and gathering information regarding his prey.

"So I want you to lay it all out for me. Tell me about his daily habits, where he goes, who he sees. Are there any patterns in his behavior and tell me about his protection." Gando sipped his coffee and leaned back in his chair waiting for a response.

Peretti cleared his throat again and began. He knew this was his chance to hook up with a big name in the industry, albeit an illegal one. And so he began with all the details that he and his small group had collected.

After almost two hours, four or five dozens "ya knows" and a few cups of coffee, Gando had learned more than he had hoped for. He knew there were either two or three large bodyguards surrounding him at all times. He was driven around in a H2 or Cadillac Escalade, each sporting tinted windows, as well as bulletproofed materials. He ate at over two dozen different restaurants in the three week period in which he was followed and had one office on the upper west side and the other on the lower east side. Both were in eight storied buildings and both were nondescript. But there was one and only one time he was alone for any period of time. He had been noticed making two trips a week to an apartment building in midtown. Each Monday and Thursday he was escorted out of his vehicle and into a secure building with a doorman. Ten hundred dollar bills had bought the name and occupation of who he was visiting. The name was not important, but the fact that two different escort services occupied the upper floors was. This was the pattern that Gando believed would afford him the opportunity of taking out Aldo. He would have to run this by Crello and come up with a plan that would be both effective and untraceable. His cockiness and experience told him that it would be totally doable.

● ● ●

As he left Harleys workstation, Davis felt the vibration of his cell phone stored in his left pocket. The caller ID appeared as restricted, but he knew who it was.

"Davis," he said, not bothering to hide the curtness in which he answered.

"It's Gasparo. I see that you called, "he responded, his tone plain and unassuming.

"Damn right I did "barked Davis. I have one dead man in my city named Jules Gando. That means I either have a dumb ass bounty hunter who still thinks Gando is in my city or someone who knows that Gando is no longer under your watchful eye. Say it ain't so, Joe." His voice tailed off, as the sarcasm dripped from his words.

The abundance of time it took Gasparo to respond had answered Davis's question.

"Ok, Stephen, this is where we stand."

Its Stephen now, Davis thought, knowing full well that his first assumption was spot on.

Without any more hesitation, Gasparo came clean.

"We lost him, but let me finish," he quickly added, knowing what Davis was mockingly planning to add. "Crello, his roommate and childhood friend put together an elaborate, well thought out plan which honestly caught us off guard. He left their condo dressed as Gando, and took us on a tour of two airports around the Miami area. During that time, Gando snuck out and flew to parts unknown with a fake I.D. We are currently reviewing all video surveillance tapes form the surrounding airports I was going to inform you as soon as we had gathered more information, but we are clueless as to where he might be. We checked the surrounding airports for any flights that had his WPP name, but came up empty. We can only assume that he has a new identity which is unknown to us and his destination is classified as unknown. Sorry for the interruption but you can understand why there was a delay in regard to informing you about this incident."

Davis was appreciative of Gasparo's honesty, but just knowing that Gando was back in circulation was a concern. Was he in Philly and killed the other Gando to take the pressure off of him? It was doubtful.

"Thanks for filling me in and I apologize for my slight hostility," Davis said with more of a remorseful tone. After all, they were playing for the same team

"Apology accepted, as well as you should accept mine for the delay in getting back to you as soon as we learned of this fuck up. I will keep you in the loop from here on in and dinner is on me on my next trip up."

Davis consented. He hung up and went back up to his office to inform his team of the latest developments. His mood darkened as he waited for the elevator back to his office.

CHAPTER 11

As Angel Almar, aka Carolyn West pulled up to the clinic, she rolled down the window for a quick cigarette. She was curious to see the new Jon Vandergriff and how adept the plastic surgeon had performed in regard to hiding his Nordic features. She took a deep inhale and thought, his blonde hair was easily changeable with dye and his blue eyes could be changed with the right color nonprescription contact lenses. She was curious how surgery would alter his prototypic narrow face and forehead, and the distinct angle of his clear cut chin. Hell, she had paid enough to this surgeon and hoped that his work fit into the "you get what you pay for" scenario.

She smiled to herself, took a short drag of her cigarette and sent a conical stream into the still air. Practicing between classes in the girl's room at high school had taught her the nuances of smoking ala film noir. She threw a smoke ring out as well, entertaining herself as she waited his release from the clinic. Her cell phone buzzed. It was George. She didn't want to be talking to him when Jon exited, so she ran her fingers across the text screen, saying she would call when her meeting was finished. When she next peered up, flicking the end of her cigarette out of the car, a tall man was seen in front of the clinic, his hands shading his eyes from the sun. When he had finally turned to face her, she knew by his lean and still intact muscular features, that it was him. But OMG, his Nordic features had been so well replaced, that she at least hoped it was him.

She knew for sure that it was when he strode over to the open driver's side window and leaned in. She had made sure to rent the same make and model car from here last visit, but she had rented this from a different company.

"So, how do I look?" Jon said, his wide and larger open mouth beaming from ear to ear. It was obvious that he approved.

"You look amazing. Not to say you were not a handsome man to begin with, but you look more confident and mature. All in a delicious way," she added, stroking his ego. "You even have a bit of a new swagger to your walk. Did they throw that in as a bonus?"

He laughed gently, thanked her for the compliments and walked around to the passenger door, which she clicked open. Before she pulled away, she turned to eye him up and down again, nodding her head in overall approval.

"I thought we would take a ride over so I can show you the ship we will be booking you on for your assignment. Haven't had any second thoughts I hope, especially after all the time, money and work we have put into this project."

It really wasn't meant to be a question but rather a statement of finality. She continued.

"They do have a tour open to the general public today but I don't want the risk the chance of anyone ever seeing you before you got to work," she said in a serious tone, then adding, "Especially with how handsome you look. We may even need to hire some body guards to keep all the females away."

She glanced at him and noticed that he was slightly blushing. She knew how to work a man.

They cruised up to the port, parking on a small incline that gave an unobstructed view of the ship. She handed him some binoculars. He scanned the ship slowly and deliberately, partially in admiration for the reconstructed vessel and partly due to his everlasting love of the ocean. She gave him a long minute and then asked, "Are you able to tell by the design if any of the internal workings of the ship might have changed over the past several years?"

He shook his head, still scanning the ship and replied that until he was able to board her, he would not be able to answer the question. After several more minutes, he put down the binoculars and faced her.

"Just in case you have any doubts, please pardon the pun, our mission is full steam ahead. With all the time I have had to contemplate your proposal, I have only become more anxious to start this plan and extract some bit of revenge. I haven't admitted this to you before, but I am a bit bitter over how the whole affair was handled in regard to my representation by Phelps and PacLantic Cruise Line. It is time to settle a score."

Out of curiosity, she hoisted the binoculars and swept them across the greeting tent area. Panning past news trucks, reporters, and some movie icons, she spotted Milton and Adriana. She saw their plastic smiles and feigned laughter, which only caused her more impetus to get their plans in gear. She tossed the binoculars onto the rear seat and proceeded down A1A, to an ocean view eatery for lunch. During their meeting, Angel and Jon, sitting in an isolated area of the restaurant, were able to throw some sabotage ideas off of each other. She and George had wanted the first "accident" to be made to look like a technical or mechanical snag which would cause the ship to abort its plans, cause no serious injuries and refund or replace passenger's tickets. If that was too complicated, maybe tampering with the food during one of the large and numerous buffets would suffice.

Angel, a Discovery ID addict, began to tell Jon about an event that occurred in Oregon in 1984. A group called the Rajneeshees, a cult that followed Bhagwan Rajneesh, a self-proclaimed 'guru' from India, had several of his follower's spray a Salmonella based liquid over a popular salad bar and eatery in Wasco County. His goal had been a trial run, with his final goal being to incapacitate the voters so that his followers could vote him into office. Over 750 in the town of 10,000 became ill. The CDC was able to bust the Bhagwan prior to his master plan of poisoning the water supply prior to the upcoming election. Although he fled the country before being captured, the event had been deemed the "largest act of terrorism on U.S. soil", by the New York Daily News. Who says you can't learn anything practical by watching television. Regardless of what means they would select to their end, they would just give the cruise line a taste of what was to follow.

After enjoying lunch, bouncing sardonic plans off each other, and Angel fending off halfhearted advances by Jon, they left the restaurant. Angel handed Jon an envelope with five thousand dollars and told him that she would be in touch shortly before he would receive a ticket on a selected cruise. She then mentioned that she had been involved with someone and apologized if she had in any way led him to believe she had led him on in any way. In reality she knew she had, but with his acceptance of her offer, she believed it was time to let him down easy. He did express disappointment and even apologized if he made her feel uncomfortable at any time. Squeezing his hand, she accepted his apologies and said that if she wasn't so involved, things might have worked out different. As stated earlier, she truly was a master manipulator. It sucked to be Jon.

Before she dropped him off at his apartment in Boynton Beach, she handed him an envelope with five large. The cruise that he would attend would be the "Great Gourmet Chef and Wine Pairing cruise. It would sail in three weeks and she had booked him a single cabin, a stateroom with balcony, on the cruise. She would run their ideas by George and decide on whatever he chose. It was not that she was subservient to him or submissive enough to let him reinforce the Alpha male species that he was, but rather that his logical mind was as succinct as that of a chess player. He could evaluate all of the scenarios of a plan along with all possible outcomes. It was a trait that served him well in the financial world and she both trusted and admired any decisions that he would choose. Angel would stay in contact with Jon on her disposable phone, for which she had purchased fifty hours on. Everything was falling into place.

● ● ●

Back in Philadelphia, the murder of the wrong Gando was progressing faster than expected. Luck must have been on their side when a print on the doorknob and outside door frame led to a low level mob wannabe named Joseph Ringoni. He had registered a nine point match on the AFIS system, which was a solid one. Davis sent two beat cops down to show his picture to some of the neighbors and as it turned out, two of them had spotted him on the day of the crime and the other a day prior to it. His rap sheet displayed a couple of drug possession charges and one for breaking and entering. He either needed to support his habit or decided it was time to move up in the world. Regardless of the reason, Davis sent two homicide detectives to pick him up at his last known address, which was in the Fairmount section of the city. When they arrived, they found him passed out on the couch with a cell phone cradled in his hand. He was profoundly intoxicated and didn't even act surprised when the two detectives entered and let themselves in.

"Are you guys here to arrest me or what," he droned and then continued. "I truly fucked up. They told me it was the wrong Gando and I ain't getting paid anything. Man, am I one fucked up dude or what?"

Grey Suit shook his head at his partner as he walked over to the couch and helped the suspect up. He removed some handcuffs from his belt and turned the docile suspect around, easily slipping the cuffs around his wrists and snapping them shut.

"Okay Joseph, let's take a ride downtown and you can tell us the whole story. Should we stop at Wawa and grab you some coffee?"

"That's cool officer", he said to grey suit, as he was led away offering no resistance whatsoever. The pair led him down the steps as he ranted. He was put into the backseat and had passed out before the car found a Wawa. Grey suit then called the Roundhouse to relay the arrest had been made and forthcoming interview that he would be given. It might have to wait till Ringoni sobered up, but it looked like one of those cases you might see on 'The First 48'. Davis gave them praise and told them to let Detective Davenport do the interview, as he had more important things on his mind.

Davis called in his brother Michael, who had been waiting until the call was finished. It had been tough over the last few months in regard to his brother. In a recent case, he had fallen in love with a female sniper that had drawn national attention to the city, the OCTF and his brother. The suspect, Jaime Valley, had fatally killed two individuals associated with the insurance company whom she had blamed for her husband's untimely and unnecessary passing. He had been waiting for approval on an upcoming procedure when he passed away. The insurance company was nickel and diming the doctor in regard to the cost of the procedure, which turned out to be vital to his survival. Jaime's demure nature was transformed into a rage against the insurance company, which later Davis and his team had solved. But it strained his relationship with his fellow officer and brother, as Michael took time both for sympathy and a romantic involvement with Jaime. Although all the evidence was compelling, she was found guilty of a lesser charge and released. She still was negotiating with the Feds who were not willing to drop this case of pure vigilantism. Lawyers had been negotiating a plea deal in lieu of a trial, but the government held steadfast in the belief that she should serve some amount of time. And although the story had faded from the news and the city of Philadelphia's short term memory loss, negotiations would produce an outcome within the next several weeks.

Michael had rejoined the OCTF the previous week. His computer skills were brilliant and he had helped the team solve several high profile murders since he joined the squad.

Stephen didn't dwell on the past, but rather on the matter at hand. He needed Michael to scan the net and theorize as to geographical areas that the real Gando might have fled to. It wasn't that he didn't trust the feds, but the truth was they liked to keep other law enforcement agencies out of the loop and steal the spotlight for their egos and the agency. All that Stephen Davis wanted to do was find Gando before he might return to his murderous ways.

"I will get on it bro. And thanks for the courtesy of bringing me back in. You know me better than anyone and it was not my intention to fall in love with a suspect. It was like "Sea of Love".

Michael had been referring to the Al Pacino movie in which he played the role of Frank Keller. Keller was a New York detective investigating a serial killer who finds her victims through lonely hearts columns. Helene then meets Keller, snubs him, but later meets again in a chance encounter. The ending was what he had hoped for, although Helene was only a suspect and not the guilty party. It was just another one of those life imitating art things.

Michael got up and Stephen told him that he would be informed of any clues or breadcrumbs the Bureau might send him.

"I don't fully trust Gasparo, but I have no other options, which is why I gave you this case. Now go find him," Davis barked in a light heated fashion that indicated Michael was temporarily forgiven. He was the only family he had.

CHAPTER 12

Gando's disposable cell phone rang, knowing that Crello was the only contact having his number. He answered, happy and anxious to fill his wing man in on what he had learned.

"That Peretti, is he some kind of character or what Julian," Crello began.

Gando paused for a few seconds before responding. In a voice as close as he could come to Peretti's, which was about an octave higher, he responded.

"Ya know, he seems to be responsible, but ya know, he does repeat himself quite a bit."

Crello laughed, knowing full well about his 'nephews' lack of creative speaking and repetition of that particular street phrase. Still, he told Crello that he had done a pretty intricate job in regard to learning the movements and habits of his prey, the elusive and cautious Aldo Mancini.

Gando went on in detail about what Peretti had told him in regards to habits, locations he frequented and his social rendezvous with some high priced hooker.

"You mean call girl. Ain't that what they call those high priced escorts that work the city?"

Gando acknowledged Crello, asking an exaggerated forgiveness for his faux pas. They remained silent for several seconds when Crello began to speak. He had been making some calls to his 'extended family' and many connections. Crello was one to think ahead, one reason he had been under the radar for most of his criminal life on the fringes of legality.

He was cerebral, convincing and cunning, three traits that enabled him to let others do his dirty work whenever necessary. He was a man that was trusted, a standup guy who did what he said. This was a trait Gando and others admired. Trust was hard to come by these days.

"Okay Julian, here are my thoughts in regard to our strategy for getting rid of this dirt bag."

Crello went on to tell him about 'another' extended family member, one who was currently serving in the military. After barely being accepted into Special Forces, he had been assigned to a group that specialized in explosive and demolition training.

"So my guy tells me about this new explosive that is being developed but is in the latter stages. He says this stuff is deadly accurate in its powers, but is harmless in its raw form. The stuff looks like silly putty, but it don't take pictures off of comic books like we used to do when we was kids."

Gando laughed, adding that as long as it peeled the skin off of Mancini's face, he could overlook its limitations. Crello continued.

"It's also undetectable by the Postal Inspectors bomb detection dogs and chemical detection equipment because it is so new. It should be arriving at Peretti's place today from Fed Ex. All you need to do is stick a nail like piece through the putty. It's not a nail though but rather a radio activated fuse that works with the cell phone device I sent you. The code is 911 for the phone trigger, and this stuff will completely vaporize everything within a 30 yard area, so make sure it's planted close to the target and that you are a safe distance away. I will be coming up soon when I think it's safe to help you with our second target. Good luck, Julian. I want to read about it in the papers."

Later that afternoon, Peretti had called Gando to tell him the Fed Ex package had arrived and asked him what to do with it. Gando told him to bring it over to the hotel and that he would explain everything. Gando had been thinking the best way to get to Mancini in lieu of all the protection that surrounded him 24/7. And although being an assassin, he did want to minimize the collateral damage to the innocent, which seemed a bit of an anomaly for a cold blooded killer. He removed a cigar from his overnight bag and decided to walk the grounds around the hotel, as a good cigar always seemed to help him focus on the business at hand. And besides, the Sopranos had been filmed right around the area he was staying. Does life ever stop imitating art?

He lit his #5 Romeo and Julieta, the 7" by 47 ring gauge cigar made famous by Winston Churchill and to a lesser degree, by Nellie Tayloe Ross, who was the first female governor in the U.S, from 1925-1927. She served the people of Wyoming for two years and lived to the ripe age of 101. And we all think that smoking kills.

Gando found the designated smoking area outside the pool and sat down in large white Adirondack chair. He held the cigar between in thumb and four fingers, inhaling fairly deep and exhaling conical plumes that meshed with the bluish grey clouds that had momentarily obscured the sun. He was beginning to focus upon how he could get the explosive near enough to his target in an undetectable fashion. His neighborhood was out of the question, as it was probably under constant surveillance. It would have to be during the course of the day when he was away from his safe haven. And then it came to him. He began to smile, as the plan unfolded like a movie scene on the big screen. It was brilliant, as long as Peretti could follow instructions and not open his mouth. He did not want Peretti to do anything but follow his instructions, as well as getting some speech lessons when the hit was completed.

"Yeah, this will work. It will definitely work," he said softly to himself.

He smiled, nodding to himself in regard to the simplicity and ease of this plan. Stubbing out the last inch of his cigar, he arose from the chair and headed back to his room.

As he approached the entrance, he saw Peretti was approaching to his right, seeming distracted and talking to himself. Maybe he would throw in some psych visits along with his language training.

Peretti caught sight of Gando, picking up his gait so he would arrive at the sliding door along with his perceived mentor. Gando noticed that he was carrying the Fed-Ex box which had remained unopened. He noted to himself that Peretti had not displayed any interest in the package, which was a sign that he was one who could probably be trusted. That was a good trait.

They nodded to each other, not speaking as they headed to the elevator bank. Once inside the elevator, Gando inserted his card, pressed the button for the ninth floor and they rode up.

Upon exiting the elevator, Gando noticed a brown bag with some green writing on it. Peretti, noticing that Gando looked curiously at the bag, told him it was a snack that he thought his superior might enjoy. Gando smiled and thanked him for the thought. He was beginning to like this kid more. Ya know.

Peretti handed Gando the bag after they had sat down and entered the room.

"I got ya some things ya might have missed from Jersey Mr. G. Check it out."

Gando slid his fingers into the bag and poured the contents on the small table. Out spilled some sharp provolone cheese, a pound of prosciutto and some hard rolls, the ones that were baked crusty on the outside, yet chewy in the middle and a staple of his youth. He was not too hungry, but told Peretti he really appreciated the thought and ripped the roll in half, adding some of the ham and cheese.

He took a small bite and put the half sandwich down. Smiling in appreciation, he looked Peretti in the eyes and began to speak. He wanted his undivided attention, a formidable task in itself. He began speaking.

"Greg. I truly appreciate not only the thoroughness in which you have done your task but also the respect you have shown me. This will not be forgotten."

"Thanks Mr. G. I am loyal to Mr. Crello, as he has done a lot for me and ya know, with yous two being such longtime friends, I will do anything ya need."

Gando nodded in appreciation, but he was more concerned with the business at hand. Today was the usual day that Mancini took his trip to Murray Hill to see his provider. And although Mancini mixed things up in regards to his schedule, he would be ready if his hormones were sending signals to his libido.

"So what's the plan Mr. G," Peretti asked.

Gando had thought this out and wanted to bounce it off of his "errand boy".

"Here are my thoughts on how we can do this hit, but feel free to chime in with your opinion."

Peretti nodded, the taught muscles in his face expressing his undivided attention. Gando continued, talking slowly so as to allow for any of Peretti's interjections and/or any confusion.

"Tonight we will take a ride into Murray Hill. There is a nice Greek dining establishment between 33rd and 34th street, caddy corner from Mancini's broad."

Gando opened the package that Peretti had delivered and showed him the contents.

"This soft clay like material is a highly powerful explosive. This small metallic object is the detonator and will receive an electronic signal from this phone when I decide our explosive is in place."

Peretti gave Gando his look of attentiveness, hanging on to his every word.

"I will be sitting across the street at a restaurant in view of the building at which Mancini will see his bitch. If the Hummer or Escalade pulls up in front, I will call you. You will be in close proximity of the building and your job will be easy. What I need you to do is casually walk down the street when Mancini's entourage pulls up to let him out. Are you with me so far?"

"You bet Mr. G.", Peretti replied, his attention hanging on every word, his body rigid, ingesting everything he was told.

Gando pressed on.

"When I give the go ahead, that's when I see the car slowing down and pulling up, I will text you. At that point, you will walk towards the car. I want you to be wearing ear buds or headphones, appearing to be, let's say, in your own little world. You will have a can of coke in your hand and toss it down behind the car. Inside the can will be this putty like material with the ignition device. It won't go off when you toss it down and this is the key,' Gando pausing slightly to emphasize the next point. "Just make sure it rolls under the car and you do it with finesse. Don't stop and aim. Just do it naturally as if you have drained the can and just want to toss it out."

Peretti smiled, hanging on every word and nodded. He was letting Gando know of both his approval and understanding of his not so complicated intentions.

"And do not, I repeat, do not say a word to anyone of his bodyguards. You must be natural and unassuming."

Not sure of Peretti's vocabulary, he repeated his instructions in a simplified manner.

"Greg. Walk down the street, casually. Make it look like you are listening to your music. Toss the can under the car and just keep walking. Can you do that exactly as I have just spelled out?"

Without hesitation, Peretti nodded. His eyes reflected a total understanding of what Gando had just explained. It was so easy, even a six year old could follow. Ya know.

● ● ●

After a couple of slices of pizza from one of Gando's childhood haunts, Peretti headed up the New Jersey Turnpike toward the Lincoln Tunnel. It was one and a half miles long, originating in the city of Weehawken, New Jersey and emerging on Tenth Avenue between 38th and 39th streets on the west side of Manhattan. They would have to cross over to the east side of Manhattan Island, the target area lying several blocks north and east between 33rd and 34th streets. If Mancini was close to following his assumed timetable, they would arrive with more than half an hour to spare. Peretti could park the car, waste some time walking around, while Gando could secure a table with a view. Before that time however, he would have to get a good estimate of the distance between the restaurant and ground zero, where the explosive would be placed. If the explosive functioned as it was designed, fifty yards give or take, would be more than sufficient.

Peretti swung the car down 33rd street and pulled into the parking garage. Before exiting the car, he went over the plan, squeezing Peretti's arm, reinforcing the importance of his explicit directions. He stared into Peretti's eyes as he reiterated the importance of not deviating from the plan. And Gando took the parking chit with him! Ya never know. He got the feeling that Greg was a cocky son-of-a bitch and stressed that he should just keep his thoughts to himself and issue no taunts to those whom were targeted. He had done all he could to make things clear and the rest was up to Peretti to follow instructions.

Gando entered the restaurant, noticing an empty table by the widow. This gave him a 'sign' that all was good. He needed the reassurance. He removed the two cell phones from his pocket and sat down. A basket of pita bread, along with several varieties of olives and some hummus were placed in front of him. Before the waiter queried his drink preference, he ordered a seven and seven. It was sort of a traditional 'thing' he would partake in before preforming an act of violence. Glancing at his watch and staring intermittently out toward the apartment building he was targeting, he sipped his drink.

He ordered the grilled octopus appetizer, telling the waiter he was not in a hurry and would place his dinner order when he had finished his appetizer. The server nodded in acknowledgement, attempting to hide his disdain for a solo diner tying up a four top table. Seeing this, Gando placed a fifty dollar bill in the waiter's palm, reassuring him that he would indeed be compensated for his patience. The waiter examined the bill, telling Gando that there was no need to rush his dining experience.

As soon as the appetizer plate was removed and another drink placed in front of him, Gando noticed a black Escalade inching toward the apartment entrance. He grabbed his cell and hit the send button, notifying Peretti that it was time. On cue, Peretti appeared turning the corner. His ear buds were in place and he held his I-Pod in one hand and the Coke can in the other. He was relieved to see that Peretti fit into the scene au natural. The timing looked perfect.

The scene began to unfold. Two large men emerged from the car. The first got out and did a quick scan of the area, paying no attention to the young looking Peretti walking towards him. Three women passed by, laughing as two walked arm in arm, European fashion. A second larger man stepped out. He too glanced at the environs before opening the front passenger door for Mancini to get out. The driver, Gando noticed, just stared straight ahead.

Some say that before a horrific act, time slows down. This was not the case. Peretti kept walking at an even pace. He raised the can to his mouth, tilting his head back as if to finish the remaining liquid. In one fluent motion, he tossed the can onto the street. It rolled toward the car as it lodged perfectly between the curb and the right rear tire. He was duly impressed.

But he became a little concerned when the steroid infused body-guard that had withdrew from the right door of the car, pointed his finger and said something to Peretti. Peretti, being a bit hot tempered and overly sensitive, removed his earbuds and said something back. Gando could only helplessly watch the scene unfurl, not being able to read lips. He sensed a concern.

Mancini emerged from the car, little concern about the exchange of words between the stranger and one of his men. Gando next noticed that Mancini was pointing and saying something to Peretti. His body language indicated that he was miffed about something that had been uttered.

Just then, Gando's memory pictured the scene in the Godfather, when Sonny was trapped at the toll booth prior to a barrage of bullets taking his life away. It was almost as if Mancini sensed a similar scenario. Gando knew his time to act was limited, but did not want to injure Peretti.

"Move your damn ass out of the way", trying to communicate tele-pathically to Peretti, his mind was racing anxiously, and knowing his window of opportunity was shrinking. Mancini picked up the pace as he seemed to be hurrying toward the building entrance. With no logic and just pure single-mindedness, Gando pressed the button on the second cell phone.

Almost as soon as he had activated the signal, a large fiery ball of energy and bright lights illuminated the greying sky. Its brightness rivaled that of a miniature sun, the heat slightly emanating from the blast and being felt at Gando's tableside. Within seconds of the blast, one that momentarily blinded his vision, the spot where the car had been was now an empty void. The sound was deafening, accompanied by flying debris containing barely visible chards of scorched metal that lay scattered about. It was vaporizing human flesh as it intensified in force. A grayish orange haze slowly dissipated. The brass poles that supported the building's red awning were melted like solder. He was far enough away from the blast site so that he was unharmed. Patrons in the restaurant dropped down on the floor. Like the old duck and cover videos that gave instructions in case we were under nuclear attack. It was pure chaos.

Gando only hoped that Peretti had somehow slipped away from the carnage. The kid had no reason to taunt Mancini if that's what he was doing. He had gone over the plan with Peretti so many times, that it became rote. There was no reason that he had to be killed, other than his cocky foolishness and tough guy attitude. And when the smoke finally dissipated, there was no form of human life to be seen whatsoever.

Diners in the restaurant had been startled by the bright light, but were now arising from the floor, absorbing what had just occurred. Some were in shock and remained motionless, while others were now racing to the widow to peer out at the large hole that now appeared on 33rd street. Loud chatter, looks of shock and even some sobbing replaced the silence. During the commotion, Gando slipped both cell phones back into his suit coat and joined the gawkers at the window. Silence filled the room of onlookers as several removed cell phones and dialed 911. Since 9/11, New Yorkers had become more involved and less standoffish in regard to reporting violent events, rather than turning a blind eye at them.

Gando found the waiter, grabbed his arm and requested a check. The waiter came back from his stupor and nodded his head. Gando told him to relax, take a deep breath and bring it over when he was ready. It would be necessary to leave the scene before the blare of sirens and the flashing of red lights would arrive on the scene. New York, a fast paced town, is known for its quick response to events such as these. That's why they call it a New York minute.

CHAPTER 13

High pitched whines from blue and white police cars, along with EMT vehicles broke the eerie silence that followed the explosion, as Gando left the restaurant. Glancing back over his shoulder and heading for the garage around the corner, he transfixed his gaze over the scene. He observed the area void of any animate life forms that surrounded the newly formed crater in front of the apartment building. Gando's experience had taught him well in regards to leaving a crime scene invisibly. When the pair had parked the car, Gando retained the parking ticket, knowing that he would be out of harm's way just in case Peretti didn't make it. It didn't look like Peretti had.

He arrived at the garage, handed the attendant the parking ticket and waited for its arrival. Not enough time had yet passed for Gando to savor part one of his revenge. He had lost his recent associate and that always bothered him. It was only the third time that a similar incident had occurred, and it never ceased to cause a tinge of remorse as well as responsibility. But he also knew that he would get over it.

When the car arrived, Gando paid the $64.00 fee with four twenty dollar bills and waved off the change. The door was held open and he entered the driver's side. Putting it in drive, he turned left and began heading up the ramp and exiting on 34th street. He would wait to call Crello as soon as he had he crossed through the Lincoln Tunnel. He would return to the hotel, check out and find another residence to secretly occupy for the next several days. Bracci was now the second and last fish that he had to fry.

• • •

The crime scene had been cordoned off. The familiar yellow colored police tape now adorned an almost one square block radius of where the explosion had occurred. A large gathering of suits, uniformed officers, crime scene investigators and EMT's now occupied the area. The investigators combed the area for any clues, but there were little to be found. Just as had been indicated, this new explosive possessed such powerful heat and force, it destroyed almost all evidence that had been there prior to the blast. But one of the suits found something. He removed a latex glove and waived a long haired crime scene investigator over.

"Take this and run it for prints and then give it to one of my homicide guys to run a DMV search on. Call the information in now," he said the final word strongly emphasized.

He had handed the investigator the remains of the once blue and orange colored New York license plate, still intact with the tag numbers almost totally disintegrated from the metal. The raised numbers and lettering were still visible, but only barely. Still crouched down in a catcher's stance, he scanned the area for any other possible clues, but the seen was almost barren and void of anything helpful. Although he hadn't inspected many homicidal bombings, this one was duly noted. It was hard to fathom, but there were almost no physical remains of any clothing, body parts or collectible evidence remaining. It was unfathomable.

News crews from every local and national cable pulled up, but the authorities were tight lipped and rightfully so. They were clueless in regards to the victims, currently being unaware as to who they were or how many there were. Investigators could only hope that the remaining New York license tag would shed some light on the investigation. New Yorkers were always hungry for news, and the more depressing, the better.

When Suit One was approached, he gave the familiar wave of his open hand along with the standard "no comment" reply. He knew it would be hours, or maybe days before the scene was processed and sorted out.

● ● ●

The warm Miami sun was just an aside for the re-launch of PacLantic's newly cruise ship, the *Adventurer,* which was the reinvented name of the same ship that had errantly strayed in St. Maarten a while back. With the bad press and publicity well behind them, Milton Phelps and his wife Adrianna, personally greeted all of those willing to shell out the minimum five thousand per room ante for the maiden voyage of his highly publicized cruise package. The first venue for the *Adventurer* was a gastronomes dream. High profile chefs such as Mario Batali, Emeril Lagasse, and Jose Garces, were only three of the gourmand chef attendees hired to give cooking demonstrations, mingle with their fans and make this voyage a once in a lifetime experience. Bobby Flay's arrogant demeanor kept him off the A-list. But there were several other Food Channel chefs, as well as those specializing in such areas as 'good old Southern BBQ', Indian fusion cuisine and even Chen Kenichi, an original Iron Chef who specialized in Szechuan cuisine, hence earning the nickname, '*The Szechuan Sage'.* He had appeared more times than any other of the original Iron Chefs from Japan, amassing 66 wins, 24 losses and three draws during the shows airings. With these superstars of culinary fame, who other than those appearing on reality shows weighing in at 600 pounds would want to attend? It would be a monumental event whose memories would last for an eternity.

Departure time was scheduled for 3:00 P.M. and all was running smoothly. Unbeknownst to owner Milton Phelps, his brother George and his significant other, Carolyn West, had made their own plans. They had their own agenda. They had reinvented former cruise ship Captain, Jon Vandergriff, as Jonathan Peterson. He was complete with a new look, style and the passport credentials to prove it. The pair sat miles away, watching as Mr. Peterson easily boarded the ship. He even shook hands with his ex-boss, Milton. He did an expert job of hiding his disdain and hatred for the man who had sold him out and sacrificed him for by spending two years in prison. Milton didn't even look twice as his former captain passed by the greeting committee as well as the ships personnel inspecting tickets. It was that easy. And it was so rewarding. Revenge would be dished up hot, not cold, as the chefs prepared their gourmet delights during the week.

It was just before three on this Friday afternoon and George needed to get back to his office in order to carry on his conceived brilliant plan. Being a financial investor and money manager, it would not suffice just to ruin his brothers operation. He would seek to amass a large profit as well, in his brother's misfortune. The more revenge, the merrier.

George happened to be a brilliant financial planner, having an un-canny ability to spot market trends for his clients. But knowing what was in store for the upcoming PacLantic maiden voyage held, it would be a no brainer to make a profit. He proceeded to purchase puts on the NASDAQ for the stock options. But not wanting to raise suspicion, he also purchased similar puts for some airlines and various transportation and entertainment related companies. A put is basically a financial in-vestment where one can "bet" that a stock will lose value over a specified period of time. If and 'when' Pac-Lantic had experienced an event that might lessen its value, all traders that had purchased these puts would see a profit. The stock had an asking price of roughly nine dollars per share. George purchased puts at five dollars and seven dollars and fifty cents. This meant that if the stock fell toward those values before a speci-fied time period, his investment would go up a considerable amount. He knew it would. The longer the time period that you 'bet' this decline will take place, the more the investment costs. He bought these puts with a short time involved. His investment dictated that the stock would lose roughly half of its value within a three month period, thereby increasing both the risk and the rewards of his gamble. But there really was no gam-ble. If the captain succeeded in his task, the cruise line would probably lose at least half of its value and become a jinx for any future investors. It was win-win.

Jon, now referred to as Jonathan, made it past security and up to his stateroom. Just the fact he was back on a cruise ship for the first time in over two years, brought back beloved memories. Since the ship had been out of commission for a while, he noticed only a few of the familiar faces from the old days. But it seemed that none had recognized him. Walking with his head down, donning a new face and consciously limiting the former swagger in his step, just added to his new persona. He was happy to notice that Angel had procured him a cabin that had a balcony. It would afford him the ability to stargaze, one of his favorite pastimes, as well as take in the salty air that had always revitalized him. The whole experience did convey a bit of irony. He had never been a passenger on a cruise, only an officer. It felt both of awkward and refreshing at the same time. Probably like a retired athlete who now sat in a broadcast booth rather than participating in the action on a playing field. But he would be participating in a way, and if all went as planned, there would be a lot of action.

The ship's horn bellowed with three short blasts, indicating it was ready to back out of its slip for departure. Vandergriff had wanted to lie low, away from all the passengers waving their goodbyes to those who remained behind. He opted to watch the view from his balcony. His goal was to just blend in as a tourist and raise as little attention as possible. Anonymity seemed to be the order of the week.

Jon was impressed with some of the upgrades that adorned his cabin. For one thing, the shower nozzle was mounted toward the top of the stall, not like the previous ones that barely lined up below his head. There were two reclining patio chairs on the outdoor deck and upon pressing down on the mattress which seemed to have some lumbar support. It was a far cry from his prison cell bed and clearly a nice touch! New carpeting in the suite mimicked the cruise lines colors; deep blue and ivory white brushstrokes in circular patterns. He assumed the influx of cash from the new investment group as well as the capital derived from its NASDAQ listing, were used wisely. And although he had yet to fully explore the upgraded vessel, he knew that it had changed in order to be more competitive in the overpopulated and flat profitable cruise market.

As the ship backed out of port toward the Atlantic, Jon began to unpack his generic suitcase. A bit anal, all of his clothes appeared as if they had just come off the rack from a department store. The shirts were pressed and the creases in his slacks were spot on. Although concentrating on setting up his wardrobe by color, his mind drifted off to the rigid schedule he had set for the week. His toiletry bag was the last item removed from his case. It contained the tainted bacterial infested dispensers he would use during one of the meals. Which meal he was not yet certain.

He picked up the colorful brochure that sat on the oak desk which outlined the week's activities and scheduled gastronomic events. Before walking out to the patio, he removed two small bottles of vodka from the small service bar, added some ice cubes to the glass and poured them both in. He squeezed a piece of fresh lime that accompanied a complimentary fruit platter which was included in his high end stateroom.

The high glossed finish on the brochure featured a group picture of a dozen chefs that had been invited on the maiden voyage of the *Adventurer.* The inside cover and first page had brief biographies of those chefs pictured, along with a list of their culinary awards, as well as the names and locations of the restaurants they had established. Although not a true 'foodie', Jon was impressed with the credentials that they had amassed. Sipping from his glass, his mind darted to the peacefulness of his surroundings and the freedom which he now realized he had missed over the past several years. He significantly knew that this trip would help to erase those sordid memories as he began his new endeavors.

The next several pages outlined each day's events. The first night was a meet and greet, featuring the chefs up close and personal. In parenthesis, it limited autographs of each to the first hundred customers, providing they purchased one of the chef's cookbooks, branded cookware or specialty seasonings. On the second and third nights, these six chefs would be in the kitchen preparing meals for the passengers, who could choose from the specialized menus. Jon put the brochure down momentarily, needing a refill on his cocktail. He completed the task at hand and returned to where he had left off.

Night four would be the "Bountiful Buffet", featuring two or three of each of the chefs specialties laid out in a stately manner. A teaser was added. Chef Garces would have his heavenly flatbread with shredded short ribs, caramelized onion and shredded Parmigiano-Reggiano, hailed by many as the "King of all cheeses". Mario Batali would offer his Polpette Alla Napoletana, his world renowned meatballs. The last headliner was Chef Kenichi's famous Mapo Tofu, minus the ground pork, so as to accommodate the vegetarian crowd's disdain of meat. It sounded like a food orgy heaven.

The final two days and nights would be cooking classes held by the dozen gastronomes, with hands on training offered to a limited number of passengers. Reporters from the Travel Channel, the Food Network and various cable news stations were all in attendance. This added free hype and publicity to the reemergence of PacLantic Cruise Lines comeback into the arena of vacation destinations.

As the third and fourth shots took their effects on Vandergriff, he slowly drifted off into sleep mode, feeling the calm effect that the briny sea air filled his lungs as it had done in his happier days.

● ● ●

Milton and Adrianna continued to mingle with the guests aboard this gourmet cruise. They made it their business to shake hands, extend air kisses and touted the intense planning that went into such a monumental event. At no time before, had so many famous culinary geniuses been gathered for such small and intimate audience. Milton silently inflated his already large ego at the brilliance of this event. Truth be told, it would go down as a major news story, but not in regard to any of the reasons that the event had been planned in the first place.

The couple excused themselves from the cameras and well-wishers, wanting to return to their room in order to freshen up for the nights festivities. Upon their return to one of the four 'presidential suites', they shared a long deep kiss prior to their assessment on the recent events.

"I just *love* the way you worked the room." Adriana began, feeding her husband's ever hungry ego.

"And you weren't too shabby either my love," he responded as he softly kissed her neck.

They pulled away from each other, still embraced, before breaking out in harmonious laughter.

"We are damn fucking good and we have this crowd eating out of our hands. I have a feeling this will be a week to be remembered. Not just by those who dished out their cash, but by the American public as well. They love those 'rags-to-riches stories.'

She nodded and backed away, mentioning they should take a quick shower, change and get back to mingle with their guests. They both oozed airs of overconfidence, partially due to their nature and the rest due to excitement that fueled the event. While Adriana took her patented thirty minute shower, Milton called his press agents back in Florida to see what he was missing. He had flipped on HLN and noticed the story running every twenty five minutes, but wanted to know if national interest was being broadcast elsewhere. His media P.R. department told him that not only was it being broadcast on all the local national affiliates, but that sales for future cruises were, as he put it, 'off the hook. He smiled to himself, mentioning that if anything monumental was broadcast, to immediately shoot him a text.

"And call in some favors we are owed, just to make sure we get more than our standard fifteen minutes of fame. Run with it."

"You got it boss," replied his main spin doctor. "Oh, and do you still want the chopper to pick you and the misses up at 22:00 on the top deck?"

"Of course," Milton replied. I think it important we make our exit from the ship in an even grander style than our entrance."

"See you then, boss."

The phone disconnected and he stripped down, wanting to join his wife for her final few minutes in her marathon shower.

● ● ●

George and Angel were also watching the events unfold on the cable networks. Living in New England, they were not privy to the same local broadcasts as his brother, but CNN and HLN gave them a fair representation of the story. Close-up interviews of Milton, arm and arm with Adriana beaming and glamorizing their new business venture made them both want to heave up their last meal. The transparent fallaciousness of their appearance was obvious to them and hopefully to others. They were as fake as fake could be. Their temporary meteoric rise before the fall was obvious to the pair, and they could only wait for that occurrence. It would only be a matter of days, if Jon completed his mission. And it would only be a matter of time before George would see a significant boom to his recent investments prophesizing the temporary demise of PacLantic stock prices. But he had learned in the past not to count on things in which he had no control over as an absolute given. He called it early flappage. The verb flappage meant to brag of not counting or obsessing about an events outcome before it happened. It basically equated to the age old adage of not counting one's chickens before they hatched. He had learned his lesson long ago. Just sit back and let the events unfold, knowing there were things you could directly influence and other things you could not.

CHAPTER 14

Jon kept a low profile during the first night of the cruise. He spent his time minimally encountering other guests. He continually carried a vodka tonic in his left hand so that his right hand was free to sample the epicurean delights that were being offered during the cocktail hour. A tuxedo clad waiter offered smoked trout in filo dough which he stabbed on three separate occasions. Baby lamb chops in a balsamic reduction was also spectacular, as well as the shrimp wrapped in Serrano ham.

Vandergriff, now known as Peterson, was truly enjoying the evening. Although he strayed from conversation, he was eyeing some of the women that were showing interest. After all, two years in prison raises the male hormone levels to a higher degree. And besides, nothing was discussed with Angel in regards to his free time. He was free and he did have time.

As the night progressed, he was able to get several names and cell phone numbers. He did not want to get 'too' well known, but he also wanted to hook up. After inspecting a sample of some single and well-endowed females, he decided to call it a night and retire for the evening. It was only the first day of his journey.

The following morning Jon slept in, waking well past nine. He was awakened by his cell phone ring. He knew it would be Angel, as she had given him the disposable phone and the only one who had that number. He grabbed the phone and pressed the green button to connect them.

They briefly spoke, she asking him about the ship, and if any of his old friends recognized him. She also fished for compliments about the accommodations she had procured for him.

"You never cease to impress me, Angel. The room is quite stately and I feel very comfortable. Today I plan to tour the ship, just to get a lay of the land. And by the way, the food is quite divine."

"That's why I am paying you the big bucks, my friend. Do you think our little proposal might be operational during your excursion, she asked, sounding more like a military planner than a saboteur.

"I will have a better idea in a day or so. The fact that a big buffet is planned for mid-week seems made to order. My future rewards more than justify the means to our end. You can count on that."

Angel hesitated a few seconds and then offered him her thanks and some encouragement.

"My people are counting on you and I have the utmost confidence in your dedication. I will speak to you in a few days after you do your deeds. Good luck, Jon and I look forward to seeing you when you safely dock."

She hung up quickly, Jon a bit surprised that he was unable to steer the conversation into a more seductive parlay, a bit horny and yet to surrender to his desires or rejections. He was still unable to read her in regards to this assignment maybe leading to a business arrangement or a personal one. He deeply wished for the latter. Either way, he would come out with more wealth from this one week of work than he amassed through almost half of his two decades of working on the high seas.

Jon reconnected the charger to the phone and arose from his bed. He stretched out his arms and contemplated what activities he might indulge in this morning. Before making any decisions, he removed some vodka and bloody Mary mix from the bar and poured the ingredients into the glass he had used the previous evening. There was still some clear liquid remaining, so why waste any. He reached for the remote, knowing that the daily activities would be listed on the ships dedicated channel, but decided it was unnecessary. A copy of the latest Daniel Silva book lay next to the television, just begging to be read. During his stay in prison, he had avoided socializing much, choosing to spend his countless hours doing some exercise or reading. It was a hobby he picked up in prison, something he had never had time to do during his long hours commanding his ship. It relaxed and interested him. That's what he would do, throw on his swimsuit and relax in a quiet corner by one of the lesser populated pools.

He downed his cocktail, grabbed a quick shower and decided to get a cup of coffee and croissant to go. Leaving the room, walked down the several flights to the nearest dining area and picked up his breakfast. Down two decks was one of the outdoor pools. If it met his approval, he would retire in a remote chair and get lost in his novel. He found one, began reading and tuned out the world.

● ● ●

Back in New York City, the horrific crime scene was being investigated by what seemed to be the entire police department. Pieces of bones, flesh, twisted metal and clothing were strewn out over the area between 33rd and 34th street. Even Homeland Security was in attendance, as bombings in the city were a rare occurrence since 9/11. Cooperation rather than competition between various law enforcement agencies had become the rule of thumb. Grey suited Homeland guy had his crime scene unit gathering the bulk of the evidence as the F.B.I. had the best database for examining the evidence now residing in clear plastic bags, all complete with photos and adhesive paper to label third contents. It had taken hours to gather the evidence, but the license tag had taken only several minutes before the vehicle was identified. It had been registered to one Aldo Mancini. It was a name well known to all New Yorkers as the son of the recently imprisoned crime boss, his father Pietro.

As a partially obscured full moon began to rise in the night sky, the heads of each investigative group stood in a semicircle around the crater that now engulfed half of the street. A captain in a once clean uniform took charge. Sipping his large Starbucks coffee, he lowered it from his lips and asked his peers for their attention.

"I want to thank all of you for both your time and cooperation in this unfolding incident. We have a lot of shit to get done. The way I see it, we first need to canvas these few restaurants, those two convenience stores and the few retail outlets surrounding this site, "he began, sweeping his hand in the direction of these businesses. "Let's see if there was anyone out of place, or anyone running away prior to the explosion. Or anyone who might have been talking some trash before the explosion occurred."

"What about these high rises," asked a stocky built man in a charcoal suit, a lanyard around his neck indicating he was with Homeland Security.

"That must be done too and hopefully before it gets past these citizens' bed times. We already have talked to the doorman to the building next to this one. He was a lucky son of a bitch. He was inside when the explosion occurred, waiting for his replacement so he could go on break. He told us that Sid, the neighboring doorman was missing. And he thinks his friend, the poor bastard, might be part of this carnage."

There were more groups involved in the investigation, their names shortened into more letters than were contained in a can of Campbell's Alphabet soup. Among those in attendance were members of the NYPD, Con Ed, the F.B.I., HLS, CSI, and even the E.P.A. The latter group was equipped with various types of equipment which could monitor the chemical composition of what, if any toxic substances might have been released into the atmosphere. After analysis they could be analyzed, high and low tech devices such as Diffusion-Detector tubes, Vapor-Monitor badges, and a variety of hand held monitors designed to test for explosives, hazardous materials and toxins. There was an array of noxious odors that had yet to dissipate from the scene. Some were recognizable such as gasoline, burnt flesh, singed cloth materials that probably emanated from the now missing awning, and the clothes that the victims had been wearing. The chemicals could be captured and preserved, much like arson investigators do, and brought into laboratories that specialized in the breaking down the smells into individual components. This too would take several days to complete.

Adding to the alphabet soup theory were the news trucks that encircled the cordoned off block. Visible letters on the news vans induced CBS, NBC, FOX, ABC, WOR, CNN and HLN. It seems only ESPN was absent, and for obvious reasons.

They all remained silent. Some shaking their heads while others scanned the onslaught, their eyes darting between the chards of sheet metal, the chunks of concrete and the streaks of blood stains on the sidewalk. It was eerily similar to what an urban graffiti artist might do on one of the many bridge overpasses around the city. Bright red, blue and yellow emergency lights danced around the crime scene, as dozens of various individuals in an array of uniforms preformed a multitude of tasks. But what was the creepiest were the gawking onlookers who huddled behind the crime scene tape. And although pushing their way to the front of the melee, reporters were banned from entering the cordoned off area, amidst decrees of no comment from those appearing to be in charge. The governor had given unequivocal orders as to avoid making any statements until more information was gathered. There would be no headlines published in the morning papers, other than mere speculation as to the nature of the event. Whether it was a terroristic attack, a psychopathic maniac or errant meteorite, there would be no confirmations for a time to come.

● ● ●

As the cool ocean breeze fluttered, the loose towels on the surrounding vacant lounge chairs created the familiar soothing sound similar to a flag rippling with intermittent flapping. It created a free feeling within Jon. He was now feeling a total sensation of relaxation, a feeling that had eluded him during his time spent incarcerated. He signaled for a drink and a scantily clad cocktail waitress arrived. She bent slightly toward him, showing the deep cleavage for which she had probably been hired, and took his order for an ice cold Heineken. He crossed his legs as she departed, hiding the slight bulge which was now stretching his swimsuit. He smirked, thinking he would be a poor choice for a Cialis commercial. When she reappeared, he peeled off a ten dollar bill and waved off the change. She thanked him with a smile as well a conscious shake of her derriere as she hustled toward another customer.

He spent the remainder of the morning and part of the afternoon, making a good dent in his novel. When it was time for lunch, he grabbed his towel and chose a table in one of the more secluded dining areas. He still wished to remain as low key as possible, at least until he felt comfortable that no one might recognize him in his 'new skin'. Knowing that the following evening would be filled with high end gastronomic delicacies, he opted for a plain cheeseburger and fries. He smothered them in ketchup and hot sauce, making sure that his rare hamburger that was cooked to perfection. He knew all too well that the dinners that lay ahead would be filled with not only exotic flavors and ingredients, but with a good deal of calories, fat, sodium and all the other non-healthy categories which made it taste oh so good. He was fit and had lost too much time eating garbage in prison. After lunch, he would work the calories from lunch off inside of the ships gymnasium and spa which contained an impressive workout area.

Hours later he arrived at the second evening's gala. The decadent offerings were accompanied by an eight piece string ensemble offering classical selections by the master composers such as Bach, Schubert, Debussy and Stravinsky. Jon was more lost in the music than by the food, having grown up with the European mindset of being in awe of these great composers. In all actuality, he was quite impressed by the way that his ex-employer Milton Phelps had been able to stage such a lavish event. He still hated the guy's guts.

Although hard to best the previous evening's production, the second evening had provided another creative theme. The food during the hors d'oeuvre hour met if not exceeded the previous ones. The hall itself morphed from is classical theme into one reflecting that of the big band era, when speakeasy's hid out in big cities. Music from the greats such as Glenn Miller, Benny Goodman, Tommy Dorsey and Artie Shaw now filled the venue. Servers wore tuxedos and zoot suited bartenders served up the liquor.

Missing from the passengers were hordes of reporters, as Phelps only invited a few, wanting his new theme cruises to embrace a bit of the mystique that would generate public interest. He wanted to start slow, having come off of a disastrous past, and wanting his new venture to erase any of the prior bad publicity he had inherited. After all, the general public is known for having a short term memory.

For the third straight day and night, Vandergriff had avoided mingling and socializing with the other passengers. Other than some small talk in regard to the food and luxury of the accommodations, he pretty much acted the loner.

He found his foot tapping to the lively horn section when he felt a vibration go off in his pants pocket. Removing his cell phone, he began to stroll to the outer deck where the noise level subsided, being replaced by the steady rhythm of the calmer ocean. He held the phone to his ear and bid a good evening to Angel.

"And to you as well, sir, "she responded in an upbeat tone. Jon had no inkling that George had his ear pressed close to the phone, honing in on every word.

"I won't keep you from the festivities my friend. I assume everything is still a go for tomorrow night's activity, she asked, her voice now taking on a bit of that seductive air she teased him with.

"It's full steam ahead," he replied, not even aware of his unconscious reply. He rolled his eyes around, making fun of himself for his oh so not witty answer.

"Good then. We will next talk again when the ship arrives and you can fill me in on what the news stories leave out. Goodnight," she ended and the phone line shut down.

● ● ●

During his past three days on the ocean, Jon was not aware, nor did he care, about the events unfolding in New York City. Two days of an intense investigation beat the norm of providing more unanswered questions than answered ones precluding any concrete facts. Down at One Police Plaza, or 1PP as it is called, the heads of the groups of cooperating investigation agencies sat in a large meeting room reviewing the facts and comparing notes. Among the group were two others, neither involved directly in the investigation.

There was a gut feeling that tugged at Davis, a feeling that he came to know and trust. Gasparo had flown up to Philadelphia and he convinced the Witness Protection agent to accompany him up to New York 'just in case'. He had called one of his old acquaintances from the academy, Sal Batella. Sal hailed from Northern Jersey but moved to Philadelphia when he was offered a position in the early days of the OCTF when he and Davis were added to that department. Batella had been instrumental in a number of arrests during the mobs heyday when it ruled South Philadelphia. Now retired, he accepted some consultant work. Sal was savvy, well experienced and his last name ended in a vowel. He had grown up with many of his friends and family members opting for work on the not so legal side of the law. His superiors were never quite sure where he stood, but his record was pretty much clean.

Standing at 5'9", his stocky frame and well chiseled good looks spoke volumes about his experience. Jovial, tough and a good listener, Sal was still called upon to offer his expertise and insight into the intricate workings of organized crime. Davis had consulted him, and after Sal's advisement, he contacted Gasparo and they joined the investigative group in New York.

On the drive up to the Big Apple, Gasparo filled Davis in on how Gando had eluded his handlers. His roommate and longtime friend, Crello had decoyed the agents and led them on a wild goose chase. They were clueless as to where and when Gando had left sunny Florida and escaped to parts unknown. Knowing now that Mancini was deceased, Davis had to explore the possibilities that Gando had a hand in the murder. He wanted in on the investigation and his reputation had gained him entrance into the investigative team.

"All you have is a theory and gut instinct. You and I both know that proves nada," said Gasparo as they approached their destination.

"No argument here. We talked theories and possibilities, so let's just wait to see what these experts lay on the table. I have an open mind and won't jump to any conclusions."

They had driven through the Holland Tunnel and were now winding their way through the lower east side, the destination being Park Row. Such landmarks as City Hall, the Brooklyn Bridge and Chinatown, came and went. After finding the elusive New York City parking spot, they flashed their creds and were directed to the meeting room. The session had yet to begin, so the two grabbed a much needed coffee and found seats toward the back of the room. Shortly thereafter, the proceedings began.

The room was filled with several dozen law enforcement individuals from the various investigative teams. A tall man with flecked gray hair, a square jaw and deep brown eyes snapped his fingers several times and the chatter within the room subsided. He slowly turned his head, glancing over the attendees before beginning his briefing. Al McGlynn, head of the New York City police department then began.

"I would like to thank everyone in the room and their teams for the quick response in gathering all pertinent information regarding this incident. The level of competency and professionalism you all displayed are very impressive. Thank you all."

He paused for several seconds making sure that he had the undivided attention of his audience. He continued.

"After this meeting, we will inform the media in regard to the basic facts of what we know, so let me fill all of you in first. The explosion that occurred several days ago was not a terrorist related action. Based on evidence recovered from the crime scene and subsequent interviews, we are now certain that the target of this event was Aldo Mancini, son of imprisoned crime boss, Pietro Mancini. He has not been seen for several days and the license plate recovered at the scene was registered to one of his businesses. Nor has he returned to his residence, according to interviews with his housekeepers and his neighbors."

He paused momentarily, scanning the room for the reaction and to see if any questions were looming. None were so he pressed on.

"All indications are that it was a mob hit and we are investigating those who might benefit from his elimination. The explosive residue found and tested indicates that it was an explosive compound used by various military factions and is not readily available, except on the black market. We are in contact with various armed forces bases to see if any of it is missing. The problem is that such a small amount was used and we are now assuming it will probably be untraceable, but we are still looking."

He took another sip of water and continued with what they had learned.

"At this point in time, we can account for at least five casualties. Mancini, his two body guards, his driver and the missing doorman. The doorman was collateral damage, a sad outcome for his family. But I for one will not mourn the loss of the four wise guys that were probably targeted. Getting scum off the street in any way is palatable."

The commissioner concluded with some peripheral details and theories before opening up the session to alternative theories and questions. Davis shot up his hand, like a third grader who knew the answer to a tough question, minus the 'oh- oh- oh' sound effects that usually accompanied the eagerness to intercede. The commissioner recognized him, asking his name and department.

"My name is Stephen Davis and I am a supervisor for the Organized Crime Task Force in the city of Philadelphia," he explained.

"Yes Mr. Davis," McGlynn began, throwing in a dig about a city that has yet to win a Super Bowl. It lightened the intensity of the room.

"There might be at least one before I die," he replied, causing a bit of laughter in the room.

"If I may be so bold, I would like to offer a theory, and mind you, I have no physical proof to substantiate it at this point in time. It's just my gut feeling, that little voice which suggests to me a possible motive."

"Proceed," McGlynn responded, his face reflecting interest in regard to the 'why and who' part of the investigation. "And by the way, I am familiar with your reputation in regards to your investigative prowess in solving some high profile cases that you had encountered. I admit I admire a job well done."

"Thank you Mr. Commissioner," Davis replied, his true modesty displayed regarding the unsolicited compliment.

"It's just a theory, and I had run it by Mr. Gasparo, sitting here next to me. I was recently informed that Julian Gando has eluded his handlers during his relocation to Florida. After several attempts were made on his life and knowing that the sons of the bosses he testified against had put out a contract on him, it might be a possibility that he is up here trying to take *them* out before they reach him. We have no proof and it's only a theory. Look, we all are involved in law enforcement and I highly doubt I am the only guy in this room that gets that gut wrenching signal on certain occasions."

The commissioner nodded as he too didn't get where he was without that instinct. He told Davis that he was more than welcome to explore his theory.

"If your superiors are willing to grant you some time, then we would welcome you aboard."

Davis made a fist and guided Gasparo's eyes down to it. He understood, clenching his fingers and following with a bump to Davis's fist. He would have no problem getting the okay to join the loosely knit investigative team.

The commissioner fielded some other questions and theories by the group open for any suggestions as to learning the how and why this crime occurred.

CHAPTER 15

Vandergriff spent a restless night despite his higher than normal intake of alcohol. It was now Wednesday and tonight was his working night. He glanced at the digital readout on the high tech Bose alarm clock which also held an I-Pod port, radio bandwidths containing A.M, F.M and even the ships special event station. The aqua blue numbers read 6:07. He knew from experience and the time of year, he had woken in time the spectacular sunrises that never ceased to awe his senses. The hues of peach, pink and aquamarine melded into a display that he had never seen captured on film or canvass. His gazed fixed on the event as if it were apocalyptic in nature. When it was over, he walked back into the room and pondered what to do so early, as he had a long day to finalize his nefarious plan.

Deciding it might be best to vent some of his nervous energy, he put on his walking shorts, a loose cotton polo shirt, embossed with an actual polo player on horseback and slipped into his Nike's before tying them up. He grabbed a room key and headed for the deck that was designated for those wanting to circle the ship. The surface was done in the same color blue as the ships logo, its surface coated with a rubber/latex composite that was friendly to joggers. One lap equaled ¼ mile and wound around the outside of the fifth deck. There were not many others out there at that time in the morning seeing how the past nights activities ran well past two in the morning.

Jon used this time to reconstruct the plans he had made for the buffet in the evening ahead. He would wear clothing that did not stand out, sunglasses to add a bit more of a disguise and plain khaki pants with a generic white polo. He would go with the alligator one rather than the polo player. He thought who on God's earth would flaunt the same designer shirt twice in one day, he bemused, not really being a fashion whore anyway.

As he walked, his mind focused on the planned instructions he had gone through with Angel countless times. They had gone through blue-prints of the main dining room where the event would be held, along with the cameras that scanned the room, as well as the whole ship. Events of 9/11 had made way for added security in every walk of life, in the name of safety and guarding our freedoms. As Monk, the famous OCD detective would say, 'it was a blessing and a curse'.

● ● ●

Gando meanwhile had found refuge a bit further south in Mercer County, New Jersey. Located north of Trenton, the state capital, it borders on the more rural counties of Burlington and Hunterdon. It also is the home of Princeton University, fast growing Trenton-Mercer Airport and the Delaware River. He had taken a room at the Hyatt Place, one of many hotels that dotted Route 1 and running parallel to the New Jersey Turnpike. Route 1 was adjacent to may high tech, pharmaceutical and chemical companies that were housed in the Garden State. It was an under the radar place to be, filled with many consultants and sales reps that conducted business with those corporations.

Crello would be taking a flight from Panama City to Trenton Mercer Airport, believing that these two airports would be less closely guarded than any of the major ones both in Florida and the New York metropolitan areas. Gando needed his help to complete the second hit and Crello was the only person he could totally depend on. It was the bond they had established, a rare trait which we all can only hope for during our lifetimes.

Crello would arrive tomorrow and Gando spent his time watching the New York news stations as well as CNN and HLN which had covered the bombing incident he created. He upped the volume and stared at the talking head.

"The commissioner of the New York City police department has issued a long awaited for statement in regard to the recent Murray Hill bombing. He was adamant that the explosion was not related to a terrorist attack. As the investigation continues, it is believed that several of the victims, including Aldo Mancini, were fatalities of a mob hit in the struggle for control of the remaining families in the five boroughs. Along with three of his associates, Pauli Dimartino, Angelo Carracci and Carlo Antuzzi, DNA evidence proved that Mancini also perished in the blast. Ray Summers, the doorman at the Murray Hill Arms was also killed. However, a sixth victim, yet to be identified, may also have been collateral damage in this violent event. Stay tuned as we will keep you up to date on this developing story."

Gando shook his head, knowing that Peretti was the sixth victim. Had it not been for his overzealous devotion and temper, there might only have been five. He liked the kid. There was no reason he had to perish other than the fact that he wanted to taunt his victims.

● ● ●

Jon spent the remainder of the afternoon just sitting on his balcony. He replayed his life, from his days growing up in Europe through his current position. As we all do, he had things which he might have done differently, but all in all, he was happy with his accomplishments and experiences. He knew all too well that after this evenings' events, his self-esteem and evaluation of his actions might change the whole way in which he viewed his life. Still, he was a man of his word and the past events of his life were now dictating his future actions. Certain events and circumstances dictate our behavior while at the same time, we are also able to choose our own paths. No one famous said that, but it does sound like a reasonable assumption.

The sun began to dip into the sea, now a greyish blue canvass in the distant horizon. Jon stared out without taking in the scene, gathering his thoughts and going through his plans for the upcoming event. He felt no angst, no guilt nor any sympathy. He separated his emotions from the results that would be caused by his hand. He was in sort of a twilight zone rerun.

Before showering and readying himself for the upcoming extravaganza, he did one last check on his arsenal. It consisted of three spray vials whose contents had been carefully loaded. Two of them held a high concentration of salmonella bacteria and the third with campylobacter jejuni, which can be transmitted through raw meat, poultry or seafood. George was able to procure this strain through another one of his clients for whom he made a great deal of money. No questions were ever asked. George also assumed that there would be other offerings other than chicken and wanted to cover the array on the menu.

He entered the shower, letting the hot spray energize him and yet distract him from the terrible thing he was about to do. He rationalized that it was directed at the bastard that had caused him the pain and incarceration he had spent over the last two years, along with the easy money he would earn. No thoughts of ethical or moral righteousness ever came into play.

Jon spent the remainder of the day alone on his balcony deck, nursing a bloody Mary, not wanting any of his thought processes to be altered. He had learned that lesson more than two years prior and was still paying for his alcohol infused miscalculation. Countless times he had run through the plan. Two of the vials were white, indicating the salmonella contained therein and the third was green. There was no room for error.

The buffet was scheduled for 7:00 P.M., and for Jon, the minutes seem to disappear at a more rapid rate than usual. It was slightly before six. He decided to take another shower, knowing that a warm shower would relax him. Actually, he was surprised that he wasn't anxious or nervous, having had more than ample time to reconsider his upcoming actions and had no intention to do so.

He took a back stairway down to the main dining area which was host-ing the buffet. Curiously, he had wanted to see the changes that Phelps had made to the ship, as well as explore any escape routes if need be. If this job went as planned and he had gotten any type of satisfaction, who knew, there might be more work for him in the future. He assumed there would be, but it all depended on the success of his mission.

Upon entering the vast room, he noticed that there was no loud music playing or themes displayed. A large octagonal arrangement of chafing dishes and Bain-Marie's had been set up so the guests could fill their plates at various stations. Tables had been arranged at various points ten or so yards away from the serving areas, so that the anticipated crowds could avoid those waiting to chow down. Scanning the 'Bountiful Buffet' as it was deemed, Jon's senses noticed not only the famous chefs stand-ing behind the serving area, but the aromas that stemmed from their creations. One station featured appetizers. Then counter clockwise there were salad and vegetable stations, main courses, one featuring meats and the other oceanic delights. Side dishes followed and a magnificent desert area, complete with a white chocolate, dark chocolate and cara-mel waterfall in which to cover any exotic fruits or decadent desserts that the diners might opt for. It truly was a gastronomic food orgy.

Jon stared at his surroundings, silently calculating and waiting for a good time to launch his plan. Subtly scanning the cameras, he noticed they were aimed toward the exit ways rather than the dining area itself. He was now satisfied. Yeah, he was sure of that.

He walked over to the area were plates were wiped down and handed to the customer. Since he was not concerned about the dining aspect of the event, he took a napkin, folded it and wrapped it around his right hand. With his left, he reached into his pocket and removed the canis-ter that held the Salmonella, transferring it into his right hand which was covered by the napkin. He walked over to the entrée section and noticed a dish called 'Chicken Vindaloo with raisins'. Moving toward the steam table which contained the dish, he grabbed the serving spoon with his right hand and ladled a spoon full on his plate. As he backed away, he depressed the nozzle, coating the rest of the dish with spray as he slowly withdrew his plate. Everyone was too excited about reading the small placards under the dishes to notice his actions. He checked a box off on the imaginary list in his head.

Moving clockwise, he repeated the process on the Mario Batali 'Pollo all Romano', as well as the 'Chicken-Chorizo Paella', and two other poultry offerings. He had emptied the contents of the two white canisters, with no one being observant of his actions.

Moving clockwise, he removed the final bottle and repeated the same process for concealing his actions. He doused Chef Kenichi's 'Chili Prawns' and its neighbor, 'New England lobster Rolls with Truffle Mayo', until the container was drained. He did make sure that he procured one of the rolls before contaminating it with his bottle.

He noticed that he never broke a sweat, his hands never trembled and his mind felt no pangs of guilt during his callous performance. Even more interesting to his mindset, was that he didn't even care why. The 'old' Vandergriff was a caring soul, barring his alcohol infused binges, and would never have perceived orchestrating an act such as the one he was performing right now. He didn't know if was the revenge motive, greed factor or adrenaline rush that erased his conscience. But he did know that the synapses in his brain that relayed any remorse were now absent. Why wonder why, he thought, as he left the gala function and returned to his stateroom.

Upon returning, he set his plate down with the chicken dish and lobster roll, both in their pre-contaminated state. He grabbed a Fiji water from the bar and set his dish down on the table angled from the television. He turned it on, more interested in the sound and light than in the shows content. It was a scrolling itemized schedule of the upcoming events for the remainder of the evening and the following day. He didn't care. After all, he damn well knew any planned events would be dropped from the venue if the contaminants which he dispensed found their human targets.

CHAPTER 16

Jon had fallen asleep in the chair, feeling like an athlete that had just finished a marathon. He was mentally spent. All of the preparation and mental toughness had finally taken its toll. The only thing inevitable for him was at this time was sleep.

Jon was woken by a bright red light on the television, accompanied by those same annoying high pitched tones we have all come to cherish, and made famous by those interruptions from the Emergency Broadcast System. Arising from the comfortable recliner, Jon grabbed the remote and increased the volume. The crawl along the bottom of the screen gave the passengers a four digit number to dial so that they would be given a place in line to see the medical staff. A half smile came over his face, being pleased that he had done his job well. He listened to the broadcast that now filled the ships public address system.

"Shortly after two this morning, a multitude of calls were received by our medical staff of two doctors and three nurses. In all of these cases, passengers have been reporting stomach pains, diarrhea, chills, fever and headaches. Preliminary findings have attributed these symptoms to either food poisoning or a possible viral infection that is being spread amongst the ship's passengers. We do not believe that any of these occurrences are life threatening, but we are urging all passengers feeling ill, to dial the numbers 199, so that we may examine you."

There was no politically correct way to convey the instructions to follow, but the medical staff did its best to convey what needed to be done.

"We urge all passengers with these symptoms to procure a stool sample prior to visiting our medical facilities located on the third deck adjacent to the health club entrance. We are currently running all possible lab work to determine the cause but our facilities are not equipped to diagnose the wide array of medical conditions in the same way that a normal hospital or lab can. We urge you all to remain calm and greatly appreciate your patience in this matter. If we see any spike in the number of cases, we will be heading back to the nearest port city in order to provide you, our valued passengers, with the best and fastest treatment possible. Please stay tuned to this channel for any updates we may discover."

It was a well phrased spin on what was developing as an epidemic of food poisoning. Although very rarely fatal, he knew that Phelps would be responsible not only for making this right, but facing another setback to his prized possession, PacLantic Cruise Lines. He chuckled to himself again, knowing that Salmonella appears between 6-48 hours post ingestion. The latter of the toxins take 2-5 days to manifest and appear. Damage control would be as challenging as the missing Malaysian Airliner flight MH370 had encountered.

● ● ●

With the advent of cell phones and real time communications, the events of the *Adventurer* became headline news on all the stations prior to 5 A.M. that Thursday morning. There were very few reporters on board, and those that were, wrote stories about dining experiences or travel excursions. Regardless of their specialties, once a reporter always a reporter and their computers and tablets were experiencing a typing frenzy. Many passengers were seen clutching their stomachs as they made their way to the already overcrowded pharmacy deck. Some screams of pain also emerged from behind closed doors and hallways. The ship's crew had not been immune to succumbing from the mass sickness and hysteria, as it spread throughout the whole ship. Phrases like 'we are all going to die' and 'pray to Jesus' only added fuel to the already contagious chaos.

When the familiar ringtone erupted from his charging cellphone on the nightstand, Phelps reached over for it. He noticed the time was slightly before 5 A.M. and tinges of concern overcame him, reminding him of that fateful call he had received over two years ago. The call had been permanently ingrained in his being.

"Phelps," he answered authoritatively, giving no indication of the deep sleep he had been awoken from only seconds before.

"It's McCain boss."

But before Phelps could hear another word, an ill feeling of dread swept over him. He turned on CNN. It was his ship. He watched in awe, now feeling fortunate that he had left the ship when he did.

"We have a situation on the *Adventurer*. During last evenings buffet, it seems some type of virus or food poisoning has been running rampant on the ship. I have several Medivac choppers en route to the ship which is still a good half day away from Miami, the closest port in the states. They have some lab testing equipment aboard as well as some of the requisite pharmaceuticals that our doctor had requested. They should land within the hour."

McCain paused for an instance, searching for a response, but it didn't immediately follow. He did hear a loud voice suddenly appear, recognizing it to be a news report with several phrases that indicated it was in regard the current story which he was filling Phelps in on.

"Meet me down at the home office. We have some serious work to do before this turns into another St Maarten."

Knowing that his orders were always met, he abruptly hung up and grabbed a quick shower. As he shaved, his mind raced in respect to what was actually happening, as well as the how and why this event could best be controlled. He would need to get a leg up on the media this time.

Fifty minutes later he arrived at his offices, accompanied by two of the lawyers and several others. Those awaiting his arrival all ended their gossiping as Phelps entered. There were no good morning greetings or acknowledgements of their presence. With a stern look, he motioned them into the large board room at the end of the hallway, with only a forward nod of his head. This is where the brainstorming would begin.

They entered fastidiously and took their seats, arranged by the corporate pecking order they were relegated to. They all knew what the boss would be opening with.

"Tell me what the fuck is going on. I pay you all a shitload of money and I need answers and solutions yesterday." It was pretty close to what they expected he would say.

McCain took the lead and brought him up to speed. He began with the early morning complaints from passengers which were mostly of the gastrointestinal variety. Each of the first dozen passengers had similar symptoms; diarrhea, vomiting, nausea and the like.

"The physicians we have on staff are very thorough and capable. They also have drawn blood as precautionary measures just in case some form of bacterial or viral organisms are the cause of these symptoms."

McCain was interrupted by his vibrating phone. Removing it from his pocket, he glanced at the number, indicating that it was the ship's infirmary. The choppers had landed and had just started running the lab work. Seeing Phelps's laser stare, he put the phone on speaker so they could all listen in.

"Even though we know the diagnosis, it might take several days to learn the origin of this illness. We have no fatalities and don't expect any. Now we need to know what caused this disaster and make sure that it was not our responsibility."

Before Phelps spoke, he motioned for McCain to cut the communications, running his finger across his throat in the universal signal to end what he was doing. He promptly did. Phelps's face had lightened from the reddened tone back to its usual tanned hue.

"This cruise featured some of the top chefs on this fuckin' planet. There can be no way that they erred in their food preparation. If it was the food, I want every invoice from every one of our suppliers."

As he spoke, the gathering noticed that the cool persona which he was publicly perceived as having, was withering away by the millisecond. Panic had set in. He continued.

"We need to trace the origin and more importantly, we must relay to the media that we are investigating the source of our food products and believe this event was due to improper food storage *prior to our receiving it.*" His emphasis was noted by all.

"What *if* it's viral", interjected Jenny Farmer of the legal team, being rhetorical. "That happens every week somewhere in the world."

Phelps then grabbed the remotes that lay next to him and turned on all three sets, which were all set on the big news stations. Fortunately, there was a Middle East cease fire broken and severe coastal flooding in California that took precedent over the cruise story. When it came on MSNBC, he tuned up the volume and focused.

"Early reports from the cruise ship *Adventurer* are coming in and there seems to be an illness affecting a large number of vacationers. Although no official statements have been made by the company, our sources tell us it is a food related illness and no one has died. We will continue to follow this story."

"That gives us some time to prepare a statement. I don't believe it would be wise at this point to presuppose or make any statements that could be construed so as to make us look responsible," Phelps stated, concluding that it was time to issue a press release.

Aboard the ship, Vandergriff sat on his patio, sipping some scotch, slowly cleaning out the mini-bar. Although screaming and panic could be heard from his perch, he blocked it out. Rather, he poignantly began focusing on the small whitecaps the ship was creating as it headed full steam back to port. He knew the ships speed just by watching the height that the waves as they crested and plunged. The motion of the sea had also become an integral a part of him. He was a bit surprised, not concerned though, of the fact that he and he alone had caused all this ballyhoo. It was a mixture of revenge, excitement and the monetary reward. It was the type of story that shows like Dateline feasted upon.

The only problem was that they usually only followed cases in which the culprit was apprehended. There was no way that he had any intention on being caught.

He continued to stare at the sea as the ship progressed toward Miami.

● ● ●

By 8 A.M. Phelps had not only called for a news conference, but had amassed much more information from the testing of this outbreak. He could spin stories with the best of them. Before he began, he noticed his wife had called several times, and even though one of his aids had called her, the calls and texts went unanswered. He also noticed a call from his brother George. What, did he want to gloat over his failure or rub it in even more? Knowing it was either one of these motives, he decided he would just ignore the calls.

Milton Phelps regained his composure, now standing tall and visibly proud. He emitted an aura displaying that he remained unruffled by the events that were slowly unfolding. His charcoal gray suit and aqua tie expressed an assured and casual confidence. His hair was slicked back, a la Gordon Gekko in 'Wall Street'. It was that overly self-possessed attitude and always in charge look that gave him what he believed to be credibility. He would soon find out if that was the case.

He was flanked by his top executives and legal experts. Most stood with stoic, serious expressions on their faces, clasping their hands in front of them in a gesture of unanimity. Broadway could not have staged it better.

Phelps went on to explain the current situation, stressing that it was being handled in a safe and judicious way. All precautions were being taken to assure the well-being and comfort of all on board, adding that all passengers would be questioned and checked out by waiting authorities. He hinted that causes of this situation might be attributed to "possible terrorist actions, poor food handling by his suppliers or by an unknown source of a disease." He suggested every excuse to blame outside sources, rather than accept responsibility for the event still in question. He concluded by adding that information would be released as it was gathered.

"The facts will be relayed in the most timely and factual manner as is humanly possible." Was this guy a politician in a past life or what?

● ● ●

The ship arrived roughly and hour and a half before schedule. The combination of calm seas and full throttle made that all possible. Phelps personally aided in the evacuation of sick passengers, making sure the camera captured his concern and self-sacrifice. He had loosened his tie, rolled up his sleeves and played the part.

It took several hours to evacuate the ship. Those unaffected were brought into small interrogation rooms and briefly questioned. Jon was briefly concerned about his new identity, but after fifteen minutes, was ushered out after answering all pertinent questions. Neither his physical appearance nor the background that Angel had created for him had raised any serious concerns.

Angel had been observing the unloading of the passengers from a safe and isolated distance. She then sent Jon a text of where to meet. After gathering his luggage, he walked in the directions she had sent him and met her by her car. She greeted him with a firm, appreciative hug.

"It's so nice to see you again. And may I say that my employers are very impressed with your work."

Jon smiled, modestly taking the credit and mentioning that it was all due in fact to the precise planning of the operation. Angel motioned him to the car and he got in.

"This is for all your hard work and diligence," she said, handing him a folded and overstuffed manila folder. She added that there was a higher sum than the agreed upon amount, which he broadly smiled about.

After discussing the events that transpired and the aftermath, Angel mentioned that she had to fly up north to meet with her clients. She asked

Jon where he would like to be dropped off, adding not to spend his new fortune like a drunken sailor. He nodded, slipping the large envelope into his carry on and thanked her again for the pleasure of doing business. Any thoughts of a more intimate relationship had been answered by her actions and he dropped the thought. After all, the hundred thousand plus could satisfy any indulgence which he might desire.

She dropped him off, asking him that if his services were needed in the future, if he would be available again. He readily agreed and bid her goodbye. He couldn't wait to indulge in several days of a hedonistic binge.

PART FOUR

CHAPTER 17

Davis was fully immersed in the New York bombing investigation. He had been given a week 'off' to pursue his theory about Gando's possible involvement. Being tangled in both high profile investigations as well as addressing the media during such crimes, he was excited to see Commissioner McGlynn in action. He respected the man and the way he was able to draw together all of the investigative agencies, making them function as close to a team as possible. Unlike the movies and television, agency cooperation has become more of a norm than the exception. He stood off to the side as McGlynn addressed the cameras and microphones that were rudely surrounding him. If anything relating to this event was the norm, it was the rudeness displayed by proud, news hungry New Yorker's.

He began by confirming that the explosive device did kill Mancini, also giving the names and occupations of the other victims. Three were connected to Mancini and the last was the doorman at the hotel. The license plate and DNA both aided in identifying what was left from the carnage. Speculating about the motive, the reasons he offered were possibly caused by the vacuum left by his father's imprisonment or a possible revenge killing. Terrorism was ruled out.

"But we are leaning towards a revenge hit, relying on some of our confidential sources close to the victims involved." Nary was a word mentioned about Gando.

McGlynn concluded with the standard clichés in regard to the progress they were making in order to identify the guilty party. Also offered up was a hotline number along with a ten thousand dollar reward 'leading to the arrest and conviction of the perpetrator of this heinous act.' He noted as well, that the murder rate in 2013 had experienced a 20% decrease, totaling only 333 murders. That was less than one per day. He fielded several questions and then left the podium, returning to his office. The media would have to either manufacture or uncover a better story to lead off the five o' clock news in the race for ratings.

Gasparo and Davis started walking away from the gathering. It was Davis's last day in New York and wanted to finalize their brainstorming on how they might draw Gando out of his seclusion, if in fact it was he who was responsible for this action. Davis stopped and grabbed Gasparo's arm. Gasparo turned and faced him, a little surprised and not knowing what his peer was thinking. With a serious face he began to speak.

"I have a wish Paul", Davis began, keeping his look serious. "You grew up in this town and I am a second class citizen from the small town of Philadelphia. I have been doing some research and although I am not of Italian heritage as you are, I have a modest request."

Gasparo had no idea where this was going, his facial features producing a puzzled look.

"Go on", Gasparo asked amused.

"Still being middle aged, I must admit, that I do have a sort of bucket list already."

"I'm listening," Gasparo said.

"The truth is, as much as I hate to admit, before I am dead and gone, I must experience the top ten pizzerias in this great city of yours. So, if at all possible, and after reading the Village Voice, I would like to stop at this place called Di Farra. It's in Brooklyn and I know it's on my way back to Philly. Besides, I promised Ashley that I would bring some back. Can we make it happen?"

Gasparo grabbed Davis's shoulder, squeezing it slightly. Smiling broadly, he muttered something in Italian and shook his head.

"It would be my pleasure and I will even buy. I will call ahead, order you a couple of pies and we can wait over at MD Kitchen. We can talk there and I am guessing it should be a couple hour wait until they are ready. Follow me when we get our cars and we can drive down there. It should take about a bit less than an hour."

Almost 45 minutes later, they arrived in Brooklyn. For those non New York natives, the Belt Parkway has one sign for entering the borough and one as you exit. One reads 'Fuhgeddaboudit' and the other, 'How sweet it is', the catch phrase of Jackie Gleason. Winding their way through the Midwood section, they arrived on Avenue J between East 14th and 15th. With the dining area's size rivaling that of the lavatory on a 767, they grabbed the two boxes and returned to where they had parked. Placing the box on the hood of Davis's car, they opened the box with the half fresh mushroom and half pepperoni, and readied their napkins. Gasparo lightly blotted the top, removing some of the oil from the cheese before it ended up on his suit jacket. Davis just dug in. At close to $30.00 for the pie, it was pricey, but more like a slice of heaven than a slice of pizza. Davis remained silent as Gasparo watched him indulge, asking if the pie was as good as oral sex. Davis gave it some thought, and after ingesting the slice, replied it was a tie. They ate, sipped their Cokes and remained silent.

"Man I owe you one," said Davis, thanking him for guiding him to pizza heaven.

"And I will call in a favor when the time comes," he shot back. They both smiled, and after a masculine fist bump, returned to their vehicles.

Gasparo suggested he haul his ass back to Philly to beat some of the traffic and see his fiancée. He added that they would talk tonight and discusses what tactics they might use to find Gando. That was if in fact he who was responsible for the hit on Mancini. But both of them had that instinct, that feeling that they were on the right track.

● ● ●

Adrianna had returned home that afternoon, wanting both to comfort Milton as well as get the facts as they trickled in. She showed genuine concern. After all, her lifestyle and income was something she cherished above all else. Milton filled her in as he paced while tightly clutching his cell phone in hand, waiting on calls that might relay any of the latest developments. He was satisfied in regard to his public statement, downplaying any fault that might be directed toward the presumed negligence of PacLantic. Adrianna agreed, mentioning the ship collision that had occurred in the past. It was a reputation that had yet to vanish from its history.

The phone rang and without examining the caller ID, Milton answered the call. He immediately regretted it when he heard the unpleasant, irritating voice on the other end, the tone containing a bit of swagger and gloating.

"Dear brother of mine, I was so sorry to see the misfortune of those poor passengers who took the highly publicized voyage you had assembled. I know how disappointed you were when I turned down the invite. What do they say, something like hindsight is 20-20?"

Carolyn was leaning in holding her ear close to the phone, while she joyfully poked his side, egging on the taunting of his brother.

"You really are an asshole, George. Sympathy I would never presume was in your repertoire, but your childish comments were something that I expected. Do you feel better now jerk-off?" Milton's inflections were even, not wanting to show the hatred he had for his brother. It was being amped up even more as his words were spoken.

George remained quiet, letting his brother vent. He momentarily held the phone away and as Carolyn watched, he wiggled his thumb over his fingertips, symbolizing the money he was making from his recent investments. He even whispered a cheerful "ching- ching", causing her to restrain from an outbreak of triumphant laugh.

With the phone close to his ear, he heard an emphatic" fuck you" from his brother and the line disconnected. George had made his point and they both knew it. They both also knew that there would be a good deal of more ill will exchanged following this incident. George's belief that his brother was responsible for his father's death and Milton's everlasting denial would fester for an eternity.

"So how is the wolf of wall street faring today," Carolyn asked, picturing the next shopping spree in her mind.

George looked at Carolyn as he began to poke his finger in the air as if punching in numbers on an imaginary calculator.

"The way I see it at this point in time, the stock in PacLantic has fallen by a third, transports are slightly down and the travel industry is slightly higher. We might be ahead roughly three to four hundred thousand," he stated, a wide shit eating grin now forming on his face.

"You are a genius, and that's just one of the reasons I love you," Carolyn said admiringly.

George knew that the financial gain added to her admiration, but he loved impressing her. She stroked his ego almost as well as his...

"And I am assuming your boy Jon was happy with his bonus?"

She nodded to confirm his assumption. He grabbed her hand and walked to the bar in the corner of the room. Grabbing a bottle of celebratory Dom Perignon Oenotheque, valued at close to $500.oo per bottle, he motioned with a nod toward the bedroom and they walked off arm and arm, two goblets in hand, for celebration sex.

"This is even better than revenge sex *or* make up sex," she whispered in his ear, and they retired to their master bedroom.

● ● ●

Gasparo was correct. Davis left almost in time to beat the traffic that formed after crossing the Verrenzano Bridge. Road construction on New York City highways was about as common as the sun rising in the east. Although he had already consumed three slices, the combination of stop and go traffic and the aroma of the New York delicacy made him give in. He slid open the box, folded the slice, a practice inherent in all New York pizza eaters, and bit off the end. Ashley would understand that the temptation was too great and besides, she could eat the last seven pieces if her heart desired.

Slightly less than three hours later, he arrived back at their condo. She was waiting outside, and approached to help as he grabbed his overnight bag from the trunk and handed her the pizza.

"I hope there is a slice or two remaining, "she said, grabbing the box and locking her lips around his lower one.

He reluctantly pulled away from the pleasured greeting and handed her the box.

"I would *never* risk our relationship over a slice of pizza, but after you try it, you will see how I fought off the urge to consume the whole thing."

She laughed as they walked arm and arm to the entrance. Although he was gone for almost a week, she mentioned how much she had missed him and promised welcome home sex would be as good, if not better than the usual. He smiled as they took the elevator up, making out as teenagers would, after discovering their hormonal awakenings.

They walked down the short hallway as Ashley opened the front door. He tossed his bag across the living room and accompanied her to the small island in the kitchen area.

"Kick the oven up to five hundred and toss three slices on that pizza stone. That's one for me and two for you. Am I generous or what? Let me shower quickly, sort out the laundry and I will join you in a few."

"Ok, love of my life," mimicking one of those black and white film noir movies from the forties, tossing her hair back in a Barbara Stanwyck kind of way.

Twenty minutes later he returned to the living room, watching a slivery wisp of smoke arise from his slice. They enjoyed the reunion, the food and just the fact they were back together. His mind darted to his brother and relationship with Jaime, wondering if he and his sibling both experienced a similar pleasure from the woman they loved. He decided that they probably did.

The seven o clock local news had concluded. After a democratic vote, they decided it best that they catch up on a lost week of passionate sex and retired to their bedroom. Is there such thing as New York pizza sex? If there wasn't, maybe now there was!

CHAPTER 18

Crello arrived on a small charter flight from Fort Myers to West Trenton airport. He had evaded any tails and decided it better to leave from the west coast of Florida where he would be both less conspicuous and edgy. He figured the feds would be all over West Palm, Orlando, Fort Lauderdale and Miami. He assumed that they lacked the manpower to cover every airport in Florida and the surrounding area. In fact, there are 19 major cities in the Sunshine State that contain larger airports, and this does not include the smaller reliever, general aviation, military and private ones. He was so right and would hopefully be so safe.

Gando was waiting in a generic Ford Taurus which had been registered under one of the fake I.D's that the late Mike Peretti had provided him. He liked the kid but his arrogance and stupidity had gotten the best of him. He was sacrificed for the cause, Gando thought, crossing himself once in a rare religious expression.

Crello emerged from the flight containing the full capacity of 12 passengers. Most were female, several had small children and he was more than confident that there were no federal agents on board the flight. Not that in these post 9/11 days were anything what it seemed anymore. He was correct as usual, as he had always erred on the side of caution.

Gando remained in the car, texting Crello from his disposable phone which car he was in and where it was located. Not until he had popped the trunk and Crello tossed in his carry on, did he enter the car. They hugged, exchanging smiles, as Crello slumped into the seat. He explained the flight was long, uncomfortable and he needed a good stiff one.

Crello proudly explained how he had eluded his tails and Gando countered with his recounting of the Mancini hit. These were the abbreviated versions and dinner would produce more in depth details. Gando concluded, mentioning that the media had just chalked the catastrophic hit up to a turf war, or a common mob hit, with nothing tied to the subplot of revenge against the man who put his father away.

"I expected no less from your sorry ass," Crello joked. He knew Gando was a professional and always made sure that his handiwork went undetected. "Where are you staying?" Crello asked, as he rested his tired eyes and body.

"I have a room up on Route 1, near Princeton in one of the many hotels along the road. Peretti secured me a fake I.D. and no one has noticed me. I am pretty sure of that."

Crello nodded.

"Let's grab a bite to eat and get back to the room. Is there any suspicion that you had a hand in this affair?"

Gando shook his head and emphasized that there were no media mentioning of his involvement and all focus was being put on a revenge hit. He truly believed that, but his underestimation of Davis was an unnoticeable fault. Or maybe it wasn't.

Gando drove up to KC Prime, a steakhouse that was off of Route 1 and the Quakerbridge Mall. It wasn't the type of high end steak house that a mob associate would ever be seen at. It was no Capital Grille, but it had dark corners and even offered, as Gando joked to Crello, a no shooting section.

They were greeted by the hostess and asked to sit in a quiet area so they could discuss business. Being only half full, they were easily accommodated. They were quickly approached by a tall brunette with the name Jessica displayed in large white letters on a name tag in the shape of a T-bone steak. Before she asked if they cared for a cocktail, Gando politely asked her to bring out two double shots of J & B scotch, breaking from the norm.

"And start us with a dozen oysters if they are fresh," he concluded. He slipped her a twenty and said that there was no rush for her to take a dinner order. Smiling, she thanked him and vanished toward the service bar.

The drinks arrived in record time, and they began to fill each other in on recent events. Gando began by asking Crello to tell him the story of how he messed up Gasparo's surveillance, which he did in Hollywood fashion. Gando smiled, with his arrogance never in question in his belief that he and his longtime friend were smarter than any cops with any acronyms attached to their department. Just as Gando was about to relay the events of the hit on Mancini's kid, the oysters arrived. Gando waited and after they were placed down, he pointed his finger to the two almost drained glasses, indicating they were ready for more.

Crello listened intently, nodding his head both in approval, as well as to take another sip of his scotch. Between their connections, patience and well thought out plans, they exuded even more confidence in regard to the upcoming hit on Marco Bracci.

"The cops don't know which end is up, Gando began. "Aldo Mancini is screaming that it was a revenge hit, Salvatore Bracci is talking power struggle and the media thinks it might even have been a suicide bomber. But that was ruled out. I will admit I have a slight concern after catching Davis from Philly in some news footage, but I have feelers out. I don't think he suspects us."

"I made some calls as well. Tomorrow some of our old friends will leak some information to the Post, saying that they know for a fact that the Chicago mob has a definite interest in moving east. Hell, with the vacuum you created by sending the two other family heads to the slammer, it reeks of realism. But I also think we should lay low for a while before proceeding with Bracci. I rented a small hunting cabin up near New Paltz. It will be close enough to our friends in Jersey, yet far enough away from our enemies in the city."

Jessica appeared with their next round and Gando then pointed to a spot just above her left breast. She shot her hand up to her shirt to make sure she was not exposing anything.

"No, no, you're fine hon. I was pointing the steak shaped name tag you were wearing. I will have a rare T-Bone and my associate would like one medium rare."

She blushed slightly, nodded and left to place the order.

During their dinner, the two discussed various scenarios for the second hit. They would finalize details at a later date. Then their conversation returned to stories from their youth, where some of their buddies were now located and how they were fairing. They skipped coffee and dessert. Crello was a little worn out from the flight and was ready to retire. Gando motioned for the check, threw two c-notes down and they left. They arrived back at the hotel ten minutes later. Gando had procured a suite for the night, and after a long day they went to separate rooms.

CHAPTER 19

Opened in June, 2004, the Riverside Correctional Facility is a medium security prison that sits roughly ten miles from the Roundhouse in Center City Philadelphia. It houses women only and is where Jaime Valley would reside for the next several years. With help and support from her boyfriend Michael Davis, she was granted incarceration in a facility close to his residence where he could visit her several times a week. It would be her home for the next several years depending on her behavior and appeals. In reality though, she was abundantly fortunate for getting such a short sentence in lieu of her murderous acts. The combination of a great attorney, sympathy from the media and the disdain of insurance companies by the general public, her sentence was immediately criticized for being too liberal.

With Michael back in the good graces of both his brother Stephen and the Philadelphia Police, he made biweekly visits to her. He made sure that her commissary account was sufficient, as well as giving her moral support.

"When this is over and you are out, we will get out of town and find a place that we can both agree upon and settle down," he would tell her.

She had no family, and other than his brother, he too had no ties to the Delaware Valley. Oscar, the curious cat and Cosmo, her extroverted canine, were being well taken care of by Michael. Trusting her best friends to him meant much to her, as well did he. Jokingly he told her that these animals cost more than children did, but the unconditional love they returned were so worth it.

"I love you so much," she would tell him, the intensity of her expression speaking more than her words. And although she still missed her husband, the man she had sacrificed her freedom for, Michael served not as a replacement, but rather a new phase in her life. Although Michael had been through a riff with his brother and the Police department, that was all behind him and the future looked positive.

Stephen and the whole OCTF stood behind Michael and Jaime. He had served his country well and never complained about the loss of his leg. He was also instrumental in solving the high profile case of Bruce Titell, the internet stalker who had inflicted fear and violence on the city several years back. Blood *was* thicker than water and whatever made his brother happy, worked for him. It always would.

● ● ●

"Did you have pizza sex or what?" echoed the familiar voice on the other end of the line.

Davis laughed to himself, wondering where that comment came from on the other end of the line. He doubted that Ashley had said anything.

"Excuse me?" Davis responded, hearing Gasparo's silent chuckling on the other end.

"That pizza you brought home. She had to love it and using my deductive powers of reasoning, and knowing that you had been gone for a week, I just figured a sexual encounter logically followed your meal."

The hesitation of a quick response told Gasparo that he was right. He also knew that Davis wouldn't admit it even if he was correct in his assumption.

"So I am down in your great city following up on some information that came in this afternoon. It's interesting but as far as I can tell, it still leads to nothing but dead ends. Now it's your turn to treat. Break out the expense account and tell me where and when you are taking me to dinner."

Davis pondered the question for a moment and thought about what he wanted for dinner. The answer was a no brainer.

"Meet me at Del Frisco's, say seven. Does that work?"

"Works for me," replied Gasparo and the call abruptly ended on that note.

Two hours later they met by the front entrance, arriving almost simultaneously. Davis held the door and they both entered the mammoth steak house. They were greeted by a young attractive Asian hostess who smiled from behind a computer screen. Davis gave his name and she nodded to another attractive young woman who grabbed two menus and led them to a downstairs table. The noise levels were tolerable due to the large cavernous ceilings and open spaces. Seconds later a waitress appeared, introducing herself and asking if they desired a cocktail. Davis ordered two Yuenling Lager's, knowing that Gasparo was a beer man and it was a great local beer. Gasparo was not shy, asking for an order of fried oysters. Davis chimed in, adding an order of cheesesteak dumplings with spicy ketchup. He would not defer to the city with the best pizza without challenging it with a Philadelphia staple. Gasparo shook his head and smiled.

"My nutritionist will have my head. I don't want to add another loop on my belt."

Davis declared that he had to return the favor, that of showing off the best pizza in New York with a dish that defined his city. The drinks arrived and they got down to business.

"A couple of interesting developments came in last night and this afternoon. Some of the uniforms canvassing the crime scene for the second time may have gotten an ID on Gando. The waiter isn't positive but he said that a guy who looked similar was having dinner at about the same time of the explosion. It's a start."

"And?" countered Davis, his eyes wide with interest.

"We showed Crello's picture around at all of the other smaller airports in Florida and may have a hit on him too. The name did not appear so we can only assume that he is traveling around with an alias. It's quite possible your hunch has some merit."

Davis smiled. His years as a detective had generated many instincts, some leading nowhere and others that were spot on. That was one of several traits that made him so successful at his job.

Davis pointed to the two nearly empty bottles, indicating another round was needed. Further discussion required another drink. Sometimes a drink cleared rather than distorted his logical train of thought.

"The bad news is that we have no leads or indications as to where they are. We have been circulating their photos to all law enforcement agencies in the Northeast, but it's early. The FBI guys have some low level guys who have infiltrated some of the mob splinter groups and they have been informed as well. So what do you think?"

Davis dipped an oyster in the tartar sauce and thought as he savored it.

"I still think Gando is responsible for the hit on Mancini and we need to find him before he takes out Bracci. Can we set up a meeting with him or do you think he is on the same page as us," Davis wondered out loud.

'I think the latter is correct. Mancini is no dummy. He went to the University of Pennsylvania down here and did a pretty damn good job of at least making his father's businesses look legit. Hell, he even set up an import business that really imports olive oil."

Gasparo laughed in agreement.

"We have all the agencies involved. We don't need this shit turning into a bloodbath. I have clearance to stay down here for a while. We need to check on all of Gando's old haunts as well as acquaintances. Maybe something will turn up."

Davis agreed that it was probably the best course of action. He had his informants and a thick file on Gando's past. Since there were no pressing cases, he would assign the OCTF to spread out and try to track him down. Michael could work his internet magic on all of Gando's past connections and locations. He loved a good challenge and was now fired up for the task.

The waitress reappeared and they both decided just to split a steak and switch over to Buffalo Trace, Davis's bourbon of choice. They both agreed on a medium rare rib eye and a shot served neat. It was characteristically, a real testosterone filled evening.

● ● ●

Jon Vandergriff was enjoying his newly found wealth. He was renting an upscale condo in Delray Beach, the kind that had the health club, pool and most important, a shitload of divorcees living on alimony payments or settlement of their ex-husbands. He spent most of his free time, which was about every waking hour, just lying at the pool, flirting and reading bestselling novels. His mind wandered between the past and present, wondering why he didn't get involved in shady activities rather than opting to captain huge cruise vessels. But then again, the opportunity had never presented itself and his love for the sea was his only concern at that particular time in his life. Clichéd as it may sound, that was then and this was now.

As he lay on his lounge chair admiring a pair of skinny thongs emerging from the pool, his cell phone rang. He had made a few friends and acquaintances since moving into his new environs, but no calls were expected. He glanced at the number and noticed it was that of Angel Almar. She did say she would check in with him.

"I hope you are enjoying that Florida sun. Hell, these New England cold spells seem to be starting earlier every year. Its only October," she began.

He smiled to himself, wondering why Americans always were so obsessed with the weather. Growing up in northern Europe he had grown used to an environ that was either cold or colder. It was inconsequential to him.

"I am quite enjoying it, as well as the lovely tropical scenery,' he replied, stills staring at the scant bikinis surrounding him.

"I assume you mean the tanned bodies rather than the sandy beaches. I get the drift" she said. "Am I right or am I right?"

"You are absolutely correct as always," he replied. "Are you checking up on me?"

"Yes and no," she began. "Yes, I want to make sure that you are enjoying your hard earned and well deserved payment, and no, because you have earned my complete trust and respect. But my employers are not sure if our actions have disrupted your ex-employer to the level which we had expected. Our dear Mr. Phelps is has proved adept at shifting the focus of his misfortune onto others. Have you been following the story?"

"Actually, after doing my job I did see that he and PacLantic were under the gun and it did give me pleasure. I just assumed that it would halt his operations for a while to come. Am I correct?" he queried, a hint of naivety engrained in his question.

"Well, the latest rumors which we have confirmed are that Phelps is suing the companies that supplied his food inventory. He is accusing all of them as being negligent in the handling and storing of product, and he has been cleared of any negligence due to the integrity of his cruise lines reputation and its famous chefs. He had offered free cruises to all those aboard and the ship will be up and running in the next several weeks. My clients are going over the schedule of events and it seems we will need your services again in the near future. Are you still interested?"

She knew the answer.

Smiling to himself, his eyes now focused on a Latina with a perfect Brazilian butt, pure You-Tube material that would go viral if he had his cell phone video ready. He returned to reality.

"Of course I am, Angel. Just fill me in on the details when you are ready and I will gladly discuss the arrangements and fees."

There was a little more cockiness, greed and eagerness in his voice. She liked what she heard.

"I will Jon. Take care of yourself and don't do anything that I wouldn't do."

It was a stupid and senseless expression, he thought, but kind of liked it anyway. He said to call in advance and would be ready for his next assignment. She said goodbye, knowing that the money was his motivating factor. It took one to know one.

George had his ear to the phone during the whole conversation and was proud of Carolyn. She played the role of Angel as well as any film noir actress from the forties. He kissed her softly on her neck, getting her attention and followed with one a bit deeper and more passionate. Smiling, he arose and walked toward his office. He emerged with a check for ten thousand dollars, mentioning that she had that shopping look in her eyes. He knew her all too well. Grabbing the check, she asked if he wanted to join her, knowing full well his disdain for watching her shop. He was a typical male in that respect, but his generosity more than made up for any short comings.

"Knock yourself out and when you get back we can go out for a nice dinner. I am going to do a little planning for our next crusade in our quest to literally and figuratively, sink my brother. But this time in a more permanent manner," he gloated.

This time he would go through the upcoming specialty cruises and manufacture an event that would sink his brother permanently. He wasn't sure yet what it would entail, but it would be the most inspiring event of his life.

CHAPTER 20

New Paltz is a village that stands roughly at the halfway point between New York City and the state capital of Albany. It houses one of New York States universities and for any movie buffs, it was where the character of Penny Johnson the 1987 film, *Dirty Dancing,* received her abortion. It is a quiet town with a population of slightly under 10,000 and is not considered one of New York's touristy highlights. That had been one of the reasons that Crello and his people chose it as a temporary safe place.

It is also adjacent to large hunting grounds, which was a hobby that Crello had enjoyed during his teens. His father would take him up toward the New York-New Jersey border to hunt, offering him the same opportunity that his father had offered him. It was ironic that Gando would tease him about it during his youth. Now, Crello hardly picked up a firearm and Gando was the one who had developed his 'hunting' skills, albeit for prey with two legs rather than four.

During their first two days at a small cabin they had rented, their time was spent with Crello teaching Gando some of the finer points about hunting, as they had obtained hunting licenses under their false credentials. The October air was crisp upstate, a refreshing change from the repetitive Florida climate that they had grown accustomed to. On the first evening they even paid a visit to the C.I.A. This was the one that they were allowed to visit safely, better known as the Culinary Institute of America. There were over 46,000 alumni spread out across the globe, each earning a degree from the most prestigious cooking school in America. The food was so good at their Italian offering, Ristorante Caterina de' Medici, they returned the following evening and took the thirty minute journey to the American Bounty Restaurant. As both were restaurant owners in what seemed like a previous life, and appreciated great food, they were blown away by the experience. If they were ready to die and go to heaven, which they were so not ready to do, they would have gladly chosen that venue if tomorrow never arrived.

On the third day, Crello received a confirmation that another group of his 'extended family' had just left North Jersey and were on their way up. Over the next several days, they would discuss various ways of eliminating Marco Bracci and anyone of his associates that stood in the way.

Gando turned to Crello, smiling and putting his cards down on the table in the middle of a cribbage game.

"I guess our meeting will be a tiny bit smaller than the one up near here in '57."

"As well as our agenda and the status of our guests," Crello replied, moving a red peg up the cribbage board.

They had been referring to the 1957 gathering at the home of Joseph , 'Joe the Barber' Barbara in Apalachin, New York, roughly 100 miles west. It was there that over 100 mafia members met, some from as far away as Sicily, to discuss operations by the recently killed Albert Anastasia. Unlike IBM, they did not discuss marketing strategies or profit and loss statements. What they mulled over was how to divide up the gambling, casino and narcotics interests left behind by Anastasia. When a local state trooper noticed a large number of high end vehicles with out of state plates converging on the tiny hamlet, law enforcement converged and detained over half of the attendees. After the deluge, then head of the F.B.I., J. Edgar Hoover had finally admitted the existence of a 'National Crime Syndicate', which was something he had denied the existence of for years. Speculation was that either he was blind, on the take or the high heels he wore in the off hours diminished his thought capabilities. Regardless of why, the event triggered a crackdown on organized crime. The upcoming meeting would indeed be a lot smaller and a lot less newsworthy, at least for now.

● ● ●

Several hours and a loss of twenty eight dollars later, Crello approached the locked cabin door upon hearing a sharp knock. Gando had his Glock out, just in case. Crello asked who it was. Chris Gary stopped his knocking, paused, and asked Crello to open up the door and have the beer ready. His high pitched scratchy voice was district enough to provide enough conformation for Crello to unlock the door.

Gando arose from the table, heading to the fridge to grab some Stella's, as the three men entered the large room. After the standard hugs and back taps, they all made themselves at home. Gando returned from the small kitchen area with an opener and a six pack. He had recognized two of the men, but the third looked eerily familiar. Crello made the introductions.

"I think you had met Chris on several occasions," he began. Gary was of stocky build, slightly balding and a wide grin graced his face. Gary had worked as a contractor having done work on several of the boss's properties. He was familiar with the layout of Marco Bracci's residence. Although he lived in Jersey, the trust he had gained, as well as his expertise in HVAC, plumbing, carpentry and security systems, deemed him a valuable asset to Bracci, and now to the group of five gathered around the table. And although he rubbed shoulders with a number of Mafioso's, he kept to himself and doled out no information to anyone, except his longtime friend Crello. Now retired, he was attracted to the money he would make by joining the group. Greed trumps loyalty.

Sal Batella was a familiar face. He retired from the force years before, but his love for the ponies and $100.00 blackjack tables in Atlantic City, inspired his current interest in this job. He made it clear that he would not break the law in this mission, but would bend it enough to help his longtime friend. He volunteered to gather information from his associates in the organized crime bureau up in North Jersey, passing it along to help the operation. He had gathered some useful information. After all, he had become privy to some inside information due to his so called allegiance with Davis and Gasparo. He loved the action and was still good enough to fool the latter.

"And this is Dave Peretti. You worked with his brother Greg, and he wanted in."

Crello had mentioned to Gando that he did not know Dave as well, also mentioning that he was wound a bit tighter than his brother. Gando shook his hand, offering his condolences for his brother Greg, adding that he was a good kid and was instrumental in the Mancini hit. Dave thanked him, offering his help in any way possible.

"I was very close to my brother and he spoke very highly of you. I want to help finish this mission with you in his memory."

Gando was moved, mentioning how not only Greg was a good partner, but also how passionate he was about his loyalty and commitment.

"He was instrumental in making things happen, and although it might be of little condolence, I will be giving you what he earned for his actions. It was more than well earned."

Dave thanked him, assuring him that his contribution to this project would be as valuable as his brothers. He owed him at least that much.

Introductions aside, the group of five sat down at the kitchen table and began to discuss their options. Crello took a long drag on his cigar, holding it like overstuffed pen, and let a large plume of smoke emerge from his mouth. Taking a deep breath, he banged the edge of the table twice with his left hand a suggested they get down to business. Gando sat with a legal pad in front of him, his right hand grasping a pen and his left hand in his lap.

"Let's start with you, Chris", Crello began. "Give us a little insight into the floor plans and any other things you had noticed about his protective precautions."

Chris nodded and began.

"So after you put the old man away," he began pointing to Gando by lifting his chin, "the kid moved to Boerum Hill, also in Brooklyn. It's near park Slope if yous guys aren't familiar, with some pretty expensive digs. He bought two connected brownstone row homes on the corner by 4th avenue". His pronunciation of the word avenue came out as "avenya". It was just the kind of accent that made a New Yorker a New Yorker or Northern New Jerseyian for that matter. He continued.

"The first level had the walls between the two units broken down, opening up a large living room and entertainment area. The kitchen is on the left, bordered by the dining area, and that flows into the two other rooms I just mentioned."

Gando was slightly nodding his head, as he both took notes and scanned the surroundings. He only trusted Crello completely and needed to get more comfortable with the others. He was a cautious man.

"The second floor has three bedrooms and the maid's quarters. And the third floor houses his office, complete with training area, steam room and Jacuzzi. His office also housed his security room where he had around the clock personnel checking the video surveillance, motion detectors and night vision equipment. It's kind of like a small fortress."

He pulled a shot of his drink before continuing.

"Oh, and there are at least two muscle heads outside the electronic gate in front as well as downstairs on the main floor at all times. After what happened to Mancini, he seems to be taking no chances."

"That's inside the compound," Gando noted. "What about his daily activities and favorite stops?"

Gando was again scanning the room, noticing the intensity and attention that emanated from the group. But the level and nervousness of Peretti seemed a bit out of place. But he didn't really know him and chalked it up as the jitters he might be feeling. He was now running with some of the bigger dogs, he thought to himself.

"I can give you some of the particulars in that regard," began Batella. "Both myself and Peretti did some loose tailing of him and his entourage."

Gando queried as to where and when, wanting to see if any patterns existed as did with Mancini.

"Well for one thing, he is a big Giant fan and has crossed the river over to MetLife Stadium for the three home games. He is surrounded by his people and gets parking near the elevators up to his box. And besides, it's too public".

Gando waved with his hand to go on, taking notes and wanting to speed things up. Batella flipped through his small Lieutenant Colombo type notebook and continued, sans the crumpled raincoat.

"He did pay several visits to his father in prison, but never at the same time or day of the week. He had dined out a dozen times over the past two months, but has yet to repeat any of his visits to any of those restaurants."

Flipping the pages back and forth, double checking his notes, he shook his head.

"In my opinion, Marco Bracci might be smarter than we think. Ya gotta figure that the killing of Mancini has made him a lot more paranoid, as well as vigilant to his surroundings. I think we need to create a diversion to draw him out."

Gando was impressed with both Batella's observation and insight. He glanced around and noticed it was time for a report from Peretti. He too had been tailing him, but kept noticing that he was touching his side now more than before. Maybe it was just a nervous habit. Maybe it was a weapon. But it was definitely not a figment of his imagination. He subtly reached behind his back and withdrew his weapon from the crick of his back.

"Nice work and damned good insight, Sal", Gando complimented him, noticing that crooked yet humble smile.

Turning to summon the information that Peretti had gathered, he looked him in the eye and asked him to relay the pertinent information.

Clearing his throat, Peretti began.

"If I may Mr. Gando,"

"Call me Julian, after all, we are all friends here" Gando said, his voice almost calming.

"Okay, Julian. With respect, would you mind filling me in on the final moments of my brother's life? I have heard so many stories, that I would just feel better hearing it from you," he asked with a little more than a hint of nervousness in his voice.

"What exactly *do* you want to know," Gando replied with more than a hint of authority.

"Like what happened in the events leading up to his death. It's just something I gotta know."

Gando looked down. He lifted his head slowly with a pensive stare at Peretti.

"Okay. I will indulge your curiosity. Your brother carried an explosive device which he was supposed to plant near Mancini's vehicle and bodyguards, which he did successfully. After that some words were exchanged, as your brother made a wide array of hand motions at the men who just happened to be minding their own business. I was across the street sitting in a restaurant watching, but was unable to hear the verbal exchange. All he needed to do was keep walking, and the both of you would be sitting here today."

Gando paused and slid back from the table several inches and then continued.

"Mancini left the car and his attention was drawn to the apparent argument. One of the three bodyguards began to speed up his pace, grabbed his arm and led him toward the entrance. The window of opportunity had now shrunk to seconds, and it was necessary to set off the explosion."

Hesitating for a brief second, Peretti than pointed an accusatory finger at Gando and said in an elevated and somewhat snappish tone, "so you killed him."

The next few seconds slowed. Gando shot a look at Crello. Peretti began to rise from his seat. Batella pushed his chair back from the table. Gary sat frozen in time. Peretti reached behind his back. Crello shot an approving look at Gando. Peretti's hand swung out from his back, a weapon brandished and then two loud shots resonated loudly in the small cabin. Two gaping holes opened in Peretti's body. One bullet entered the center of his chest, the other over his left eye. Spatters of

Tuscan red flowed from the newly created wounds that now appeared in a body that had been full of life only seconds before.

The room was now filled with an air of silence and the distinctive odor of cordite. Crello moved toward the body and instinctively kicked the gun across the hardwood floor. Peretti's shirt was torn and Crello reached down toward a group of wires that now lay exposed through his shirt. Following them, he tugged, exposing a small recording device. Anger and concern were expressed in Crello's face, his mind racing. He looked at the three men, all now staring down at the dead body. He bent down on one knee and rolled the body over, taking out his wallet, some keys, his cellular phone and the recorder that was now detached from the tape formerly securing it to his side.

"This doesn't look like any device used by law enforcement."

He showed it around as the heads raised and continued.

"It is my belief that this guy was working for Bracci and if we hadn't found this device, we would all be walking with targets on our backs."

There were no objections or hints of disagreement.

"We need to bury this dirt bag and speed up this meeting."

Batella grabbed an old blanket from the couch and laid it out on the wooden floor. As he and Gary rolled the body up, Gando headed toward the kitchen to grab whatever cleaning products might be there. Knowing it was a hunting area and animal blood was omnipresent, he knew if they were able to clean up a majority of the human blood, there would be little suspicion.

Over the course of the next two hours, they drove several miles to a secluded spot in the large acres of forest, located a softer spot of earth and deposited the body in the freshly dug hole. Batella even joked about hopefully not having to come back up to move the body, referring to the scene in Goodfellas after Pesci and his crew had to do just that. The comment eased the tension a bit, which had pretty much dissipated from the four remaining men.

Upon returning from the now moonlit sky, they poured some stiff drinks and did a pretty thorough cleanup. Gando's gun was a 'throwaway' and the two spent casings were picked up and flushed down the toilet. Both bullets remained inside of Peretti as they had found no exit wounds. Gando was experienced and knew what ammunition was right for what location. He was the David Tutera of hit men. So what if it was a murder rather than a wedding.

Gary volunteered to run into town to grab some dinner.

"Get some Italian food or some sandwiches. I wouldn't trust anything else up here."

He nodded and left.

While he was out, Crello scrolled through the phone as Gando recorded the text messages and Batella recorded the phone numbers that corresponded to each of them. He then listed all the numbers, which Batella could pass on to one of his buddies still on the force and get the corresponding names. Two large would be a nice donation for an hour's work, tracing the numbers that were stored in the cell phones memory. Some had names and some just letters, but within hours they would have all the names and addresses of Peretti's phone book.

"Hey Sal," Gando called out. "Tell your guy we will make it four large if he has the names to us tonight."

Batella nodded and called his boy at the station.

● ● ●

After a dinner of Manhattan clam chowder, roast beef sandwiches and chips, they sat around the table, waiting for the call. The card game now included four, so it transformed from Cribbage to hearts, the stakes remaining low. They all agreed that once the phone identifications returned, they would text a message back to Bracci, if it were in fact Bracci who had put Peretti up to spying, and text him that he had found Gando and wanted to meet up for his payment. All were in agreement that they should try and schedule a meet with Bracci, exchanging the tape of Gando's plan for the agreed amount of cash. If everything went according to plan, Bracci would be dead within 48 hours.

● ● ●

Slightly less than two hours later, with all the beer drained, the disposable phone rang. It was a call for Batella, the one who would provide the information as to all stored and incoming numbers that landed on Peretti's phone. Batella answered, scribbling down notes prior to relaying the information to his associates.

"The good news is that I have a list of mostly all of the numbers on the phone. A couple of calls were made to a known betting service, several to some takeout restaurants and the last one to his place of employment. The bad news is that there are two numbers which correspond to separate generic throw away types, neither containing any GPS tracking. That's why they are used by every criminal regardless of their felony preferences."

Crello thought for a moment and then posed a question.

"Can we text the phone from his without giving up our location?"

"That's what I would do. And I promised my guy that someone would drop off a small donation for his troubles. I will do it myself tomorrow."

Gando then motioned with his finger for Crello to hand him the phone, Crello querying what he was about to do.

"I am going to send a text to the first of the untraceable numbers and see how it plays out."

"And your text will say," Crello asked, knowing what he would type in, pretending to be Peretti

"Let's mention that he has the tape and needs to deliver it as soon as possible. We can send it to the first number, wait several minutes, and if there is no response, send it to the other one. We can keep it short and sweet."

Crello nodded and Gando tried the first number. A call was out of the question, the reason being that he was no Rich little and couldn't imitate Peretti's voice. He highlighted the phone number and typed in the text, his dexterity falling way short of a teenage girl's nimble fingers. "We have Gando and his plan on tape and you need to hear it. He is a sitting duck. When can we meet?"

They patiently waited. After several minutes a reply came back.

"With whom am I texting?"

"Peretti" he typed and then waited again.

Seconds later the text notification sound beeped and they read it.

"Hey idiot," the text began, "I gave you a code for a reason and you are not the only lackey that I have on this phone."

Gando winced at the obvious belligerence that he showed his hired help. He did have a reputation for arrogance and it came through loud and clear even on his messages. Gando went to the message screen, hoping to find the code in a past message, but all had been deleted. Peretti wasn't quite the idiot that Bracci thought he was. The screen was void of past messages and there was no code to be found. He momentarily fumbled the phone, recovered and then replied.

"I lost the freakin code. It's me. Who else would contact you?"

Gando prayed it would work. His prayers went unanswered and no response was to follow. He threw the phone across the room. It hit a large piece of stone on the fireplace that ran from floor to ceiling, proceeding to shatter into countless shards of plastic and microchips.

With that, the group decided to call it a night and discuss any other ideas the following morning. They all arose around the same time, sounds of gunshots and nearby sounds of ATV's resounding in the open woods from nearby hunters. Crello told Chris and Sal that they should try and hunt down any more leads through their contacts. He and Gando would remain for the next several days.

"We need to decompress a bit and I have an idea that might work. Julian and I will toss it around and if we need your help before returning to Jersey, we will contact you."

They exchanged the customary hugs and handshakes outside. Chris and Sal headed toward the vehicle, one passenger short from their arrival and drove off the site. Crello and Gando returned to the cabin, Gando showing interest in Crello's comment about an alternative plan. Nothing had been mentioned, but he knew it was probably well thought out.

● ● ●

The next day, a pair of visitors followed their GPS to the location that Gando had rented up in New Paltz. Upon hearing the killing of a large engine, the recognizable macho hum of the H4, the pair exited the cabin to meet their guests. The leaves made the old familiar crunching noises associated with fall in the Northeast portion of the country, a sound Gando strangely missed during his time in Florida. The H4 was charcoal grey in color with a blue cross painted on the side, the logo used to represent their firm, Blue Cross Security. The car sported Delaware tags, the reasons being the low fee to set up a corporation there, as well as hide their New Jersey home office. If ever checked, their corporate address would lead to a storage facility outside of Newark, Delaware. Hell, at least both of their home bases were in one of the two Newark's.

Anthony and Santee Giaboni exited their car as they approached Gando and Crello. Through the vast underground network that lived in the metropolitan New York-New Jersey area, the four had previously done business and even spent some social time together. They shook Anthony's hand and kissed Santee on the cheek prior to inviting them in.

Blue Cross Security offered various services in the area of both active and passive undertakings. They were experts in technological information gathering, trained guard and attack dogs, had several contacts with mercenary types and had a fair amount of varied independent contractors on retainer. It reminded Gando of his old friend Rick Grosse and his firm, 'Full Service Concierges.' Rick had been a useful resource to Gando until his demise in the name of love, another victim to a woman scorned. He too almost had fallen prey to a similar scenario.

Upon entering, Crello motioned for the pair to relax on the over-stuffed couch and offered them a cocktail. Santee accepted for both, requesting two beers.

"We need to be back in Jersey for a client dinner meeting by seven. Otherwise we would partake in a bit more of a serious drinking mode."

Gando disappeared into the kitchen and emerged with four bottles of Birra Poretti, a beer from northern Italy first brewed in the late 1800's. Gando smiled to himself, finding irony in the name of the beer and its similarity to the man he had killed the previous day. What's in a name?

Crello skipped small talk and got down to business.

"As you probably have heard, myself and Gando have skipped out on our witness protection detail and have returned to put an end to those who seek our demise. One of our problems has been solved but we need help in eliminating the other. That is why I asked you two here."

Crello paused momentarily, sipping some of the cold lager before continuing.

"Cutting to the chase, we need to eliminate Marco Bracci before he does the same to either of us."

Crello went on to explain the series of events, beginning with the elimination of Mancini and leading up to failure to flush Bracci out of his protection by texting him with the now deceased Peretti's cell phone.

Santee and Anthony listened intently, each formulating ideas that would help the pair accomplish their end results. Utmost was the fact that their target be eliminated and secondly, no forensic evidence would link the pair to the crime.

After discussing various methods and scenarios, they suggested a plan which would meet both criteria.

"We have a pair of killers that will get the job done and leave no trace. We have employed this method before and our track record remains perfect. However," Santee continued, her intensity rising, "you will have to obtain some items for our plan to succeed. If you can, *and do*, your problem will be solved. What we will need is about a month after you get us the required items to make this work."

Santee and Anthony went on, explaining the how, what and why as to how their plan would be foolproof. When they were done, Crello and Gando loved the simplicity and safety of their agenda. It took less than an hour of conversation to hammer out the details, as well as agree upon the $20,000 fee. When they returned to Jersey, they would work at Godspeed in obtaining the required items needed for the plan to come to fruition.

In less than two hours and three beers, the pair departed. A retainer of five large was handed to Anthony and they shook hands, cementing the transaction. Gando and Crello just had to remain invisible for the next month and change. After that, they would not be hunted men. When the Blue Cross H4's tail lights disappeared, the pair returned to the cabin and made the requisite calls to put the plan into action.

"How about one more dinner at the C.I.A.," Gando said. "Ya never know if we will be back here again and I think we deserve it."

Crello agreed and they both freshened up for a final dinner in the mountains. Before they left, Gando called the rent a car company to extend his lease. The following morning, Crello would make the necessary calls to put the wheels in motion.

Over dinner, they decided to embark upon a road trip, through New York State and the Berkshires that bordered on western Massachusetts. By the next morning, they packed what they had brought, wiped the cabin down for prints and began their soiree. As they entered the car, Crello's phone alerted him to a new text. He read it to himself, smiled and placed it in his pocket. From the other pocket he removed two Cuban cigars from their white containers and handed one to Gando.

He accepted, nodding to his closest lifelong BFF, and the road trip began.

PART FIVE

CHAPTER 21

About 4 weeks later

"I think that I am *just* beginning to feel some of that nervous energy and apprehension finally leaving my body," Bryant said reflectively. She was staring out as the sun began to take its nightly dip into the slightly choppy Atlantic. "What is it, like two weeks from tomorrow?"

"Exactly," replied Abby, squeezing her best friends hand in a confident manner. "And we *so* deserve it. And it's a business trip. And a write off and," they both laughed as Abby's voice trailed off.

They were talking about the working/pleasure cruise they would be taking aboard the Adventurer. Upon the pair moving down to Florida several years back, they had opened an adult store called 'Toys O Joy', which had taken off and grown to include two franchisees. Both had become friends in Philadelphia through a common acquaintance named Julian Gando. He was the man that Bryant had dated and was now on the run from federal authorities in the Witness Protection Program. Other than an accidental meeting about a year ago, the pair had done everything to avoid ever running into him, or his associates, any time in the future.

They had been invited as paying guests aboard the Adventurer's 'Venue Six', a cruise for swingers and those with 'voyeuristic sexual curiosity and experience', as it was labeled in the brochure. Their role would be to exhibit their extensive and original line of items such as leather fashions, pleasuring devices and various aphrodisiacal scents and gels. They would set up a display and talk to the passengers for three days, and then spend the final three as vacationers, while a second group of exhibitors displayed their own specialties.

"Best case scenario is that we take lots of orders for our merchandise and maybe even get some interest from those who are interested in a franchise," pointed out Abby.

"And an even better scenario would be to meet some hot dude to hook up with, nothing serious ya know," Bryant added, accompanied by schoolgirl type giggles.

Abby held up two fingers, indicating to Andrew, their waiter, that they were ready for two more drinks. Andrew was in his mid-forties they assumed, sporting long brown hair in a ponytail, and making up for his receding hairline. They were regulars and Andrew was always cordial, his flirtatious lines had been repelled when the trio first met. But they still liked to flirt and bounce ideas for new products off him. They *loved* teasing him and he loved the attention.

Abby grabbed the final proof for the catalog they had prepared for the voyage. Pulling her chair closer to Bryant, she eagerly began to elicit her approval for the go ahead to have them printed. It was an eight page glossy brochure, the cover containing images that left little to the imagination. The back page contained an order form, offering a 15% discount to any cruise members who chose to purchase any of their wares. All that was needed was to enter promo code 'Venue Six' on the order form that was inserted into the center section. Abby was so proud of the quote underneath the 'Toys O' Joy' logo, touting their new sensual gels and body rubs. It read ' Special Lotions for the Motions of the Oceans'.

"I think that we should also offer an additional 5% discount to those who might share our catalog with their friends not on the cruise. We can put a small box on the order sheet, asking the passenger to enter their room number, so that they can get the additional offering back on any future orders."

"I *love* that idea, girlfriend," Abby said, adding that she knew there was some reason that she kept her around. The relationship and bond they had formed in during their time in Philadelphia was as tight as super glue holding a construction worker in the old television ads. It was a special one.

Bryant had not seen that new addition. She shoved her friend, rolled her eyes and told her she was such a nerd. They both laughed as Andrew carried their drinks over to them. He placed them down and before asking what all the commotion was about, a rude customer in a leisure suit with white shoes rudely snapped to gain his attention. Now his eyes rolled and the three of them laughed.

After discussing and finalizing the new catalog, the pair agreed that it was fit for distribution, with an X rating of course, and decided to order 500 copies, about one for each passenger on board.

"Next week will be here before we know it," Abby said with encouragement. She held her glass up for a toast. They clinked the rims of their cocktails and turned to watch the daily picturesque sunset. It was a sight that those who lived by the oceans never would tire of.

● ● ●

Jon had learned well from his dealings with Angel Almar. He had observed her precautionary cloak and dagger activities that she had employed whenever they were together. And although he never questioned them, he now knew that he had committed a criminal act and taking more safeguards would reduce the waning bit of paranoia that accompanied his illegal activities. So when his phone received a cryptic text the previous week about retaining his services for an upcoming project, he was ready. His rented Nissan Altima sat in the cell phone lot adjacent to Miami International Airport, waiting for the call that denoted her plane had landed. He no longer had any sexual interest in Angel, realizing it was fruitless, but the economic aspect had replaced it tenfold. With the money he would receive, he could have any two twenty year old women found on the multitude of websites and still have a shitload of cash remaining. It was now all about the holy buck.

The message on his cell simply read, "Am out front of terminal", and he was on his way. He started the car and headed toward the arriving passenger area. He slowed when he noticed her sleek figure, carrying only a small travel bag. He pulled up and popped the passenger door, allowing her to get in. She greeted him with a small kiss on the cheek, a friendly, non-sexual gesture, and mentioned that her time was limited.

"My employer has a lot on his plate, actually too much, so I will be in and out of here rather quickly. I have an offer for you and hope you can free up time for me next week. This offer will be much more lucrative than your past one. My flight leaves in four hours, so let's grab a drink somewhere close and I can go over the details."

He nodded, playing his excitement close to the vest and not expressing any eagerness or anxiety. He was losing his moral fiber and replacing it with sheer greed. It was the true American way.

They made small talk as Jon headed toward one of the nicer hotels that skirted the airport area. Angel teased him by mentioning that both the payoff and the assignment would both prove quite exciting. Jon smiled, knowing that she would probably not mention more until they arrived and had ordered their first drink. Minutes later, they arrived at a Marriott and pulled up for valet parking. Her door was immediately opened first and the pair made their way through the sliding glass doors and to the lounge area that lie ahead. They proceeded ahead and entered the dimly lit bar, the televisions tuned to various college games. Opting for a table away from the sparse crowd, they slid into a leather booth and noticed the approaching waitress.

Introducing herself as Joanne, she asked if they had wanted the bar menu, followed by asking if they knew what they wanted to drink. Angel asked for a dirty martini with blue cheese olives and Jon requested a Heineken. She diligently scribbled the order down on the check and disappeared toward the bar. When she was out of site, Angel began to remove a folder from her attaché. Removing a file, she began to remove several documents and stared into his eyes. She had his undivided attention.

"Next Saturday, PacLantic is running what they call Venue 6. It is a 6 day cruise which hosts various activities, items and lectures, for those into what we might call an alternative life style. Its main targets are swingers, BDSM and those with sexual appetites for new experiences."

As the waitress approached with their drinks, Angel halted her explanation until the server had vanished. She continued.

"Unlike our last venture, we are leaving this project up to your own creativity and the opportunities which may arise. The way my employers see this, is that there will be a lot of those who will wish to remain anonymous for obvious reasons. Take pictures. Buy passengers drinks and loosen them up. Whatever it takes and what you deem appropriate to our project. Your fee will double and depending upon your success, may even triple. Is that satisfactory," she asked, putting her hand over his, adding a tiny squeeze.

His mind raced through the math, which was more than compensatory for the weeklong cruise of sexual adventures. He thought about her suggestions, which were both nonviolent and sensible. During the cruise, he would get a better feel as well as more ideas to make his assignment work.

"That is acceptable," Jon said, pulling his hand slowly away and reaching for his drink. She grinned and thanked him with a non-verbal wink and smile. She also removed an envelope which she placed on the table. It contained twenty five thousand dollars as well as a new identity, tickets and passport.

"Examine this in the privacy of your home. You have a week to prepare and we will not speak until your return."

He nodded in agreement and pulled the envelope into his lap. Angel downed the rest of her drink in one long motion and rose from the table.

"I am sorry to cut this short, but as I had mentioned, I am on a tight schedule. Let's head back to the airport and say our goodbyes. My people are very proud and impressed with your work. I know you will not disappoint us this time as well."

He rose as well and headed toward the valet. The ride back to the airport was mostly silent. She had made her point, laid out the logistics and it was now up to him to make the plan succeed. He still loved a good challenge.

Fifteen minutes later they arrived at the departure area. She kissed him lightly on the cheek, reaffirmed her confidence in his abilities and left for the gate. She even blew a kiss just for the effect. In two weeks, she would have results.

● ● ●

Milton and Adrianna were enjoying a quiet dinner, away from the press, the limelight and the daily grind. The past five weeks since the disastrous gourmet cruise was now well behind them. Between placing blame on his distributors, the Board of Health's inspection, which they passed with flying colors and his expert public relations staff's spin, he was back in business. Surprisingly, the negative media actually attracted even more curious followers who wanted to see what his cruises were all about. He likened it to rubberneckers who slowed down to gawk at horrific collisions that held up commuters for hours. Or those who were obsessed with stories of serial or spree killers. The macabre sold, and it sold very well.

"Maybe I should invite that bastard brother of mine. He would probably learn more than he did in the back of our dad's old Impala he used to use as his bedroom," Milton chided, smiling as he brought the single aged malt to his lips.

"It's getting kind of old with your competitive nature and derisiveness toward him. After all, he was a help in your investments and some of the business planning," Adrianna mentioned in a soft and concerned tone.

Milton's face began to redden slightly. His lips formed a flat and slightly crooked feature before he replied. Adrianna knew that a demeaning and cutting reply would shortly follow. She sat back, holding her drink. He leaned forward, placing his drink down on the white tablecloth with an attention getting din.

"Firstly, you are the last person I need to tell me how to interact with my brother. Secondly," he added, grabbing a second finger of his left hand while clenching them in his right, "I don't hear you complaining about the generous lifestyle in which you have grown accustomed to and third, it goes well beyond the scope of what you know about us. Do I make myself clear?"

As her mind shot an array of silent expletives at his rant, her head slowly nodded, acknowledging and hopefully silencing his wrath. The remainder of the meal was spent in total silence. Acclimated to these types of outbursts, her actions impeded any more of his patronizing demeanor. Adding insult to the already condescending nature of his behavior, he concluded with an arrogant smirk on his face, knowing it would piss her off even more. That was a side of Phelps that was familiar to his inner circle.

CHAPTER 22

Gando and Crello had taken a most enjoyable road trip through the New England area, awaiting the call from Anthony and Santee. They had caught the tail end of the foliage in New Hampshire, dined on lobsters and whole bellied fried clams in Essex and visited some of their connected 'extended family' in Providence. All of their activities were low key, looking forward to the big show that would soon take place back in New York. The disposable phone finally chirped its ring tone. They would shortly know the when, how and where part of the plan that lie ahead.

"I hope someone had a nice month long vacation, seeing as my wife and I have put together an ingenious, well orchestrated plan. Hell, this might even be some of our best work ever," Anthony began, a bit of swagger in his voice.

"Would you like to fill me in on some of the details," Crello asked, masking the enthusiasm in his tone.

"Let's just say you two can start heading back. I would like to get this thing done tomorrow evening. They are calling for light showers, and since it's a new moon, witnesses will probably be at a desired minimum. I will fill yous two in tomorrow at lunch, but the two killers have honed their skills well and will make you proud. They are actually quite impressive. We will see you say around two at that luncheonette in Newark, you know where I mean."

"We will see you then, "Crello replied.

He placed the small cell phone back in his coat pocket and smiled at Gando, tossing in a small nod indicating his approval. A wide grin graced

Gando's face and the two headed back to their vehicle. Their questions would be answered at their meeting.

During their ride back, Gando called one of the smaller chain motels and secured two rooms for the night up near the New York-New Jersey border, which was on the way home. They could kick back, grab a bottle of Seagram's 7 and discuss future plans after the killing was done. They were both still fugitives and even if they were caught, there would be no threats to their freedom as long as they could not be tied into these murders. So far they could not, but might have some explaining to do to the feds on their past whereabouts and escape from the program if they were.

When they arrived at the hotel, they brought only their small over-night bags in. Although a bit weary from the prolonged travel, they were also feeling rejuvenated by tomorrow's meeting. On the ride home they had speculated about the how part of the plan. They were teased by the information that there were two well-trained killers, but also knew, or at least assumed, that the Giaboni's would be wise enough not to leave any loose ends, which was why they were getting the big bucks. And their reputation was stellar. Crello had used them because they had clean records and flew well under the radar, an admirable trait in these days of high technology and the density of government agencies having multitudes of initials.

The next morning Gando's phone rang. It was Crello saying that he was getting a shower and would come and get him for breakfast in half an hour. He had slept well, partially due to the almost empty bottle of whis-key that glared back at him from his nightstand. It was slightly after nine and as Gando prepared for his morning shower, his mind was racing. He was the one who had always planned the hits and had been an active par-ticipant. His gut told him that this would be an event that he would have to become a spectator for and he wasn't too keen on that factor. But he would hear Anthony out before his perceptions got the better of him.

On time as usual, Crello rapped three times lightly on the door of room 320. He took a precautionary look through the peephole only to find his friend's smiling and anxious face staring back. Although he and Crello had shared their youthful mischievous experiences, he knew that his best friend was now crossing the line he had avoided for his whole existence. He could have remained in Florida, but Gando had the feeling that Crello was bored and was ready to step out of his comfort zone, as well as standing by his BFF. He appreciated it and would do everything in his power to protect Crello, as he would do the same for him. He opened the door.

"I suggest we eat light. I can't even remember the last time we had been to the Tops, "Crello exclaimed, his hand rubbing his nonexistent and flat stomach.

The Tops Diner had been founded in 1972 and memories of their families once a month Sunday dinner was fresh in both of their minds. Although New Jersey is trashed for everything from its exorbitant tolls to its crime infested cities, there are no better diners anywhere in the free world. Built in the art-deco fashion to resemble streamlined trains, such as the Burlington Zephyr, there are few places remaining that offer early bird special served by a gum smacking waitress that calls you 'hon'.

The Tops diner was one of these classics.

The pair grabbed some food from the generic buffet at the generic hotel, which carried the usual undercooked scrambled eggs and over cooked, extra crispy bacon. Picking at the food, they discussed the up-coming meeting and future plans. All talk was moot, as the days upcoming events would dictate their future.

Gando pushed away his half eaten plate and motioned with his head that it was time to take a walk. His right hand clutched two cigars which they would smoke outside while they walked. Winter was settling in and forecast called for intermittent showers, barring a dip in temperature which might cause some brief flurries. The sky was grey and the crisp and clean smell of snow permeated the late October day.

● ● ●

At the designated time, they arrived at the Tops, parking toward the rear, adjacent to a minivan with tinted, smoked black windows. As they emerged, so did the occupants of the van. It was Anthony and Santee, and the four walked toward the entrance together.

Upon entering, the diner was pretty much familiar as it was back in the 70's, barring the newly fabricated seating, the menu selections and the revolving pastry carousel. They requested a table toward the back and were led there by an attractive brunette with a European look. As they took their seats, they were graciously handed menus. They were told that their waitress would be Kimberly, and would be arriving shortly to take their order. Excluding Santee, three of the four pair of eyes watched the slinky hostess retreat to her station. It is said that when you stop noticing those slight innuendos, it's time to hang it up. It was obvious that these three men were not quite ready.

Kimberly appeared shortly thereafter, and with pen in hand, queried if they would like a beverage. The three men opted for cocktails, while Santee requested a cup of hot tea. They bantered with small talk, electing to get down to business after their orders were placed. The drinks were correctly distributed to the foursome and they promptly ordered. Other than choosing their side dishes, all went smoothly and Kimberly scribbled on her pad and sauntered off to the kitchen. Her movements mimicked the hostess, Crello wondering if there was a local college class for 'diner body language.'

Anthony leaned in and began to speak.

"While you two were touring the country, Santee and my associates were framing our plan, and it's a damn good one. And although we had to conduct some questionable activities, we firmly believe that they are far beyond any suspicions."

Gando and Crello just nodded, focusing intense attention to Anthony's explanation, not questioning any of his cryptic elucidations. Anthony continued.

"I believe that our plan is simple, foolproof and quite deadly."

Turning to Gando, he directed the next statement right at him, knowing his penchant for being directly involved in killings.

"Our two trained killers *will* get this job done and in a manner that will be untraceable. All I ask is that you sit back, relax, maybe even catch a movie or nice dinner...and leave the work to us. There is no need for you to get involved or take any unnecessary risks." But that type of overly confident arrogance slightly unnerved Gando. And Anthony knew all too well that Gando was said to enjoy watching people die.

Anthony immediately recognized that Gando was uncomfortable with his ambiguous explanation. He was a stone cold killer and realized he needed a better justification.

As his eyes shot an ominous glare at Anthony, he spoke.

"So tell me the where, when and how this plan of yours will transpire," Gando said his manner both authoritative and unyielding.

"The when is tonight, and the other two factors are better unknown. This is solely for your protection and safety."

"Not pleased", Gando countered, adding, "I paid this fee and only *I* will decide what is relevant to my safety. Give me a little more credit," he added, his tone becoming even more obtrusive.

Anthony held his hands up in a gesture for Gando to calm down and hear him out. Santee knew better than to come to her husband's aid. Crello just remained a bystander.

The conversation was temporarily halted by Kimberly, setting her tray down on the stand and doling out the requested dishes.

"Would any of yous care for anything else?" she asked, oblivious to the intensity at the table.

Gando waived her off, politely stating that they would call for her if they needed anything else. She left in a heartbeat, unnoticed and knowing that she was intruding. Maybe she did take that course, Crello thought, smiling as she exited.

Grasping his fork like a pen and pointing it at Gando, he answered another one of the questions.

"As I said earlier, it will be going down tonight and will happen when Mr. Bracci steps out for his habitual Saturday night journeys."

"Good. And you are still omitting the how?" Gando asked, having had two of his three questions.

"This I cannot and *will not* divulge," countered Anthony, his demeanor emphasizing his point and stubbornness, adding it was for his safety, as well as having any prior knowledge in case if he was linked to the crime and if polygraphs were to follow.

Good enough, Gando thought silently. He knew where Bracci resided and would wait patiently all evening down the block, only to witness the job he had generously paid for. He disregarded Anthony's words about protection safety and anonymity. It was the proverbial thrill of the kill.

Gando nodded and consented, agreeing with Anthony's plan.

"It's all in your hands and I trust you implicitly," he conceded. Better to give the impression of a concession than to show his hand. He would wait down the block from Bracci, just to see what these two Belgians could accomplish, and with how much violent passion they could wield upon their victim. Had to be more than a Belgian waffle exerted on ice cream, he assumed.

● ● ●

Gando and Crello left New Jersey with more than enough time to spare.

"I noticed you were not too thrilled with the way that Antony is handling things," Crello stated. He knew all of Gando's moods and facial expressions well enough to make that assumption.

"Does this effin prick know who I am and what I expect," Gando stated with an air of cockiness. He shook his head, squeezing his lips and moving it from side to side. Crello knew that it was his expression indicating insubordination and a perceived disrespect shown by Giaboni.

"Give the guy a chance, Julian", Crello suggested in a tone he knew would not be taken by his friend as a sign of weakness or concession.

"Either way, we will be planting ourselves down at the end of the block to watch. Let's just say that I too want to make sure that our money is being spent to get the desired results."

Crello knew that there was no use arguing with his hard headed friend. Yeah, he could have brought up the fact that word might have leaked and extra protection might be present. Or, one of the multitudes of Federal agencies might also be staking out the residence. Either way, it seemed the evening was preplanned and it was chiseled in stone, much the same way as the newspaper read by Fred Flintstone in the town of Bedrock.

● ● ●

The pair spent the next several hours driving around, but not before Gando requested that Crello call Batella.

"Ask Sal to pick me up a piece, just in case any complications might arise. Crello consented again, made the call and Batella acquiesced. They drove south down the New Jersey Turnpike and exited at mile marker 92.9, the Thomas Edison rest area in Woodbridge Township. The early darkness was descending upon the area, as the 24 hour day produced more darkness than daylight. They pulled up to the center of the parking area, adjacent to the car with Batella. His timing was as precise as any Rolex ever constructed. Giving an acknowledging wave, he opened the car door and approached the passenger window. Crello toggled it down with the button. Sal leaned in.

"It was the best I could do with the short notice. It's a semi-automatic, serial number has been removed with acid and it works. That's all I know and all I wanna know," he said with the gruff voice and kid smile on his face. It was quite an anomaly.

Gando nodded in appreciation as Crello took the brown paper lunch bag it was contained in.

"This is for your trouble," Gando said, passing an envelope through to the window. "And there will be no refusals. I appreciate both your promptness *and* respect."

Sal held out his hand and shook with Gando, knowing better than to argue. Hell, the piece cost him five hundred and knew that the envelope would be more than sufficient. The ten hundred dollar bills proved him correct. Sal turned and walked back to the car as Gando and Crello pulled out hurriedly. He could settle with his bookie now.

It was a shade past five and they could be at their destination in Brooklyn within the hour. They would hop over the Outerbridge Crossing, cruise through Staten Island and cross onto the Brooklyn-Queens Expressway. Remembering the major arteries in the metropolitan area were like riding a bike, they were things that remained within ones memories for a lifetime.

Crello and Gando chatted on the drive, conversing about everything other than their upcoming rendezvous with the eventual demise of Bracci. They recounted sexual encounters with the same woman, practical jokes made on their friends and sprinkled in a dash of what lie ahead. At one point during a merge in traffic, Gando even pulled Crello over and kissed him on the head, a well understood sign of the tight bond which existed between the two best friends.

Slightly after 6:00 P.M., they arrived at the destination. For good measure, as well as a touch of paranoia, they circled the block several times. They noticed all of the cars had N.Y plates, as well as the fact that none of them jived with their perception of federal surveillance vehicles. Out of touch for a while, Gando would later realize that his perception of such vehicles was quite outdated.

On the second trip around the residence, they found a spot several hundred feet from Bracci's residence. Directly in front was the Cadillac Escalade. Gando removed the gun from the bag, flicked on the safety and slid it barrel first between his legs. He then once again checked the safety.

Seconds later a large blue minivan crept slowly down the street, its rear windows tinted so as to remain anonymous. It too had New York tags, albeit stolen ones just for an extra measure of security. What transpired in the next several minutes was the stuff that a Tarantino movie was made of

Two large men emerged from the front of Bracci's residence, their heads turning in a motion that depicted their eyes were scanning the immediate surroundings. One was extra-large, wearing a dark overcoat. It looked more like a tent than an outer garment. The other was taller and broader, more of his bulk emanating from his upper body rather than his midsection.

The light emanating from the doorway behind produced a smaller man, Bracci, whose head also turned to scan the street. He threw a white scarf around his neck, placed his hands in his deep pockets, and followed two steps behind his protectors. The damp, foggy atmosphere that framed the scene embedded a surrealistic sequence in Gando's keen observations.

Out of the corner of his eye, Gando noticed the blue van momentarily speed up and then slow down, the timing orchestrated in sync to the trio descending the steps. One man separated from the others and trotted toward the passenger door of the Escalade. He began to open it, synchronized with doors in the van sliding open. Within seconds, two figures emerged from the van, running so fast, they appeared as a blur. Like well-trained thoroughbreds, their speed gained momentum as they approached the target.

Tent sized overcoat was as fast as he looked, which was slow as shit. Startled, he turned, his face consumed with panic as he heard loud, violent snarls approaching. Noticing the dogs were upon his boss, he jerked the car door open wide and slid in, slamming it shut in microseconds. He put the keys in the ignition and started the car. He rolled down the windows to get a shot at the canines, but they moved in a blur. He fired aimlessly. Tall and broad seemed to be undecided between covering his boss or running back to the condo. He chose the latter.

Belgian Malinois, pronounced 'maelinwa', are also known as Belgian Shepherd's. Their energy drive ranks among the highest of all breeds, and they are primarily used for detection, police work, search and protection. The Navy Seals employed one in Operation Neptune Spear, the secret mission in which bin Laden was taken down. In this instance, the Giaboni's had trained them, using the scent of clothes obtained from Bracci's dry cleaner. They would mount a relentless attack, with no concern for their lives. They were trained killing machines with no conscience.

As Gando and Crello watched from their vantage point, the two dogs chose two different attack points. The first leaped several feet in the air and dug his piercing teeth around Bracci's neck. The second stayed closer to the ground, launching himself toward the fleshy part of Bracci's leg, the area that contained his vital femoral artery. Both Gando and Crello stared silently as they watched the dogs tear at their target, confiscating chunks of flesh from what was soon to be a lifeless body. Even from a distance, they noticed a body ravaged by killers with an animal instinct, in quite a literal way. Gando was now satisfied that he got what he paid for.

Then several shots emerged from the Escalade which set a plethora of actions into precise movements. Several car doors opened and one of the men closest to overcoat fired two large shotgun blasts through the driver's side window. Those were the last shots fired

Almost instantaneously, a car with blue lights and a shrill siren approached the scene. Men were scurrying around the developing crime scene. Then two men and one woman emerged, guns drawn and pumping their handgun projectiles toward the pair of attack dogs, but the enveloping darkness a speed of the dogs proved fruitless. All that the agents saw were the dogs tearing down the street, oblivious to the silent, high pitched dog whistle of which the dogs had been trained to respond to. With their door up, Anthony and Santee waited for the killers to leap in and sped away in apparent anonymity.

A second car crept toward the scene. As it passed the vehicle that Gando was driving, the eyes of Gasparo met those of Gando's. It was a hunch, but Gasparo, as well as the regularly assigned agents, had been staking out the residence of Bracci. Just in case Gando appeared, he could possibly tie up a loose end. He had believed that Gando was the driving force responsible for the bomb that killed Mancini and his instincts had again served him well.

Gando looked at Crello, who had realized who it was at the same time. He threw the car into gear and accelerated down the street. Gasparo did the same, pressing the pedal down as his left hand reached out the window to mount the blue flashing light that was used to indicate an emergency. This was an emergency and he would do whatever it took to take Gando back into custody.

Gando cautiously sped down a one way street he was on, hoping to get to the Williamsburg Bridge, Manhattan Bridge, or Brooklyn-Queens Expressway and eventually cross back into his familiar turf of New Jersey. He ran several red lights, but Gasparo and his passenger stayed close behind, lights emitting blue strobe flashes into the night. Crello put his left hand on the dashboard and turned to look through the rear window. Gando's eyes alternated between the obstacles ahead and the rear view mirror. With his hands intensely gripping the wheel, he maneuvered his car through the unfamiliar side streets. Eventually a sign for the BQE appeared and he swerved over several lanes to enter the ramp.

The bright blue light continued its ever present flashing in the rear view mirror, even as he tried to shake the tail. As he approached the entrance ramp, a large tractor trailer did the same, merging from a separate highway. Approaching seventy miles per hour on the ramp, the truck, which was slightly ahead of him, began to swerve toward the shoulder. Gando slammed on the brakes, his car fishtailing toward the right, his control severely compromised.

With a will of its own, the car skidded right, even as Gando pulled the steering wheel left. In an almost perfectly symmetric fashion, the right half of the car struck the left rear end of the truck, sheering of the whole right side of the automobile like scissors through paper. The last memory that Gando would later recall, was the feeling of warm liquid covering him and seeing a severed torso being thrown from the car. He would not recall the car rolling over three times or the arrival of the EMS and emergency vehicles that would transport him to the emergency room. Almost two days, nine and a half hours of which was spent in the operating room later, he would finally realize the severity of what had occurred. He was now handcuffed to the I.C.U bed and after regaining full consciousness, would have a shitload of questions to answer.

CHAPTER 23

"I think its several blocks up. I can see the ship from here," Bryant said, as Abby followed her lead.

The big day had finally arrived and the pair was more than prepared for the new experiences that lie ahead. They had deposited their display and merchandise at the PacLantic loading dock the previous day, and were told that it would be placed by their assigned exhibit area in the large convention area. Their car contained two sets of roll on luggage and carry-ons, which they would bring directly to their stateroom. Over the past several years they had worked hard and smart, earning a nice living. If all went well on this cruise, they might be able to procure some investors and start a franchise.

The hoopla surrounding this event was quite overwhelming but precautionary as well. Milton Phelps had a tunnel erected covered in a dark impervious material so as to block out the curious onlookers and photographers. Some guests were even transported right to the deck via helicopter, adding to the already over the top circuslike atmosphere .Abby and Bryant got into the spirit, lowering their designer sunglasses and blowing air kisses to their imagined public admirers. They were giggling like school girls.

Other passengers took to their boarding, appearing more like public officials or well-known sports figures who were preparing to face an indictment. Like those we see on CNN walking with their heads down or covered with manila folders, all in the spirit of avoiding publicity.

Milton Phelps was slightly peeved at the attempted upstaging of what he hoped would be his signature cruise venue. Adjacent to their departure area lie the *Goddess of the Seas*, one of his competitor's new ships that was now the largest in size, tonnage and occupancy in the world. It boasted new innovations such as PSV's or Personal Submergible Vehicles, which could hold between six and ten occupants in a sustainable environment about 100 feet below sea level. It also sported several tennis courts, a hot air balloon which was tied to the stern and a revolving gourmet restaurant shaped like the Seattle Space Needle. Even Phelps awestruck, setting his sights on surpassing all of his competitors one day in the future. He counted on it.

The boarding of the ship began at noon, a long line of those bold enough to admit their interest in the cruise, who were not intimidated by the circles of flashbulbs and microphone booms.

Jon Vandergriff waited patiently in line, donning a hat which mirrored that of Indiana Jones. It was tipped slightly down and even with the top part of his aviator framed dark glasses. He wore jeans with a light brown sport coat, his eggshell colored shirt open at the neck.

In his right hand was his boarding pass and faux passport, while he carried a small black duffle in his left. Fifteen minutes later he was greeted by a courteous member of the staff, wearing a scantily clad outfit which fit in with the theme of the cruise. It was befitting and he bestowed a secretive rising approval, but it was hidden behind his carry on blocking his private areas. He was given his room assignment, key and all other pertinent forms and questionaires for his trip. His arm was lightly touched by another of the hostesses, and after examining his room assignment, she directed him to the appropriate elevator.

He was getting into cruise mode. But not like he had in the past as the captain. Instead, it was as a vacationer, having one ulterior motive that had yet to be formulated. And although his motive was clear, his plan was yet to be formulated. As he walked toward the elevator, he took in all of the cameras, furnishings and blind spots that occupied the room.

Not that he was paranoid, but he knew all too well of the security system that graced these vessels. Headlines of missing passengers and the lack of safety had now been addressed by all of the prominent cruise lines. His past incompetent behavior and the eventual events which led to his incarceration were probably a contributing factor.

Jon rode the elevator up to the 9th floor, the suites just below the ridiculously priced penthouse ones. He slid the card into the horizontal slit, knowing that each time he did, it would be recorded by the ships security log. Being conscious of the secure monitoring of the passengers would only work in his favor.

He entered the room, impressed with the upgrades that Phelps had during the past several years. Tossing his tote on the large king-sized bed, his first action was to inspect the mini bar that graced the state-room. He nodded in approval. Grabbing a bottle of tonic water, he filled the empty glass that sat adjacent to a full bucket of ice. Pouring in what he knew to be a sufficient amount, he walked to his bag and removed a bottle of Grey Goose that he had purchased prior to his journey. Even though the trip was gratis, he despised paying twelve bucks for a shot and a half of his pick-me-up of choice.

After filling his glass, he proceeded to the sliding glass door, taking in a profound breath and view of the ocean air that had become an integral part of his past existence. As he sipped his cocktail, his mind wandered to where it had been over the past several days. If he accomplished his task of disbarring PacLantic of scheduling any future cruises, his stipend would be in the low six-figures. However, if the line was banned for a period of over six months, the figure would double. It would increase four-fold if the time period exceeds one year and a day. George had done the math and the lack of his brothers generating income for such a prolonged period, would most likely bankrupt his venture. And if he could pull the latter off, he would be set for quite a long period of time. All he needed to do was come up with a game plan. He had six more days.

● ● ●

Abby and Bryant patiently waited as the line progressed at an unhurried yet tolerable pace. Twenty minutes passed and they were finally admitted off the gangplank and onto the ship. Their credentials were checked with minimum scrutiny and were passed on to the host. Men were greeted by women in scantily dressed outfits, while the women were greeted by broad chested men in tightly fit tee's that bore both the logo of PacLantic and the outline of tightened abs.

Bryant glanced at their itinerary and programs, while Abby assiduously led the way to their rooms.

"They put us in room 817. That is so awesome and coincidental", Abby exclaimed.

"And why is that," countered Bryant, as the two hustled toward to bank of elevators.

"Duh," Abby said in a way that mimicked a 'bimbette' hired by MTV might respond. "Isn't that your day and month of birth?"

"Duh, back at ya," Bryant replied, oblivious to the meaning of the number until Abby brought it up.

Both were believers in the 'there is no such thing as a coincidence' theory.

"Que sera, sera," Abby snickered, and they both entered the arriving elevator to their room.

● ● ●

After the mandatory muster drill, a mandatory exercise which prepares passengers for a safe evacuation in the event of an emergency, the cruise got down to business. There was a 6:00 P.M. happy hour, not as happy as one might have liked to believe, that offered ½ priced drinks and complimentary appetizers. The passengers didn't seem too shy about consuming any of the free samples passing by, their memories erased in regard to the food poisoning episode that had occurred several months before.

The drill was scheduled for 2:30 and depending how long it lasted, they would be allowed to set up their displays. It took roughly an hour, so they headed down to the convention area to set things up.

They had chosen some of their more popular items. Included were multidirectional vibrators, their signature tie-died lingerie, going under the moniker, 'The 60's free love generation line', and some flavored lubricants and stimulation gels. They chatted with several other vendors, noticing the fact that no one else had been exhibiting similar wares up to their standards. Finishing up, they secured the booth with a curtain constructed of flogging whips, and hustled off to their room to ready themselves for the evening's upcoming gala.

The evening flowed smoothly. Abby and Bryant worked their flirtatious interludes around the room, trying to gather interest in their wares, and possibly some stud. Vandergriff remained aloof, taking in the security safeguards and geography of the ship, during his pre happy hour perusal of the ship prior to happy hour. He knew he would remain alert and awake until he had either formulated a plan or passed out from an overabundance of alcohol.

At several points during the course of the night, during Jon's scanning of the room, his eyes met with Abby's, a stranger to him but definitely one he wanted to meet. Hell, Angel had put no social restraints upon him and he wouldn't have cared less if she did. It was all about accomplishing a goal. Although no words were exchanged, subtle, yet sexual innuendos emanated between the pair. While turning to see if Bryant had caught any of the exchange, Abby noticed that she had apparently left, and was in conversation with a couple standing near the bar. A slight but telling nod from Abby prompted Jon to raise his glass, knowing the two would meet during the week ahead.

Jon turned and walked away, playing the 'hard to get' scenario. He took the long way back, taking the stairs that he could study the walkways that encompassed the ship. Still having no plan as to what monumental event he could concoct for his employers, he hoped it would come to him in one of those unanticipated moments of realization, of 'seeing the light'. He walked, observed and challenged his mind as to what he would do. Maybe it was time to lie down and let his mind wander into the devious and darkest domains of his head.

After reaching the top level of the ship, he turned and took the elevator down to his suite. After a day of observations, he was confident he knew where the blind spots of the ship would hide his deceitful actions to follow.

As he lie in bed, his mind racing, he decided to approach the dilemma of how and what to do in order to wreak havoc on the ship. We all approach problems from different angles, in various thought process levels. And this one needed that type of attention.

PacLantic had shaped this cruise for a distinct type of clientele. They were after those with self-indulgent, narcissistic tendencies and hedonists. Realizing this, he then assumed that pretty much all of the travelers would be self-absorbed in the multitude of events, as well as the eye candy that inhabited the ship. Following this path of logic, whatever he may eventually do, would probably go unnoticed by those, whom like himself, were following their own agenda. Yes, he would still need to exercise caution, but there would be so many events occurring, that many would be oblivious to what others were doing.

With his new methodology in regard to his approach, he drifted off to sleep and a peaceful REM sleep in minutes.

CHAPTER 24

The following morning, Bryant and Abby awoke with an energetic attitude, precipitated by the day's events that were to follow. It was 5:30 A.M. and after adhering to their plans of not over-indulging on the first night, they donned some workout pants and tops and headed for a half hour workout in the ships exercise room. They were not overly surprised to see it pretty empty, which suited them all the better. After some light strength activities and cardio, they took the stairs up to the outer deck where continental breakfast was available. Sipping coffee and picking at chocolate croissants, they planned the day's activities, which would consist of talking to the hundreds of guests that would be assembling in the convention area.

"I am so psyched, girlfriend," Bryant said, the second cup of coffee adding to her excitement.

"The truth is that I am too. Hell, it's a new experience and I love entering the unknown, ya know things and places I have never experienced."

"And you *are* a 'been there, done that' kind of gal," Bryant added and they both laughed, expelling some pent up nervous energy.

They finished up, slid a tip down, and headed back to shower up and change for the 8:00 exhibitor meeting. Doors would open at 9:00.

After showering, the pair dressed in sexy lingerie that they would be displaying. Abby, who was much less modest than Bryant, wore fishnet stockings with a laced top that exposed very tip of her nipples. She covered it with a sheer shawl. It was something that would be hard not to focus on. Bryant donned a long black negligee along with a pair of spiked silver tipped heels, but covered it with a beach sun rap. She left it open, feeling more secluded with it on.

At 8:00, all exhibitors were gathered in the large display room. Dressed smartly in a shirt and tie, the tall man with a graying pony tail and high cheekbones addressed the gathering.

"I would first like to thank you all for participating in our special event, which I hope will both raise the bar for cruise ship themes, as well as being profitable for all of you involved. It took both a lot of initiative and balls to sign up, ladies excluded," which drew a small cackle from the crowd. "Our guests will be allowed in shortly and I know that you can all give them the show that they paid their spendable income for."

Again, a smattering of anxious merriment filled the room.

"My name is Robert Farley. I will be circulating around and please feel free to ask for my assistance in any matter that comes to your attention, no matter how inconsequential. I am at your service."

Brief applause filled the room and Robert exited the stage area. As if prompted, the representatives of the various displays began to attend to their exhibitions. The room contained a fascinating and diverse consortium of interests.

A variety of internet websites promoted such services as website design, porn site advertising and the sale and promotion of homemade sex tapes. There were movie production companies seeking the next hot porn stars, as well as one exhibit that offered you a chance to film your own movies with your favorite 'actresses' and performers. Domination and submission booths displayed the latest 'tools of the trade' and a host of other related subject matters were addressed by these small companies. The Rolling Stones were dead wrong. You *can* always get what you want.

The doors opened promptly, and like a high powered Dyson, the crowd was sucked in en masse. Abby and Bryant's area was quickly populated by women who were attracted to the bright, seductive colors of their wares. They fielded questions, complimented their customers on their choices and started selling. They made sure to compile both mailing addresses and an e-mail list. Their names would be entered into their database and all who signed up would receive catalogs with discount coupons, wanting to strike while interest was peeking.

It seemed as if they were mobbed for an eternity. Neither Abby nor Bryant had time to breathe or catch up with each other. They were surprised how many women had attended and without either realizing, how their sales were accumulating. When the noon hour arrived, the crowd started to thin out. Shopping is one of the many reasons one needs to eat and gain strength so they could shop more.

Food was set up for the exhibitors and as they gathered around the buffet, the hot topic of conversation was how successful they all had been during the first morning.

"If this keeps up for two more days, I am so set for life," came a line from the far end.

"Remember when they called it free sex back in the sixties? Now its expensive sex," bellowed another comment from the group.

Abby wondered why that hot guy she had made eye contact with the previous evening went unseen. Maybe he already had a hookup? Brought his wife or girlfriend? Or maybe he was a late riser?

The afternoon session rivaled the previous one. Business and traffic were brisk, as were sales and catalog sign ups. Toward the late afternoon, Abby caught sight of her possible current crush and evening fling. He was walking around the room, stopping at various vendors and chatting with several of them. He turned as she was staring him down and their eyes met. He walked toward the exit, still locked in eye contact, offering a slight nod as he disappeared from sight. Not subtle but effective.

● ● ●

Jon returned to his room. He had spent the morning hours trying to formulate a tactic that would stop the ship in its tracks, or at least in its wake. He considered tampering with the engine, but the entrance to the room was secured with a fingerprint entry system. Maybe he would call in a terrorist threat, but that would be traceable. He finally decided that he would just clear his mind for the evening and peruse the woman that he had been successfully flirting with.

Checking his watch, he noticed that it was approaching 4:00. He decided to shower and approach, or at least contact the mysterious woman prior to the afternoon session ending at 5:30. He jumped into the shower, letting the hot water cleanse his body and mind. He would dress to impress and somehow make contact with his hopeful conquest.

He decided upon his new ass hugging Guess jeans, an eggshell colored chambray shirt and a black leather blazer. He applied a touch of Bvlagari 'Man', hoping to add to his machismo presence. After lightly spraying his hair with spray, he tugged his coat down. Both he and the full length mirror approved of the final product.

He left the room, heading for the elevator to bring him to the convention floor. Upon arriving, he noticed that the crowd was still dense amongst the exhibits. Standing on his toes, he gazed in the direction of the 'Toys O Joy' booth. His eyes once again met those of Abby's, although he would not learn her name until later. He nodded, holding up seven fingers and then pointing to his wrist indicating a time. She caught his signal and nodded, not demonstrating an overly enthused response, but rather one of curious interest. Holding up her hands, elbows bent and palms parallel to the floor, she displayed the universal signal inquiring as to where. He mouthed the words 'lounge on deck seven', holding up his fingers to confirm that she understood. Abby nodded and turned back to a customer that had been patiently waiting on her. Bryant had been engaged in an intense conversation with another patron, and oblivious to the silent conversation that had just transpired. Although partners in business and being BFFs', certain things remained secretive.

Jon silently praised himself for the perceived smoothness of his subtle, yet direct actions, as well as the confidence that she was interested. He spent the next hour and change walking past the shops of duty free wares, cruise excursions and viewing the restaurant menus. He pretended to be interested, even after reviewing these attractions several times be-fore. Familiarizing himself with every aspect of his surroundings would only add to the success of his final mission.

● ● ●

Slightly past 7:00, Jon stood with a double vodka tonic in his hand, glanc-ing at the entrance to the lounge at where he and mystery women were to meet up. Like most men who carried some old school chauvinistic pre-judgments, he assumed that she would arrive fashionable late. He was right and at 7:15 she entered the room. She approached him, noticing a confident air in which she carried herself. He loved confidence. He loved *women* with confidence.

"So princess, may I offer to buy you a drink," was his opening line,

Had it not been for his piercing blue eyes, radiating an intense sensual stare, she might have already written him off. She had countless numbers of lovers, dating back to her days as a 'provider' in Philadelphia. At this point in her life, her sexual preferences leaned more to men who had dif-ferent physical attributes and vibes than the faceless and nameless Johns she had serviced in her past. Jon was one that fit her requirements. Let's hear the next line, she thought, hoping it would be a vast improvement over the opening one.

"Make it a silver Patron, a double while you are at it. It might last me a bit longer," Abby aid, trying to gauge a reaction to her obvious taste for high end spirits.

"I figured you for at least a triple shot," he replied, seeing how she would reply.

She liked his directness.

"It's my first drink all day and it's still early," she countered, liking his blunt and anything but subtle counter.

He went to the bar, ordered and returned with her drink. He pre-sented it to her with a slight bow. Holding out his hand, he introduced himself as Jonathan Peterson, his new identity that Angel had obtained for him. By now, he had even convinced himself that he had morphed into that new persona.

"And I am Abby Road, like as in the Beatles. I kind of adopted that as my stage name."

"And I love the Beatles, so as far as I can see, we are off to a bloody good start," he bemused, doing a pretty good British accent.

She raised her glass. He followed and they toasted, as Jon wished her a week of success in all business and social endeavors, regardless of all and any expectations.

She liked his voice, his accent and his boyish good looks. She smiled, thinking that this guy might just fill her needs and the desires that might emerge in the hours that lie ahead.

During the next hour, they talked, drank and flirted with an array of innuendos, some subtle and others more of direct nature. Both of them tried to disguise the definite physical attraction that pierced the space between them. Each knew it existed but neither wanted to appear too anxious or needy. After the fourth or fifth round, Jon suggested they take a walk and get a taste of the crisp ocean air. Abby approved.

Jon slipped his hand into hers and their fingers locked. He suggested they go up one flight, where there was less light and the night sky would reveal its stellar grandeur.

Jon led her up to the predetermined spot which lacked any video monitoring, or at least any that he could detect. As they walked along the railing, the deck was pretty much deserted. One couple walked hand in hand as they headed toward the same stairway that Jon and Abby had previously ascended. Jon put his hand on her waist, stopping her and suggested this was a good place to stare out over the dark ocean and admire the night canopy of stellar brilliance. He pointed and spoke.

"And that is Taurus the bull", he said softly, his finger outlining the shape of the astrologic constellation.

"And I see you are quite an eclectic man about town, Mr. Peterson," Abby said in an almost mocking fashion. She was testy this evening, but that was Abby being Abby.

Jon left the rail and faced her, slightly pushing her against the railing as he leaned to kiss her neck. She wriggled out of harm's way.

"Slow down, cowboy," she muttered. "I am one of the women who like to play, but also like the domineering roll and I would prefer to be the aggressor."

But Jon also liked to play rough. He spun her around into his original aggressive positon and again leaned in, but this time was met by two pounding fists against his chest and a knee that landed south of his groin area. Maybe it was the pressure of not having a direct plan, or possibly the fact that he wasn't used to women physically fighting off his advances. Or maybe, he began to consider, this is who he was now.

Regardless of the reason, a searing rage overcame his persona. Placing his hands under her armpits and lifting her off the deck, he tossed her over the rail. It was an endorphin filled, mindless moment. For only a few seconds, he noticed the panicked flailing of her arms and the delayed shrillness of her scream. A second later, the scream was drowned out by loud, ear piercing sirens, accompanied by white lights that pointed off the side of the ship like cannon turrets. He had not accounted for the motion detectors that had been placed at one foot intervals around the circumference of the vessel's lowest level.

Without a second look or thought to his actions, survival mode kicked in. Jon bolted for the stairway leading upward, knowing the lounge was one floor below. He could then take the elevator up to his room from that point. As he ran, he heard a monotone announcement pierce the oceans peace and quiet.

"This is an announcement of high security. Our alarm system has alerted us to the fact that either a large object or person has broken our detection field and gone overboard. We ask you all to remain calm. If you are near the aft side of the ship, please look out toward the ocean to see if there is anything out of the ordinary below where you are stationed. Also, please check to see if all the members of your party are accounted for. We greatly appreciate your help. You can alert us by picking up any of the many courtesy phones scattered on the walls of most areas of the ship. Thank you for your cooperation."

Jon felt the ship cut its engines and slow down incrementally. Life boats with their search crews were rapidly lowered down into the dark ocean, as their halogen fog lights scanned the immediate area designated by the sensors. Vandergriff broke into a faster pace as he emerged from the elevator and slipped his card in the slot of his stateroom door. It opened and he headed straight for the mini bar. With hands shaking, he grabbed the first two shot bottles he encountered. Twisting the caps off, he poured the liquid down his throat, hoping it would steady his nerves. Beads of sweat began dropping off his forehead, stinging his eyes, as he reached for another pair of random plastic bottles.

He took them with him as he slid open the door to the patio and tossed the empty bottles overboard. No new alarms sounded. Gripping the handrail and staring out, he reflected in fast forward mode, the thoughts as to what his life had become since the accident at sea which had caused his life to alter its course. The innocence was long gone, as well as any threads of moral fiber. Greed and revenge had led him astray. They had become so consuming and perverse, that he realized the heinous act he had just committed had solved his problem in regard to his deal with Angel. It was a sad state of affairs. He was ashamed, as the feeling of guilt now totally consumed his fragile, emotional state.

Turning around, with his back toward the calm waters which gently lapped the ship in rhythmic pulses, he gripped the handrail. He closed his eyes and in one fluent motion, leaned as far back as possible until he lost his grip on the bar. He tumbled backward, freefalling with no control, as he was enveloped into the darkness of the night.

● ● ●

Milton Phelps was sipping his single malt scotch and watching reruns of Law and Order. It was one of the few ways in which he was able to escape the everyday pressures he either encountered or caused by his own doings. He got up to pour several more fingers when the cell phone rang. It was probably Adrianna saying she would be late. Looking at the digital display, he cringed when he learned he was incorrect. The name came up Doug McCain and calls from his right hand man were usually ugly. He turned on CNN prior to answering the call. They *always* were the bearer of such 'wonderful' news stories.

"Ok McCain, what's the good news," Phelps queried, hoping it was.

"It's the Adventurer. They have encountered a problem."

Milton was reading the crawl while trying to focus on McCain's concerned tone, as well as the reporter's serious facial features.

"Hang on Doug, I am trying."

"We've lost a passenger and all hell is breaking loose on the ship. I'm getting a chopper and heading over there. I will give you the long and short of it when I arrive or get something else."

McCain listened for a minute but there was no reply coming from the other end of the line. He knew the story was breaking on all major networks. He hung up.

Phelps listened.

"CNN has just learned of a pending situation aboard the troubled PacLantic cruise ship, the Adventurer. Reports coming in have confirmed to us, that at least one passenger is currently missing and presumed to have gone overboard. No other sources have been able to confirm or deny if any foul play was involved."

The serious brunette paused for effect before continuing.

"This is the third incident that has plagued the rebounding company in the past three years. The first involved an accident which occurred as the ship was docking in the island of St. Maarten. The second took place several months ago and involved severe bouts of food poisoning that occurred on a gourmet cruise. If confirmed, this will be the first mishap involving a death occurring. During the past several years, other cruise lines have experienced similar incidents but the track record for PacLantic may have just experienced the final misfortune that just may sink this seemingly cursed enterprise."

Phelps tossed his highball glass across the room just after emptying its contents. It was his way to calm his angst. He had done everything right to patch up past events and dealing with a new a disaster wrought with death could eventually prove catastrophic. He could only watch and wait as the events played out. He detested the feeling of helplessness.

● ● ●

Up the eastern seaboard, George and Carolyn were in a different frame of mind. They too were following the news, preferring to open a bottle of Crystal, their libation of choice served during special occasions. This event would most probably warrant a second bottle as well.

"It is disturbing though that Jon isn't answering his calls on the secure phone. I have tried him at least a half a dozen times,'" Carolyn said with a suggestion of concern.

"Knowing my brother, he might be jamming all of the phone lines or is blacking out the Wi-Fi service. Jon will see you called and get in touch. You picked such a fine and clever man to do our dirty work. He has been extraordinary in his success," George said in palpable sarcasm, raising his glass. They drank.

"Assuming this was Jon, he will be well rewarded for his work."

They toasted again.

Speculation rather than facts would dominate the story until the truth could be sorted out.

CHAPTER 25

The next morning, the mood of the ship had taken on a solemn presence. With the excitement and expectations of a wild hedonistic week, reality had stepped in, and it would be ending in several hours. During the pre-dawn hours, stewards had slipped memos under the guests' doors, stating that Pac-Lantic would be offering either full refunds or vouchers for a future cruise. One would not expect the latter to be the choice of many.

Since the midnight hour, McCain had held meetings and interviews with the staff, gone over surveillance tapes and accommodated some of the guest who had offered up theories regarding some of the passengers' peculiar behavior. Hell, it was a pretty odd group to start, so his expectations were pretty limited. He had already learned the identity of the missing passenger, Jessica Rand, who had been using the name Abby Road during the convention. Bryant was located and questioned, relaying a pretty precise time line to the ships investigating team. She had last seen her roommate finishing up her makeup prior to leaving the room. She had not mentioned to Bryant who she might be seeing or where she might be going. That is how the pair rolled at times. Her concern was genuine to a fault, but her help was not.

At 4 A.M., McCain ordered one last search of the ship prior to arriving back in Florida. He prayed to God that she might be passed out in some area that had been overlooked by the staff. He also ordered the crew to recheck all of the alarm systems, life boats and surveillance equipment, being proactive just in case the seeming curse of the cruise line reared its head once again.

He and Mack Logan, a fair haired Irish lad from South Boston, continued their search. Mack was his 'go to guy'. He was familiar with all of the ships protocols and logistics. As they walked several feet apart, McCain felt a sticky feel underfoot. He shone the high halogen beam of his flashlight down toward the spot, noticing an amorphous shaped crimson spot. Surrounding the small puddle were a spattering of what appeared to be single blood droplets. There was concern in each other faces as they began following the trail of several droplets that were dotting the walls of the inner deck.

"They were probably blown by the wind against the wahl," said Logan with his still distinctive New England accent.

Silently, their flashlights took separate pathways as they followed the random blood droplets. In seconds, the pair of beams halted at a human hand hanging over the side of one of the low lying life boats. Glancing at each other, the pair took off to the nearest stairwell to get a glimpse from above. The only sound came from the waves gently caressing the ship's hull. As they approached the upper deck which would offer a more complete view, they could only hope that their missing passenger was alive and far from any critical state.

Upon arriving, their overhead view revealed what appeared to be a lifeless body, but Logan's beam detected some slight movement on two fingers of the left hand. McCain aimed his light at the head. To his freakish astonishment, the face, albeit distorted with bloody wounds, was doubtlessly that of a male. He nudged Logan to take a look. He pushed the phone button that would directly alert the ship's doctor.

"Hey Doc, get down to Level 2 ASAP. And bring every freaking thing you have in the infirmary. We have a male victim on lifeboat 6. He is cut up pretty bad. His legs seem to have crashed through the windshield of the life boat and it appears to be the only thing that kept him from tumbling into the sea."

"On my way," Doctor Heflat responded swiftly, tipping his head indicating he wanted Nurse Lisa Sue to accompany him.

Both McCain and Logan agreed not to alert other search teams. Firstly, they had been, and still were, looking for a female, and secondly, they did not want the word to leak out amongst the passengers. That would cause even more panic.

When the other pair arrived, the four climbed down the ladder that led the passengers to the safety of the life boat. Now the three lights illuminated the figure. Breathing was shallow. Heflat took out his scissors and began to cut slits in the pant legs, the area where the darkest concentration of blood had been visible. Lisa Sue raised his head and rested it on a pillow. She then hooked up a blood pressure monitor and gently tried to revive the victim.

Stirring almost without notice, his head turned to see what was happening. The last thing he remembered was falling overboard and then seconds later, a sharp, paralyzing pain engulfing him, prior to his blackening out. As his eyes opened, he took in four faces, which focused in like a Hitchcock classic.

"Who," he began, in a barely audible volume.

"Am I," was his next utterance, thriving to form words that would coincide with his lack of ability to form whole sentences or thoughts.

"Just lay still," Heflat calmly began. "Can you tell me who you are or where you are," he whispered, the volume of voice slowly tailing off.

He remained speechless for several minutes, before flashes of events and who he was began to emerge. His head turned to McCain and their eyes met. McCain was struck with that 'familiar face' thing which we all experience on occasion.

"Blood pressure 70 over 54," stated Lisa Sue with obvious concern.

McCain struggled with this man stretched out in front of him. His intuition kept reinforcing that he *knew* this man. His mind raced to identify him. But Jon made it easy for him.

"Hey McCain," said the unidentified man, his voice growing in clarity.

And then it struck him. The hair was darker, the eyes more raised and the lips fuller. But the voice struck a chord and chills ran down the length of his body, as did the words that followed.

"McCain, I believe there are rough seas ahead."

"Vandergriff...are you Captain Jon Vandergriff?"

"A painful smile creased the injured man's lips, followed by a slight nod of his head. And then he passed out.

McCain stood up and left the rest of the group to make a painful call. He held the phone up to his line of vision, ready to press call, and then dropped his arm to his side. He needed to explain the situation to Phelps in such a way as not to raise his perceived level of disquiet. Regaining his composure, he raised the phone again and hit send. It was answered on the first ring, or maybe even before that. McCain took the lead.

"First, we have yet to find any trace of Jessica Rand, the one who is being highlighted in the news. What I just stumbled upon was another passenger, who is in critical condition found face up. Sir, it's quite strange," McCain said, his voice sounding like he had seen a ghost.

"Spit it the fuck out, Doug," came the expectant, arrogant and demeaning tone of Phelps.

"The injured man is one of your former employees. The injured man is ex-Captain Jon Vandergriff".

McCain then ceased to utter another word. He knew it would take time for Phelps to process the information he had just received. Phelps took a long minute and half to reply.

"I haven't seen or heard anything about that bastard since he was released. I was told he had gone back to Europe, that son of a bitch. How could he afford that cruise and why the hell had he not been stopped by the TSA or our people?"

"The thing is, he looks nothing at all like he had in the past. He must have had some facial reconstruction. Hopefully we can learn more in the coming hours. We have a chopper on the way to get him to the nearest triage center. That is, if he can hang on that long. The doc is working on him now. He is a fucking mess."

CHAPTER 26

After hearing about Gando's near fatal car accident and the preceding events, Gasparo called Davis. He knew that he would be interested, but mentioned that at this particular time, there was no need for him to make the two hour trip up north. Gasparo gave him the details but omitted certain leads regarding the full blown investigation that was now in progress.

Behind the scenes, police had a multitude of leads to follow. The bodyguard who bolted was now in custody and being interrogated. Did he turn on his boss? Calls were going out to track down dog breeders who specialized in attack dogs. Residents were being questioned in regard to noticing any persons or vehicles that seemed out of place. Bracci was dead, one of his bodyguards was dead, and the suspect list was growing, rivaling the size of a New York City phone book. The case would grow cold very quickly unless they got lucky. Mob killings tended to make those witnesses with 20-20 vision temporarily go blind.

Davis, at home with Ashely Stone, told her about the melee. She knew his obsession with Gando's past actions, and would do anything to be involved in his permanent incarceration. She played the sex card, distracting his preoccupation to get involved, for at least for the current evening.

● ● ●

Jon had survived the airlift from the ship to the nearest hospital. During that period of time, he had never regained consciousness. From early that morning to early the same evening, surgeons and specialists did the best they could with a body that had fallen almost seventy feet and survived. There were broken vertebrae, damage to several of his vital organs, yet not as much head trauma as one might have expected. Doctors came out after the procedure with the prognosis that his life and survival would be touch and go for the next 48 hours. The police needed to question him, as well as the ships security personnel. When the news finally revealed the name of the second victim, Carolyn knew why her calls had gone unanswered.

"What the hell happened to our mole, Jon? Was he a victim or did he just slip? There is no way in the world that he would sacrifice himself when all that money was at stake. There would be no guaranteed outcome if he had decided to take a leap off of the deck," Carolyn queried George.

"All we can do is to wait and see how it plays out. Latest reports on CNN say that the girl is still missing and the injured man is in critical condition. Did you try him again?"

"Many times, she replied nervously, adding, "Do you think I should take a trip down to Florida and visit him or just wait for a call?"

George weighed the pros and cons of the suggestion for a while, tilting his head, appearing as if was forming a mental plus and minus column.

"Let's give it a day or two and go from there. He might call if he's up to it. He knows your number and how many dollars are at stake here."

As Carolyn arose, George's arm shot out and grabbed her in a dominant fashion, pulling her back on the couch. She looked surprised and a bit miffed. "What is it now?" she said with a touch of anger.

"Wait. We need some insurance for when you go back down to Florida," he said in a somewhat apologetic tone, now realizing he had been a bit too overbearing. He went on.

Brenda Mays, a longtime school friend of Carolyn was living down in Florida. The two were high school friends, bad girls during their wonder years. Although Carolyn had eventually outgrown her bad habits and actions, Brenda had not. She had continue to hang with a bad crowd, spending some time in prison for check forging, and a second stint for drug possession. The two remained friends and Carolyn had even visited her within the past year. She had cleaned up her act a bit, now going to nursing school and completing a drug rehab assignment which limited her second jail time for the second offense. George knew her too, and although wasn't too fond of her, believed she could be of some help to his plan if the monetary reward was incentive enough for her to return to her ways.

Carolyn listened as George formulated a plan, just in case their captain had decided to stray. Unlike George, Carolyn did not like to use people for personal gain. But she did hear him out. When he finished bouncing some ideas off of her as a backup plan, she sat in disbelief about how cruel his mind could work. The only coaxing it took to get her on the same page was bribing her with a new car and a trip to Vegas. Money spoke louder than morals. She agreed to propose his plan to Brenda and try to sell her on it. After a five minute call, they had enlisted Brenda's cooperation.

Meanwhile back down the coast, Milton Phelps was locked behind closed doors with his team of legal and public relation gurus. They had been successful in their two previous surgical repairs of the company's previous disasters, but the third time is not always the charm. What irked Phelps the most, was what Vandergriff was doing on the ship, why he was not recognized and who, if anyone, put him up to his apparent suicide attempt. That's what it had been labeled according to reports he was getting from his inside man within the Coast Guard. He and the team anxiously awaited the results of interrogation as soon as he was able to speak. He had been informed moments before, that he was.

A group of varying law enforcement agencies were gathered around the bedside of Vandergriff, or Jonathan Peterson, the alias he had taken on according to the documents found in his stateroom. Representatives from the FBI, Homeland Security, FDLE and the Coast Guard were all in attendance. They had a multitude of question for him to answer. Although conscious and awake, the morphine drips along with the multitude of tubes and machines that he was connected to, might interfere with the clarity and truthfulness of his responses. He sat up with an expression mixed with pain and curiosity. He took a sip of water with his left hand, barely able to lift it to his parched lips. Swallowing hard and seeming to have trouble speaking, words emerged from his mouth.

"So what do I owe all of this attention to," he asked the group that surrounded him.

Lou Chambers, the FBI station chief in south Florida took the lead. Since the FBI has a fair amount of leeway in regards to the crimes that it may investigate, they could label this a terrorist crime, due to the fact an American citizen was injured. Or use the fact that the incident occurred on a vessel registered in the U.S.A. Regardless, no one argued with the 6'4" federal agent who also had the respect of everyone in attendance.

In a calm and probing tone, Chambers began the interview.

"Let me first offer you my best wishes for a speedy recovery. My name is Lou Chambers and I am the FBI station chief here in the Southern Florida District."

Before continuing, he flipped open his credentials. Jon nodded, acknowledging what he had been shown.

"So what would you gentlemen like to know," Jon said, resigned to the fact that it was game over. Not only due to his incapacitated state, but because his guilty conscience needed to be extricated.

"Start from the beginning and please try to be thorough. I realize it may be difficult, but we need to know the sequence of events that led to your current state."

Jon sighed and began.

He took them through the accident on the ship, his conviction and incarceration. He told them about a woman who had contacted him toward the end of his sentence to sabotage PacLantic cruise lines for a considerable amount of money.

"I had no job prospects and at that time, I still harbored, excuse the pun, some hatred for Milton Phelps, the man who threw me under the bus."

He paused, sipping some more water as he winced in pain from almost every movement made by his shattered body. He pressed on.

"I was the one who tainted the food on the first PacLantic cruise, the gourmet food tour extravaganza. It was not due to any mistakes by the distributors. It was Phelps doing what he does best, and that is to misrepresent the facts to everyone. He is a pure narcissist.

"And how was that accomplished," asked Chambers, showing genuine concern and interest.

"Way too easily," he began. "All I had to do was spray the food with a viral contaminate that I had been given. I knew neither what it was nor what it would do to the passengers. I *was* informed that there would be no toxic effects, and thank God that there were none."

"So you went on another cruise because your first act of sabotage failed," inquired Chambers, taking notes as he spoke. His mind was trying to piece together the how and why as to Jon's current state of mind. He would learn soon enough.

"And how did you end up here?"

Jon forced a grin, still displaying his pain.

"Her name was Angel Almar, and she explained to me that she represented a nameless group that was interested in destroying PacLantic. I really had no concern as to their identity or their motives. After the punishment and public humiliation I went through, I became intrigued in helping her. Don't get me wrong, by nature I am not a vengeful person, but the circumstances and lack of employment options that seemed nonexistent, drove me to helping her."

Chambers nodded, exhibiting the optimum expression of empathy he could muster. He scribbled down the word group, wondering if there was more than one party involved. He waved Jon on to continue the story.

"This cruise that I signed up for was a high profile and ground breaking event. Add in the fact that PacLantic had survived both my mishap and the food incident. I was obsessed with success in lieu of my previous failures. Add to that, the fact I was offered a large sum of money if my goal was accomplished."

"And that goal was?"

"The goal was to put the PacLantic line out of business on a permanent basis. Since I am a success oriented man, I would try again to destroy Milton Phelps. After all, he did destroy me and the life that I loved."

"And how did you plan to accomplish that on this journey?"

"To tell you the truth, I had yet to formulate the how part."

Jon needed a moment to regroup. His severe injuries made it difficult to hold his concentration and formulate his thoughts. Chambers understood this.

The nurse returned to check his vitals, mentioning to the group that he was being pushed to a point that could yield serious and possibly fatal consequences. Chambers acknowledged that, mentioning that he would be done shortly.

He asked the others to wait outside and would inform them of all relative information and facts that he would learn. He believed that one individual would be easier to address than four. They agreed and filed out of the small hospital room.

Chambers waited patiently, not rushing his subject, who was displaying obvious discomfort from his injury. When Jon's eyes once again opened with apparent clarity, Chambers continued the interrogation.

"And how did you meet this Angel Almar," his notebook filling up with notes only legible to himself.

She found me. I didn't ask the how or why. Understand this. I was unemployed, depressed and had nowhere to turn. But she must have known about my past, obviously," Jon stated, which was a fact that he never really dwelled upon or questioned. He smiled, as if he was just realizing what a fool he had been, adding, "I felt that I was played and formed like a lump of Silly Putty."

Jon kept up the pace and timeline of the events that landed him in his current, crippled state. He had a very notable memory considering the condition he was in. When he was finally done with the details, Chambers pulled a phone out of his pocket. It was the phone that had been gathered along with all of Jon's belongings from his stateroom. Chambers took it out and shook it at him, while Jon's eyes followed it flawlessly. Chambers spoke.

"There are only two numbers on this phone, which tells me it's probably disposable and contains a secure line. Both came up as "Private". Neither yielded any results. This led him to assume that these people were tech savvy, disabling the GPS feature. Tracing the serial number, it was purchased somewhere in or near Boston and we don't want to tip her off that we have questioned you. I need you to call her and get her down here."

Jon again nodded and Chambers continued, knowing the number by heart.

"As we sit here, we are in the process of releasing a story regarding your injury. It will mention that you were a passenger, name withheld, who had too much to drink and fell off his balcony. Fortunately, the injuries were minor and after being questioned, it was determined that there was no connection to the missing woman."

Jon followed his every word.

"I want you to tell this 'Angel' that the report was true and the authorities were satisfied that you had no role in the woman's disappearance. Stress to her that you are due to be released within 72 hours and are expecting a visit from her with payment in full. We will take care of the details."

"Are you going to arrest me?"

Chambers shook his head to indicate they were not.

"Your condition and prognosis are not good. The doctor filled me in. The bottom line is that you are guilty of several crimes, but with your cooperation and hopeful recovery, we can minimize or possibly eliminate your sentence if you fully cooperate. Do you comprehend the implications of your cooperation?"

He nodded sullenly, indicating that he did.

The nurse entered the room as if staged, and told Chambers he would need to leave. He had been given much more time with the patient than he should have been. As he turned to leave, Jon said he would call Angel before they sedated him.

Chambers smiled and thanked him before leaving. He didn't quite catch the stern look he was given by the LPN.

When she left, after handing him the standard paper medication cup, he downed the pain killers and thanked her. He quickly dialed Angel. He insisted on being direct and to the point, exchanging no formalities.

"Be here within 24 hours or I will go to the police."

Before a word came through on the other end, the call was terminated. Jon drifted out of consciousness in less than five minutes.

Carolyn quickly dialed a number and spoke.

"He is getting tough in his old age and growing a set of balls."

This worried George, the person on the receiving end of the call. Up until this point, there plan had gone off so well, they had become a bit complacent and cocky.

"Just take care of it. When I get home we can further discuss and plan accordingly. We must remain anonymous."

And with that, the line went dead.

Carolyn was having a bad phone day.

The group of four decided to find a place for lunch that had eluded them due to the circumstances. They would discuss what Chambers had heard and before returning to the Federal building in Miami, each man representing his agency would form a team to carry out the specifics. With the help of the GPS on his Samsung Note, they decided to meet at the Gator Diner, located about ten minutes away.

The group met outside, and upon entering, they were taken to a large booth in the back away from the doorway. Their shoes alone communicated they were involved in some type of law enforcement group and the hostess did not want to alert or scare away any local patrons.

Menus were doled out, four coffees ordered and the waitress returned for their food requests. FDLE went with the Chicken Fried steak, which complimented his figure. Coast Guard went with a cheese omelet and grits. Homeland and Chambers opted for the burger and fries, Chambers joking that the extra greasy food stimulated his thought processes. They all laughed.

Being an alpha male, which all four seemed to be, Chambers spoke first, deciding usurp his privilege of being the lead investigator. He was practical, with a calming voice and displayed no obvious arrogance or overbearing mannerisms. No one questioned his unspoken lead.

As the quartet ate, Chambers ran through the whole story that Vandergriff had told to him. Before the last refill of coffee he was done and presented several theories to the group. He held out his right hand, palm up, as he began.

"Guys, feel free to interrupt, but here is how I see it."

He grabbed his index finger and continued.

"One, this might be a small terrorist group, interested in some type of experiment to see the feasibility of attacking a large number of Americans in a fashion yet to be attempted."

Grabbing his second finger he continued, mentioning that this might be an attempt to publicly humiliate Phelps for his arrogance, or more possibly, someone with a grudge. His third finger and theory was blackmail and the fourth, saving his thumb just in case he formulated a fifth theory, might be a plot by one of the larger cruise lines to once and for all, put him out of business.

All nodded their heads in agreement. Coast Guard chimed in.

"What if on a larger scale, the ship was to be occupied or hijacked by one of our enemies and subsequently armed with some powerful armaments or nuclear devices?"

Coast Guard got a slight nod from Homeland, but Chambers disagreed.

"If that were the case, they might have chosen a larger vessel, and as we are in the process of doing background checks on the crew and passengers, so far that idea might be a little obtuse. And the one thing that keeps gnawing at me is the phrase Jon used. He intimated that she was working for a group of people and not just one." He shook his head perplexed, adding that it might just be a ruse.

They remained five minutes longer and discussed what aspect of the investigation each would be involved in. A lot of variables were still in play. Learning of who Angel was, who she worked for and what her motives were, was the biggest by far.

Chambers picked up the check and they all headed out. And then his cell phone rang.

"Yes Jon. Yes. That is awesome. What time? So she is? How much so?"

The three stood there, having no clue about the conversation coming through from the other end, but the grin that emerged on Chambers face spoke volumes. He pressed the end key. The group huddled together.

"Our Angel has just returned Jon's earlier call and told him that should would be down by 6:00 P.M. And yes, she sounds worried. She asked him countless times if he had contacted the police and he assured her that he was questioned and they were satisfied. He mentioned it was being treated as an accident. End of story, and she bought it. I am going to get a team over to the hospital for surveillance. I want to know how she arrives, what she is driving and get some photos that we can run through the system. We will get some prints in the room and wire it, in order to tape the conversation. It looks like we are in business. Let's get it done and close this fuckin ugly case.

215

● ● ●

Before even starting the car, Chambers was on the phone doling out assignments for the staging of the afternoon's events. Three agents were immediately requisitioned to the hospital where Jon was being monitored. One was to pose as an orderly, another as a nurse and the third a doctor. His room was wired with video and sound, which was so inconspicuous due to all the electronic monitors and wires keeping Jon alive and conscious. Seeking revenge for the man that Angel had made him become, he summoned all his strength to put on a convincing performance.

Chambers set up shop in the typical minivan familiar to all those that watch any of the current crime genres. Agents from all four investigating agencies were posted around the hospital in order to gain information leading to a swift identification of this woman.

Slightly after 6:00, a woman arrived in a black Lincoln, indicating she had the bucks for a car service and the anonymity she perceived accompanied the fee. She talked to the driver briefly before shutting the door and then proceeded to an area which allowed parking. Before she had come to a halt, Chambers knew the name of the fare as well as her starting point. That point was Miami International Airport.

Checking further, there had been an Angel Almar that had arrived on a Jet Blue flight from Beantown. The list of all Angel Almars produced none residing in the Boston area. It was an obvious alias. Now they had to find out whose alias it was.

She entered the hospital and a call was placed to Chambers which indicated that the visitor had requested the room of Jonathan Peterson. They were now 2 for 2.

What they didn't know was that Angel lacked no flair for the dramatic. She had come as Carolyn, wanting to make sure that she was not being sought after. She carried the Angel Almar wig and disguises in her large purse. If all seemed safe, she would find a stall in a nearby bathroom and change into her alter ego.

After several passes by his room, she decided that it seemed safe. Besides, she gave Jon little credit for creativity and had no reason to doubt the truth of his story. She proceeded to enter the ladies room and change.

She a stopped at the nurses desk and after several minutes, was given a pass to the patient's room. That call too confirmed her name and destination, but did not match the description given by Jon. It was noted by one of her tails, that she appeared nervous. Her gate was hurried and she habitually glanced behind her and from side to side. Her designer purse swung loosely by her side. The agent posing as the doctor confirmed that she was entering Jon's room.

She walked in gingerly and abruptly stopped. Although the news had said his injuries were minor, they appeared anything but that. Picking up on this, Jon beckoned her over and sat up. It was a struggle but he had been practicing. Her pace resumed and she dragged a chair up to his bedside.

"Are you alright," she asked, her concern almost convincing.

"Yes, yes I am fine Angel. But I must apologize for ignoring your calls. The phone had sustained some damage, but one of the nurses was kind enough to tinker with it and now it works."

"Thank God for that," she countered. Her sincerity was now wavering. Jon got to the point, as per instructions he had received from Chambers and his team.

"We don't have long to talk so let's keep this brief and to the point."

This was a side of Jon that was new to Angel. He had always been more timid and passive. She was momentarily taken aback.

"I have completed my part of the bargain and our business relationship can be considered terminated. Without any plans, I pushed a woman overboard in the heat of the moment. Up until that point, I was clueless to how I would sabotage the event. So you brought the payment I assume?"

Angel, without any thought or resistance, removed an envelope from her purse.

"Hold on," said Jon nippily. "This does me no good here. Too many people are in and out."

He leaned over to grab the notepad and pencil that had been conveniently left for him. He scribbled down a name and number.

"When you leave here, you are to wire the money into this account at this bank," he ordered. "I will call them to see if has cleared. They are open until 8:00, which gives you ample time to do this. Now please go do your business and I will say it again, consider our business relationship over."

Angel reached out and softly squeezed his forearm.

"If that's how you feel, I understand. Just realize that if my people do not see the company go under, your future bonus will be terminated."

"And I understand that. I have successfully completed all three assignments and you have paid me the agreed upon amount. Am I correct?" he asked forcefully.

"You are correct and if it is your decision to sever any future contact or agreements, then so be it."

With that said she got up and headed toward the door. Turning she added, "The money will be in your account as requested, so just don't do anything stupid like going to the authorities. I need not mention that my people would frown upon that with severe consequences."

Those were the last words she said and the investigation started in full gear. The beauty was that Chambers now had probable cause after her identity was discovered. The next hours would hopefully yield her location and answers to that nagging phrase, my people.

● ● ●

The events began to unfold as soon as the woman known only as Angel had left the hospital. The black Town Car made a U turn and pulled up in front of her. She got in. By the time it had pulled away from the curb, roughly fifteen minutes after she had entered, the Feds had the company, drivers name, background and the person who had hired the car. The name again came up as Angel Almar. At least they knew through airline flight logs that her flight had originated out of Logan International. They had sent in a team to gather prints she had left on the railing of his hospital bed.

"This bitch is good. Pretty well prepared and covering her cute ass," commented Chambers to the junior agent who was sitting with him in the vans' control center.

After locating the bank, Angel ran in, filled out a deposit slip and waited for a receipt. No questions were asked regarding the large deposit, per orders given by the F.B.I. Having handled large sums of Georges' cash many times, she thought nothing of it. The car then entered the interstate which led to the airport. As it weaved through moderate traffic, no fewer than ten cars alternately had her in view, along with her exact location. Before the car pulled up to the Jet Blue terminal, Angel placed a phone call to Brenda, putting the plan that George had concocted into motion. Brenda appeared hesitant, but when the fee was doubled, she readily agreed. One FBI and one Homeland Security agent had already boarded the plane in first class. Just another example of our hard earned tax dollars at work. The flight was due in at 11:19. Agents would be waiting.

Chambers called Jon to get more details, also querying if she had touched anything in the room with her hands.

"She sat up straight, hands folded in her lap like a good Catholic schoolgirl. And the fact the door was half open, negated her touching the doorknob. But she did grab the railing of his bed. Your people already lifted her prints."

"You are becoming quite an observant detective, Jon. Now why couldn't you have put your hidden talents to a better use?"

He heard a slight chuckle emerge from Jon. He liked the guy and although Jon had made some bad choices, landing him where he lay now, he did believe there was hope. That is, if he would survive.

● ● ●

Meanwhile, Milton Phelps had spent the day doing something very foreign to him. He remained silent and under the radar as news of the cruise ships were dribbling out. There were still no hard core facts that he had learned and the varied reports were all speculative at best. Not until he could substantiate fact from fiction, would he address the ever present public that seemed to thrive on bad news. The following morning would not be a good one.

CHAPTER 27

The suburbs of Wellesley Massachusetts are roughly 18 miles from Logan Airport. Its median household income is nearing $200,000 and the residences average slightly over four times that amount. George Phelps liked both the proximity to the city as well as the snootiness of that address. That was the destination of Angel and the black limo that picked her up at the airport. She was glad that it was finally over. She would no longer have to worry about 'her people' or pleasing 'them', but only George. She let out a sigh of relief as she arrived.

Almost on cue, when the door to the car was slammed shut, a massive array of vehicles converged on the residence. Blue and red lights from cruisers, unmarked government sedans and even a SWAT truck were now surrounding her. Lights went on in almost every house on the block and doors opened. Residents shielded their eyes from the blinding lights as they finished tying the strings around their robes. Rather than storming the house and causing an even greater headline grabbing scene, several of the agents approached the front door and knocked.

Seconds later a man's voice said to hold on and he would be there in a minute.

The voice on the other side of the door yelled back in an obviously urgent manner.

"I said now or the door will be shattered in ten seconds."

It swung open as George Phelps stood there, his slacks and buttoned white shirt remaining unruffled. His hands were held high. Oddly, he did not ask anyone what this was about, which is the normal reaction from someone who would lawyer up as soon as he was spoken to. The agent continued.

"We have a warrant to search the premises and would prefer to ask you politely to join us down at the federal building to answer some questions."

He nodded his head and gave a three word reply, a favorite phrase of the criminal set.

"Call my attorney."

While George was cuffed and led away towards one of the unmarked sedans, he scanned the area for Carolyn. It was obvious that whichever arm of law enforcement was here, he rightfully assumed that they had learned something. Still, he was dumbfounded as to what they had learned or how they had learned it. Before he entered the car he caught a glimpse of Carolyn as she was being driven away. She was hunched over and her body was jerking in a manner that told him she was crying. Under her hardened exterior, there existed an oversensitive and childlike side. He could only pray that she reverted to the former.

The motorcade that originally stormed the house was now reduced to three. Those vehicles would shortly arrive at their destination in downtown Boston. All of the others remained behind to exercise the search warrant. George let out a sigh of relief, knowing that his 'business computer' was locked behind a hidden safe in the basement of the building where he rented space in Boston.

The couple had been separated since they were picked up and they both sat in separate interrogation rooms. Chambers had caught an FBI jet after the now identified Carolyn West had boarded the flight to Boston. He would question her. Boston agent in charge, Scott Berlin, would interrogate George.

Chambers grabbed the now thick manila folder prior to entering the room where Carolyn was being held. He brought agent Marge Holly along, just in case he needed to revert to that woman to woman, good cop bad cop technique. He would get to the bottom of this in a New York hour.

"Anything I can get for you Miss West," he began. He opted on taking an approach used to gain trust and confidence, rather than the rubber hose thing.

"Just a coffee, please," she said timidly. She was not in charge now, a far cry from her dominant role with Jon.

Chambers nodded and Holly left the room to get her a cup. She knew the drill, taking her time to let Chambers gain some of that trust.

He opened the folder, as she silently sat across from him, head down and eyes fixed on nothing in particular. He tapped on the table, getting her attention and bringing her back to reality. He spoke.

"You know why you are here. You also know what you have done, as well as to whom and the reason behind it. So let me tell you what we know *and* what you need to tell us now."

She sat frozen as she listened, her hands visibly trembling.

"The former sea captain Jon Vandergriff, whom you renamed Johnathan Peterson has told us pretty much everything. He talked about the food contamination scheme, the payment, and pretty much everything else. We have you on tape visiting the hospital and agreeing to place his fee into his account. We have you on the bank video as well."

The trembling was now accompanied by her arms now wrapping themselves around her small frame. It was classic body language that indicated guilt.

The door opened and Holly returned with her coffee, setting it in front of her. She had not been cuffed to the metal link that protruded from the table. It was another technique to put her at ease. Chambers continued. Carolyn picked up her coffee.

"So up to this point we have a laundry list of charges that are being filed as we speak. We have attempted murder, conspiracy to commit murder, several public safety issues, bribery and with a little finagling, and we might be able to top it off with some terroristic threat issues. But the extent and vigor in which we prosecute you is all in your hands. It all depends on the degree of your cooperation and how truthful you are in answering my questions."

During that short speech, Carolyn had lost all color, in her face and her whole body was beginning to tremble. She put her hands together and buried her head in them, as tears accompanied the irregular breathing which now consumed her. Holly handed her a tissue and tried to comfort her, spouting some bullshit that the truth would set her free.

Chambers waited a moment before asking her the money question, wanting to know who 'her people' were. Over the next hour several things happened, the most unexpected beginning with Carolyn never requesting a lawyer even though she had been Mirandized. She then went on to give the complete background in regards to who planned it, the reasons why and the coup de grace, who 'her people' were. Chambers learned that her boyfriend George was the mastermind but was taken aback by the fact that there was no conspiracy. It was George and him alone with the help of his dependent and greedy significant other. He relayed information to the bureau chief in Washington, sending the recordings in close to real time.

George on the other hand had little to say, waiting for his mouthpiece to show up. Scott Berlin tried his best tactics. Taunting his subject initially and then building up his ego and finally reading the same laundry list of charges that Carolyn was facing. For good measure he added insider trading, fraudulent trading and, money laundering to boot. Still he remained silent as he waited for his lawyer.

Forty minutes and three cups of coffee later, his lawyer arrived. He was given some time with George and then summoned in Berlin.

"My client realizes the severity of his actions and wishes to offer his deepest remorse for his crimes. But at the same time, my client can be an invaluable asset in helping our government ebb the flow of massive amounts of funding that are being used by our foreign adversaries. He is willing to name names and companies. It is his wish to speak to someone high up in the Justice Departments food chain in exchange for considerations involving his past actions."

Berlin shook his head in disbelief. This man, who had a hand in attempted murder, deflating the travel industry for a short time and was now hinting at the knowledge of anti- American activities, really had some set of balls.

"Listen asshole," he began, as Scott was known for telling people what he thought, "this decision is above my head. I will relay your request to my superiors, but for now," he added, nodding to the guards stationed in the interrogation room," get this dirt bag into a cell and out of my sight."

And with that, the interview was concluded.

● ● ●

In Florida, Milton Phelps awoke to the constant ringing of both his cell phone and land line, two distractions that had eluded him the previous evening. His wife was nowhere to be found. McCain had nothing to report and his cocktails of Johnny Walker Black and Xanax had put him in a rough state. He answered the phone, slurring his words. The only words he could make out were for him to turn on the news. He did. He listened and watched. All three stations were focusing on the breaking news of his sinking cruise line.

The familiar sound of a key turning in his locked door briefly caught his attention. Adrianna stood with a takeout bag of lunch, procured from his favorite eating establishment. She was well aware of the breaking news regarding her husband's latest predicament. The Peking duck and stone crab egg rolls would either cheer him up or provide no distraction to the intense guise that sprang from his face. In all the years they had been together, sharing the ups and downs of his obsessive drive toward success, she had never seen this particular look that he now projected. Concern filled her whole presence. Her gaze then switched to the voluminous voice and live broadcast of the reporter by which he was seemingly being hypnotized.

"In a coordinated and swift action, state and federal law enforcement agencies have now connected a Massachusetts couple in the string of attacks aimed at PacLantic Cruise Lines."

Two pictures appeared on the screen, both familiar to Milton.

"George Phelps and his live in companion, Carolyn West, both of Wellesley, Massachusetts, have been charged in a host of crimes leading to the sabotaging of the business owned by his brother, entrepreneur Milton Phelps."

Milton backed up to the bar and took a large swig off the half full/half empty bottle. This was no indication of his optimism or pessimism in regard to how he viewed the contents of the liquid that remained in the bottle. Milton sat motionless and rigid on a stool by the bar, his mind now processing the event. He questioned his perceptiveness regarding how he missed the capabilities and hatred that his brother had unleashed. He took another large gulp, oblivious to the concerned look that Adrianna now wore.

"Milton, my love, talk to me. We can and will get through this. We always have," she began, her voice quivering with fear. It was a fear that arose from her emotional depths, those of which she had never felt.

"You have never given up or backed down. We can work through this together, just as we always have."

He did not hear a word.

Being caught up in a large ego and drive for success, these traits were now blinding him to the not so obvious events that were unfolding around him. He arose from the stool and opened the large window which gave him a high level view of the smaller residences and expansive blue ocean that lay in front of him. His lust for power, control and fame had blinded him to the small vignettes that he had become oblivious to.

A tear trickled down from his cheek, partially due to his failure and more dramatically, due to the repressed guilt he was now feeling in regards to his role in the death of his father. In a robotic, zombie-like fashion, he arose and opened the cabinet beneath the bottles of alcohol that adorned the shelf on the credenza. His eyes darted back and forth, unevenly between the television, his wife and the bar he sat behind.

His hand fumbled through the drawer and he emerged with a large heavy object. In a fluent motion and with no thought, he held the large caliber gun to his head and pulled the trigger. The story would run for several days as, it tied up all the loose ends of the small group of individuals involved. Adrianna would be torn with guilt, eternally fixated on what she might have done.

● ● ●

Later that night, an observant detective stationed by a video monitor panning Jon Vandergriff's bedside, leaped from his post. He left the neighboring empty hospital room and was able to apprehend a nurse that had not been cleared for access regarding his monitoring. In the right side of her pocket was a syringe that was loaded with Ethylene Glycol. If she had successfully injected it into an I.V. bag, Vandergriff would have not survived the evening. It was not his time, and upon learning of this attempt, he became even more confident he made the right choice in cooperating with the authorities. He knew there would be hope for him after all. George Phelps would later have several more charges added to his indictment. The woman arrested was named Brenda Mays.

● ● ●

Over the next week, the players were sorted out as their roles in this heinous plot became better defined. Due to his full cooperation and heartfelt remorse, Captain Jon Vandergriff, aka Jonathan Peterson, pleaded down and received the lightest sentence. Carolyn West would face more serious charges and would be remanded prior to the trial. The government was in no rush to schedule a trial date.

The arrogant Mr. George Phelps made his request to a pair of high ranking U.S Attorney's, one in the Justice Department and the other from Homeland Security. His pleas fell on deaf ears. They could and would not trust a sociopath who was only looking to plead down his charges and there was no proof that he had any useful information at all.

The cases would take over a year to get to trial and the media frenzy would report on the progress as the case progressed. It took some time, but the cruise industry would rebound to levels above those which it had attained prior to the incidents which had occurred.

Eventually, all of the motives came to light regarding the players involved. Carolyn West had gotten caught up in the monetary gain aspect. Like George Costanza in front of a potato chip bowl at a party, she was double dipping, consumed with gifts and spending cash that George used to manipulate her.

George's motive was both biblical and greed filled. He was willing to sacrifice his brother, in the business sense, as well as gain revenge for his lifelong obsession with placing the blame of his father's death on Milton. Milton had overworked his father, and refused to sell out while the profits were high. Avenging his father's death had led to his own downfall. It was an outcome he would never have expected.

● ● ●

Bryant Merril would eventually sell the business. It took a while for her to recover from the loss of her best friend. In that regard, she pushed for more safety and security measures to be introduced in the travel industry. It was a cause that would help her friend's memory live on and hopefully diminish the likelihood of such events from occurring in the future.

CHAPTER 28

Davis and Gasparo stared down at the man who lie handcuffed to his hospital bed. He had been in a coma for several days. Upon awakening, the following days were rough, laden with the guilt that he now blamed himself for the death of his best friend, Jake Crello.

"You do understand Julian, that there will be some consequences for you deserting the program," began Gasparo. "Maybe some jail time. And I hope you will be so kind as to fill us in on the untimely deaths of the younger Bracci and Mancini." His tone was official.

"I understand," said Gando. "But in regard to their untimely deaths as you stated, I don't believe I can be of much help there," smiling his trademark smile. It was the kind that was a cross between self-satisfaction and a child-like innocence.

Gasparo and Davis shook their heads, both smiling as well. And although Gando was a cold blooded killer, they had both come to like his style. Maybe it was the fact he remained modest and loyal to himself and those he respected.

"We will be back when you are feeling better and talk some more, hash out some details," said Davis. "Take care, Julian," he added, with a bit of sincerity detectable in his voice.

"I understand," Gando acknowledged.

It was time for a cheesesteak, and with that, the pair left the room.

Made in the USA
Charleston, SC
26 May 2015